On Becoming Us

A Story of Lifelong Friendship

Guy S. Fasciana
A Novel

Published by
Tenor Publishing, LLC
304 Hidden Hills Drive
Greenville, SC 29605
Internet: guysfasciana.com
Email: info@guysfasciana.com
Printed in the United States of America

ISBN Number: 978-0-935929-02-7

Library of Congress Control Number: 2016900401

Disclaimer
This book is a work of fiction. The names, characters,
places, incidents, and dialogue either are products of the
author's imagination or are used fictitiously. Any resemblance
to actual events, locales, or persons, living or dead, is entirely
coincidental.

Acknowledgements

Most importantly, I want to thank my wife and best friend, Jane V. Gwinn, for her support writing this book. Her daily comments, "How do you come up with these things?" and "I don't know where you get those ideas." were very flattering. I don't have a clue.

Jane read each revision without going to the loony farm--love gives you the strength to do many things. She was my alpha reader (tells you how well you're doing) and my beta reader (tells it like it is). I thank her for her effort.

I also want to thank Jennifer (Jennie) Moore who read my book and was strong enough to tell me when it didn't flow or when it didn't make sense.

Thanks to International Plastics' David Elliott (cover formatting) and Eric Wood (website creation).

Special thanks to Bill Burns, instructor at OLLI / Furman.

On the first day of class, Bill gave us our first assignment. Write a one-two page story that could serve as a basis for a full novel. I wrote that story and more. He gave specific instructions how to write a fiction novel: *Let the story go where it wants to go and don't discuss the story with anyone.*

As any good student, I listened to my teacher. The story didn't go where I thought it would but I kept writing. Only once did I get "writer's block"—it was when I tried to steer the story in a different direction. After four days, I let the story "loose" and the block went away.

After nine months, I had completed a 77,000-word novel. I didn't think I had that many words in my head but they were there waiting to get out.

I also want to thank Lynn Mayberry and John Maietta who listened to various readings and commented on my story throughout our study group.

On a clear day, you could see New York City. Even from New Jersey!

The gusty winds have swept away the summer smog, and made way for crisp, clean, winter air, and deep, blue skies.

Is there a better place for a fresh start than in New York City in the fall?

Chapter 1

The Art Exhibition

October 12, 1984

MY MOTHER IS CATHOLIC. My father is Jewish. She's Sicilian; he's German. Oil and water!

They married in Pittston in the late-1930s at a time when everyone looked unfavorably on "mixed marriages." Despite that fact, my neighbors were my extended family. That's the way it was in our small, northeastern Pennsylvania town.

I always had dreams. Big dreams! While most kids in elementary school played baseball and basketball in their back yards, I contemplated about my life while sitting on the porch watching them play. Thoughts of my future consumed me until I discovered exactly what I wanted out of life: a big-deal career, a "goddess" who loved me more than life itself, and a large family.

I wasn't asking for the moon, I just wanted regular stuff!

What could possibly go wrong?

My name is Jeffrey Rosenbloom. I'm the youngest offspring of the unlikely marriage between Levi Rosenbloom and Rose Agostino. My family gave me the tools—culture and work ethic—with which to accomplish my dreams and to create a life of which they would be proud.

I worked hard building that life. I became a famous forensic artist by contributing to the arrest, conviction, and incarceration of many notorious criminals. However, my illustrious dream career ended prematurely. During extensive rehab, I reinvented

5

myself.

I'm hosting an art exhibition showing off my "reinvented" me to reconnect with the world. At the New York Hilton on the Avenues of the Americas, my staff and I arranged the main section of a conference room to display my new art--watercolors. In another section, we staged my pen-and-ink drawings, some of which I sketched as far back as grade school.

Within minutes of opening the doors, the room filled with friends, family, business associates, and onlookers. They acted as if at a party celebrating a long-awaited World Series win by the New York Yankees. I was very flattered.

Servers in formal dress provided wine and snacks to my guests. Some of the wandering souls may have come here only for the food and drink. You know how an event like this draws a group who will use the occasion to overindulge, thinking no one is watching; no one is keeping tabs. Most, however, came to see my new work.

Twenty watercolor paintings sat on easels throughout the room, mostly landscapes in and around the Pocono Mountains southeast of Scranton, Pennsylvania. Attached to the watercolors, in the lower right hand corner, were discrete labels--price tags-- on which were hand written numbers. Several "reserve" pen-and-ink sketches of celebrities, politicians, criminals, and a few friends hung in the corner—under the radar. They had no such tags and were not for sale.

Prominently displayed on the wall, straight in from the entry was a painting, entitled "You May Kiss the Bride," of a young couple kissing after a marriage ceremony at The Camelback Inn in Tannersville, Pennsylvania. The backdrop for the romantic joining of two lovers contained mountains of leaves bursting with reds, yellows, and tans.

One man asked his wife, "Do we know them?"

"It's Jeffrey and his wife. Jeffrey painted it from one of their wedding photographs."

"It's beautiful!"

Almost instantly, a hush came over the room. At first, at the door leading from the foyer into the conference room and, then, like a wave, the silence spread throughout the room. The disturbance was a young lady who slowly, but confidently, moved through the room looking at the paintings. The tall lady in a basic, black dress sashayed past men and women alike, taking time to pause and unpretentiously connect with each one who made eye contact with her. Her smile was more engaging than flirty. She wore dark sunglasses making her facial expression difficult to assess fully.

Her flowing black hair, skin tone, and ruby red lipstick made her look "ethnic" — possibly Greek or Israeli. Her figure was one upon which an ordinary dress could be hung and look expensive. She was dazzling.

As she moved past me, my eyes locked onto her like a magnet. I felt an instant connection. She wore a distinct, but unfamiliar, perfume. I noticed the slight sway to her hips. As my eyes followed her movement through the room, the expressions on the faces of other guests seemed to beg an answer to the question: "Who *is* she?" As she leaned toward the people she acknowledged, I pictured her as a kid showing off in front of her friends, pretending to be a movie star.

She paused at the pen-and-ink sketches for a minute, walked away, and returned for another look... a long look.

I thought, "Who is the 'Black Dress'? Perhaps, she's a model who became curious about the crowd or the paintings."

The "Black Dress" disappeared as quickly as she appeared.

Once she left, everyone began to circulate again.

Three of my best friends from as far back as Cub Scouts just arrived.

Mike Costanzo, who slowly looked around said, "I had no idea you could paint like this. All these years, you hid the good stuff from us! Well, I'm impressed. I wish you well."

Ted Mosconi recognized some of the pen-and-ink sketches as those of my ex-girlfriends. He smiled and gave his signature giggle, as would the cat that ate the canary.

Sal Greco, saw a large group of people huddled around a more colorful painting, a scene entitled "Early Morning," of a waterfall along the Delaware Water Gap. Rushing water, a yellow morning sunrise with bluish-gray fog, and droplets of dew on the dark green vegetation filled the canvas. He looked at me and said, "Perfect!"

I interacted with my guests and my friends. We shared stories about growing up and about my work. Seeing everyone communicating warmed my soul. Levi and Rose reaped the rewards of good parenthood. My appreciation for my friend's support was palpable.

The time was 4:30 p.m. Mike drove home to Philadelphia. Ted took a cab to JFK Airport to fly home to Atlanta. Sal drove back to Springfield, Massachusetts.

During the past three hours, I sold sixteen of my twenty watercolors and received critical acclaim for my new medium. The afternoon was a success by any standards.

I reflected on my life. "My parents seemed to have an easy time meeting, falling in love, and raising a family. They educated themselves and had good careers. I wondered, "Was their success luck or was it by design?"

"If luck did play a part, did I share in their good fortune?

"Were the negative events in my life bad luck or bad decisions?

"I heard my parents' story hundreds of times. Their story is a good one. I can repeat it word by word!

On Becoming Us

Henry Ford invented the Model T Ford for the working class. Ford's Working Class had good jobs and cash to buy a Ford of their own.

When people weren't working, they went to the movies to see "The Great Train Robbery," the first silent movie. They also got help with their laundry, washing their clothes in the Thor Electric Washing Machine.

The working class was moving on up. However, if they wanted to celebrate their elevation, they had to get illegal booze because Prohibition was the law.

People from all parts of the world wanted to escape their poor living and working conditions and come to America, the land of opportunity.

For those immigrants who came to America, worked hard, bought homes, and started businesses, success was their prize.

Chapter 2

Levi and Rose

First Half of the Twentieth Century

MY FATHER, LEVI, told me how he met my mother, Rose. He told his story at birthday parties, anniversaries, holidays, and every other occasion during which anyone would listen. I heard it so many times I know it by heart.

He said, "Your grandparents, Ira and Sylvia, along with other Europeans, emigrated to Pittston, Pennsylvania to get away from poor working conditions at home. A year later, they opened a clothing store, "Rosenblooms," in Wilkes-Barre, Pennsylvania, a prime shopping location. Four years after that, they had their first son, Levi, who would eventually inherit the clothing store."

In Jewish families, the first-born male typically inherited his father's business. Subsequent males, if there were any, chose professions—doctors, lawyers, dentists, or the arts. Female offspring studied liberal arts in college to prepare for marriage to someone who had inherited their father's business or to someone who had become a doctor, lawyer, or dentist.

When Levi was of age, Ira told him, "I think you should study business. It will prepare you to run the clothing store." Bucknell University had recently chartered a business school.

My other grandparents, Dominic and Concetta Agostino, were Sicilians who came to America in their early 20s to start a new life and a raise a family. They were devout Catholics deeply involved in their church. Dominic opened a restaurant, Coccina Italiano, in West Pittston, Pennsylvania.

When she was of age, Rose Agostino said to her father, "I want to go to the new business school in Wilkes-Barre so that I can get an accounting degree like Mr. Giggarelli next door."

Dominic was so proud that Rose wanted to go to school. "A girl, mind you, going to college!"

Levi Rosenbloom and Rose Agostino attended the first class offered by the new school.

Both were studying business. Both were late for their first class. Both sat next to each other in the last two empty seats in the front row. Rose smiled at Levi and Levi smiled back.

"Hello, my name is Levi Rosenbloom."

"Hi, I'm Rose Agostino."

"I know of your family. Your father has the restaurant in West Pittston."

"Yes, have you been there?"

"Yes, I've been there a few times with my parents. The food is good."

"I've seen you around Pittston a few times, but I don't think we've met before."

"No, I don't remember meeting you."

For their second class, Levi motioned to Rose to sit next to him.

"Hello again," Rose said.

Levi said, "Are you following me around?"

"Actually, yes I am. I like the way you smile at me."

"I smile at everyone. What makes you think you're so special?"

"You may smile at everyone, but I'm the one you asked to sit next to you."

"This was the only seat left."

"Really?" Then Rose looked around the room and said, "I guess you're right."

A fly on the wall could see, Rose and Levi were attracted to each other, but, because he was Jewish and she was Catholic, each of them knew pursuing a relationship with each other would be fruitless.

Even though America was a melting pot, during the 1930's people paid attention to each other's names and were always aware of nationality and religion. Rose knew Levi was Jewish and Levi knew Rose was Catholic. It was easy to keep track of names and religions because new arrivals to the "Melting Pot" (the United States) had not yet "melted."

Levi and Rose continued to sit next to each other during the first semester. They often smiled and innocently flirted with each other, neither intending nor expecting anything beyond friendship during school.

During the second semester, Levi and Rose were in the same class and, again, sat next to each other. Levi smiled and flirted with Rose and she reciprocated. He seemed to like her more than she liked him. However, he always chose to sit next to her. Perhaps Rose held back her expression of affection since she knew her father and knew how upset he would be if he thought they liked each other. Really, a Catholic and a Jew?

Levi and Rose worked together on group class projects. They often drove across the Market Street Bridge to Kingston to get sandwiches at Levi's favorite delicatessen, "Goldstein's," to discuss their projects. This was looking more like romance than friendship.

They kept telling themselves, "Nothing is going on here; we're just friends."

They knew if they got involved, their parents would kill them—literally kill them!

During summer break after their first year at Bucknell, Levi and Rose didn't see each other and their mutual interest waned. Levi worked in his father's clothing store and Rose worked in her neighbor's accounting office.

Sometimes feelings lessen; sometimes feelings intensify. Who knows why that happens?

The second year started with another class in which Levi and Rose were together. When Levi saw Rose, he got up to sit next to her.

Rose remembered Levi accused her of following him around and she quickly said, "Are you following me around?"

"No, this seat has a better view."

"Better view of what?"

"You!"

The feelings developing between these two seemed to rush back as if they'd never been apart. Levi and Rose continued to talk and smile at each other. Soon came the group assignments and they volunteered to work together again. Their friendship grew as time went on, a friendship on which both had placed a boundary. During downtime with their projects, there were many discussions about life, religion, and politics. They seemed to enjoy their time together, especially their philosophical discussions.

One day after class, Levi asked Rose if he could take her to dinner.

"Levi, you know we can't do that. What will our parents say?"

"Neither of us knows what they would say. It's only dinner."

"I don't think it's a good idea."

The next day, Levi repeated his request. Again, Rose turned him down.

Levi decided to give it some time before asking again.

A week later, Levi asked Rose to dinner again. Rose declined once more.

He thought, "In the beginning, when Rose said 'no,' her tone implied 'absolutely not,' but now her 'no' sounds more like 'I don't think so.' In fact, she was starting to be less emphatic and 'no' was starting to sound like, 'Maybe.' "

Levi believed he was making progress in his pursuit of Rose. So, he decided he would ask her out to dinner again the following week.

He thought, "Surely she can't keep saying no. Maybe I need to be more formal so she knows I'm serious. Maybe then, she'll say yes."

So he asked her, "Rose, will you honor me with the presence of your company at dinner Saturday night?"

"No!"

"Rose, you know I'll keep asking until you agree to go out with me."

"What about religion?" Rose said to Levi. "We don't believe in the same thing."

"Perhaps but we're not that far off--we both believe in God, we both believe in the Golden Rule, we both believe if we're good and honest people we'll go to Heaven. I don't think God distinguishes whom He lets into Heaven based on the circumstances in which they were born or raised, but by their deeds. He doesn't only let Catholics in, only let Jews in, or only let Protestants in for that matter. From our conversations, you know this is my belief."

"I agree with you."

"If you believe what I believe, why won't you go out with me?" Levi asked.

Rose said, "But you 'know' how our parents 'think.' "

Rose thought for a minute. "OK. If we go out, it'll be only one time. You'll see that being together outside of school will not be as great as you think. One date and you'll get it out of your system. Promise you won't ask me to go for dinner again. Just once!"

"OK. We aren't getting married. We'll eat, we'll talk, and we'll enjoy each other's company."

"We can go out to dinner, but we just can't get serious about this."

This was the first step toward becoming more than friends.

Levi told Rose, "I'm very happy about all we have in

common. We have the same outlook on life; we share the same view of the world; we like the same recreational activities; and we like the same music."

That weekend, they went out for dinner.

After dinner, Levi told Rose, "I had a very good time tonight."

"I had a good time as well."

"How about going to a movie with me next Saturday?"

"I thought we agreed we would go out one time."

"We said we would only go for dinner one time. Now I'm asking you to go out for a movie."

"I'll think about it."

As anticipated, Levi and Rose went out again.

After the third date, Levi decided it was time to kiss Rose. He walked her to the door and just stood there. He was leaning toward her when the porch light went on. They both smiled and got embarrassed. "OK," he thought, "Maybe next time."

On the next date, Levi decided to kiss Rose in the car before they walked to the door. After they kissed, they both knew they were in trouble. Rose thought, "There's no turning back now!"

As the dates—dinner, movies, sporting events-- continued over the next few months, discussions about religious similarities replaced "arguments" about religious differences. Then, there were discussions about raising children.

One day after class, Levi said to Rose, "I was thinking it would be nice for you to come to my house for dinner."

"Are your parents going to be OK with this?

"Yes. My father is a businessman and has many good ideas and I'd like for you to meet him."

"What does your family talk about during dinner?" Rose asked. "Do they talk about religion?"

"We talk about business, world events, growing up. Regular stuff like that. We **never** talk about religion."

"OK, then I'll come to dinner."

"What does your family talk about during dinner?"

"My parents talk about their friends, the old country, cooking at the restaurant, and how good or bad business has been."

"See, our families talk about the same thing—friends and business" said Levi.

Before dinner at the Rosenblooms and just before Levi left to pick up Rose for dinner, he cautioned his parents about the imminent dinner conversation.

Levi told his parents, "When Rose is here, let's talk about the usual things we talk about, but let's not talk about religion. I don't want to scare her away."

His mother Sylvia said,

"Levi, are you ashamed of your family?"

"Are you ashamed of our religion or our beliefs?"

"No," said Levi. "I just don't want to talk about religion tonight!"

During dinner at the Rosenblooms, there was the usual small talk about people the Rosenblooms and the Agostinos knew in common, talk about Rose's career plans, and some talk about running a business. It went well. Ira and Sylvia behaved. Levi was very pleased and so proud of his parents because religion never came up in the conversation, not even once!

Over the next few months, there were many discussions about mixed faith marriages—as if there ever was to be a marriage.

Levi and Rose soon finished their studies at Bucknell Junior College. Levi went to work in his father's store. Rose continued studying toward a degree in accounting.

One night at dinner, Ira, Sylvia, and Levi were discussing marriage and children. Ira told Levi, "I expect my grandsons to be raised Jewish. I'm less interested in what religion my granddaughters would follow."

Levi was upset but didn't say anything. He knew that Judaism revolves around the men. Levi didn't care what his father wanted; he just wanted to marry Rose.

During dinner one night, Levi said to Rose, "If we ever decide to get married, I would be OK to raise our children Catholic."

Rose said, "Are we having a philosophical discussion or are you asking me to marry you?"

"Yes. Let me make it official. Rose, will you marry me?"

"Yes."

Levi jumped out of his chair and hugged Rose. "I can't believe you said yes! After all this time, you gave me the impression that you didn't care for me, you said yes. I bet you knew all along I would ask you to marry me and you knew all along that you would say yes. I can't believe it. I'm so happy!"

"Me too."

Overhearing Levi and Rose's conversation, the other customers at the restaurant started clapping. Some of the women got up and hugged her; some of the men got up and shook hands with Levi.

Levi told Rose he wanted to take her shopping for an engagement ring. Before they would go though, Rose wanted Levi to ask her father if he could have her hand in marriage, as was the custom at the time. After all, Levi knew the Agostinos because his family often ate dinner at the restaurant.

Rose suggested, "I'd like you to say hello to my father in Italian. That'll "break the ice' and show a willingness to meet halfway."

Levi thought Rose's suggestion was good. He heard Rose greeting some of her friends in Italian. He could recite the greetings and could almost sound like an Italian. He just had to throw in some hand jesters as he spoke.

They left the restaurant holding hands and smiling from ear to ear. They were ecstatic; their feet hardly touched the ground.

A few days later, after Levi gathered enough courage and after he and Rose practiced what he would say, he went to

Dominic's restaurant, Coccina Italiano. He walked into the restaurant early in the morning and asked one of the waiters if he could speak with Mr. Agostino. Although he and his family had eaten at the restaurant many times, he'd never been in the kitchen.

As soon as Levi entered the kitchen, the cooking odors instantly distracted him. He loved Italian food and loved the sweet smell of simmering tomato sauce.

Dominic Agostino was preparing food on the island.

"Buongiorno, Mr. Agostino."

Hey Levi, "Buongiorno, Como stai?"

"Bene. Bene."

Once Levi said hello in Italian, he almost forgot what else he was supposed to say next.

He hesitated... and then said, "Mr. Agostino, I want to speak with you about something important."

"Sure, Levi, what can I do for you?"

Levi couldn't remember how he was to ask Mr. Agostino for Rose's hand. He and Rose practiced it but because of the sauce and because he was so nervous, he forgot.

Finally, Levi said, "Mr. Agostino, You know I'm fond of Rose and I love Italian food...I want to marry Rose..."

"What?" Dominic breaks in. "You want to marry my Rose?"

Levi reached into his pocket for his handkerchief and, wiped his forehead, "What do you think?"

"What do I think?"

"You're Jewish, that's what I think."

"Mr. Agostino, please let me finish. I can provide for Rose. Our clothing store is doing well. I promise to honor and respect her. I promise to honor and respect you and your family. I promise to be a good husband for her ...I'll be a good husband! You don't have to worry."

Dominic froze as if a robber came out of the alley with a gun and demanded all his money. His neurons just held onto the

19

words in his head and they couldn't come out.

He said, "We're Catholic. You're Jewish. We're not the same 'kind.' We don't think the same. What makes you think a mixed marriage like this would work?"

"Both our families believe in God, both our families believe in the Golden Rule, we believe if we're good people we'll get to Heaven. God looks to see if you've been a good person and treats everyone with respect. We aren't so different!"

Levi took a deep breath and wiped his forehead again. This time, he kept the handkerchief in his hand.

Dominic was quiet for a while, obviously thinking about what Levi said and returned to preparing the food.

Levi glanced at the door as if he were about to run out of the restaurant and wiped his forehead again.

"I know you can provide for my Rose. I'm not blind. I've seen how the two of you look at each other--I've watched Rose. She's happy, she smiles all the time, and she walks as if she's, and how do you say, in the clouds. But what about important things like children?"

"Will my grandchildren go to Catholic Church? Will they go to Catholic school?"

"Rose and I talked about children. We want to raise our children in the Catholic faith."

Dominic took his time thinking about what Levi asked. Thinking and chopping. At one point, he almost cut his finger chopping the onions.

One of the workers came in from the restaurant to ask Dominic a question.

It seemed like an eternity since Levi asked his question as he waited for Dominic's response.

While the waiter was asking *his* question, Dominic wasn't completely listening to the waiter.

Dominic said to Levi, "I have to sleep on it. Come back tomorrow morning."

"OK. Is 9 a.m. convenient?"

"Yes."

When Dominic got home from work, he woke up Concetta, Rose's mother, to talk about Levi's question.

Dominic said, "Levi Rosenbloom came to the restaurant this morning and asked me if he could marry our Rose. I knew they were going out but I hoped they wouldn't get serious. I didn't expect it to go this far."

"What did you tell him?"

"I didn't know what to tell him. I told him to come back tomorrow and I'd let him know."

"What are you going to tell him?"

"I don't like it—a Jew and a Catholic. What's this world coming to? What do his parents think about this? Do you think his parents are happy with this? Why didn't they stop him?"

Concetta said, "They're a nice family—I never heard anything bad about them."

"We're not going to marry his family, we're talking about our Rose and the problems she and her children are going to have with a mixed marriage."

"Let's try not to get too emotional. These kids have known each other for a couple of years since college and have been dating for a while. Nothing we said to Rose has discouraged her from wanting to be with Levi. They're going to do this whether we like it or not, with or without our blessing. You remember the Volpe girl. Her parents didn't want her to marry that Irish boy, she eloped, and now she doesn't even visit them at Christmas. I believe it's better to accept their love and have a good relationship with them than to say 'no' and risk losing our daughter. Other than being Jewish, what don't you like about him?"

"I like him OK. He talks about educated things though— [he's] not down-to-earth like us. I don't know if he's 'stuck up.' If they promise to raise the kids Catholic, our decision is easier."

21

"Do you think they'll promise to raise the kids Catholic?"

"He said they would."

"Do you trust him?"

"Yes, I trust him. He's a good man. I can tell."

The next morning at the restaurant, Levi talked with Dominic.

Because Dominic was nervous, his broken English was more broken than usual, He said, "Rose's mother and I talked last night. We know your father is honorable. Your family is nice. We like them. They come to the restaurant and are good customers. I like you but I want to be sure you respect my daughter and my family. Remember, honor and respect is the most important thing. If you promise to do this, I'll give you my blessing and hope you have a good marriage with lotsa bambinos--Catholic bambinos."

Six months later, Levi and Rose were married in the Catholic Church. It was a nice wedding. The bride was pretty, the groom was handsome, and the families were happy—even the Agostinos. The reception was at Coccina Italiano with practically everyone who lived in Northeast Pennsylvania attending. The couple went to the Poconos for their honeymoon and set up housekeeping on Swallow Street in Pittston.

In 1941, Levi and Rose gave birth to a son. In keeping with Italian tradition, they named their first son Dominic after Rose's father. He would be the successor to the Rosenbloom clothing store when he became of age.

In 1942, there was another child, Maria Concetta.

A year later, in 1943, I was born.

***

History of Wyoming Valley

WYOMING VALLEY consisted of Scranton, Wilkes-Barre, Pittston, and adjacent towns, along a section of the Susquehanna

River, which flows from Upstate New York to Northern Maryland.

Farms were scattered on the hills of both sides of the river; coalmines were located in the valleys. Many immigrants from Italy, Germany, Poland, Ireland, and Scotland found this area attractive because they could use the farming and mining skills they knew well. In addition to job opportunities, the countryside with its rolling hills resembled the rolling hills of Europe, which made them feel at home.

Farming, done mostly by German settlers, provided food needed for the growing population. Some immigrants were fortunate to buy some land; others worked for landowners until they could save enough to buy their own land.

Wyoming Valley was rich in highly sought after Anthracite coal used by industry because it was clean-burning and hotter than bituminous coal found in Virginia and West Virginia. The history of the mines in Wyoming Valley began with the Welch and Irish who arrived early on to create companies in charge of working the mines. Many of them were experienced miners; some were merely laborers.

Soon after the first wave of immigrants settled in the area, Italians and Slovaks immigrated to claim their share of this opportunity. In addition to the need for coal miners, was the need for support services such as grocery stores, clothing stores, tailors, shoemakers, doctors, and carpenters. This need presented special opportunities for skilled laborers as well as miners.

Jews from Germany and Poland were the last to immigrate to Wyoming Valley. This group came from a wealthier class, was more educated, and had some "seed" money. With their seed money, they opened businesses such as clothing stores, dress factories, and textile mills.

Once the men found their way in the new country, they sent for their wives and families. Wives and daughters found jobs in some of the mills and in the garment industry.

After World War II, jobs were available for anyone who wanted to work—things were good! People bought homes. Detroit automakers created the "buy now, pay later" mentality, so people bought cars to park in front of their new homes.

Inside their homes, they had washing machines, transistor radios, and television sets— at first black and white and then color. Seventy-five percent of households watched shows such as "I Love Lucy" and soap operas (so named because soap companies sponsored them).

Consumer products became more creative: The Polaroid Camera, Ban Roll-On deodorant, and Playboy Magazine with Marilyn Monroe on the cover girl and as the nude centerfold.

Women expected to be married and ready to have children by twenty. If they worked, they happily gave up their jobs once they started a family.

Chapter 3

Elementary School

1948-1955

MY TWO SIBLINGS ATTENDED Saint Rocco's Elementary School. Every morning, my mother drove us to school and then went to mass. After mass, she visited the Rectory (Priest's home) or the Convent (Nun's home) to say hello and to see if anyone needed help with shopping or cooking. That was her daily routine.

Although we lived on Swallow Street, a few blocks away from Saint Rocco's, we couldn't walk to school. Main Street crossed between our house and the school and it was too dangerous to cross the street alone.

My first day at school was not as scary as it was for some of the other kids. My older brother, Dominic, and my sister, Maria, minimized the scary part—leaving my mother, finding the bathroom, and waiting for lunch. When you're a kid, you focus on different things.

I didn't know anyone. Most of the kids were from the surrounding area, a few blocks away. Some of them lived far away in West Pittston. They all had Italian last names; I was the only one in my class whose name didn't end with a vowel.

Of course, I felt a little awkward. I stood out in my class because, before my parents married, they agreed to raise their children Catholic and for them to attend Catholic school. However, this wasn't a problem since I was flexible. I quickly made friends and easily adjusted to new surroundings.

Two weeks after starting first grade, I joined the Cub Scouts. Den 303 met every Tuesday in the basement of Saint Rocco's Church. There I saw Sal Greco and Ted Mosconi both of whom were in my class. Mike Costanzo, my neighbor on Swallow Street, was also a Cub Scout. Mike went to the Pittston School District. During our first Cub Scout meeting, the four of us instantly became friends. It was then we made a pact to "be friends for life."

After the meeting, we talked about our first day of school.

Ted lived on Main Street about five blocks from school.

He said, "I didn't have any problem since my father drove me to school. Some other kids from where I live also come to Saint Rocco's Church, Saint Rocco's School, and are in the Cub Scouts."

Sal said, "I don't have any brothers or sisters. Even though I was only two blocks from school, I didn't want to leave my mother."

"My mother, Katie, walked me all the way to school. I cried all the way. She cried all the way. I didn't want to let go of her hand. She held on to my hand as tightly as she could. My sweaty hands felt glued to hers. The second day my mother told me she would walk with me to the end of Railroad Street and I had to walk the rest of the way on Tompkins Street to school. She promised she would stand on the corner and watch until I got to school. Every few steps, I turned around to see if she was still watching--she was. Each time I turned around, she waved."

Mike didn't have a problem making the transition to school.

He said, "What's the big deal? At some point, you have to come out from behind your mother's apron and leave the house."

So, we successfully managed our first major task of "cutting the cord" and leaving our mothers.

Grade school was straight forward—reading, writing, arithmetic, and games. There were opportunities to participate in art and music. It was easy stuff, fun stuff.

In 1950, when Sal was seven, his parents bought a store on Main Street with an apartment behind it, three doors away from his father's barbershop. They moved from Railroad Street and lived behind the store. Sal and Ted now lived across the street from each other on Main Street; Mike and I lived a few doors away from each other on Swallow Street.

Our world, where we hung out, consisted of three-square blocks--less than one square mile of learning opportunities. Our neighborhood offered us a chance to learn about things—life things, not academic things. Our parents looked at it as "less than one square mile of places to get into trouble."

Main Street had many small businesses including a sheet metal shop, a taxi company, a vending machine company, and a social club--the Serradifalco Society. There were two butcher shops, a bakeshop, a supermarket, Il Primo Ristorante, and the Slocum Dress company. Uncles Mike and Sam Piazza owned Il Primo Ristorante.

These were Sal's uncles. We always referred to our friend's aunts and uncles as if they were our own.

Across the street from Pittston Taxi was Mack's Department Store owned by Ted's grandparents. Ted and his family lived in an apartment above the store.

In an alley behind Sal's apartment were a lumberyard, the taxi repair shop, and a "junk yard."

Like most kid's, we were curious about everything. We learned how to fix cars at the taxi repair shop. The mechanic even let Sal drive the taxis up and down the alley. Sal knew this "experience" would prepare him to drive once he was old enough to get his license. One time he hit the wall head on when he was parking the car. It was only the bumper and there wasn't any damage to the car. You had to get close to the wall to see the crack. Well, he was just learning!

The lumberyard supervisor, Mr. Johnson, taught us about building materials and tools. Next to the taxi garage and across from the lumberyard lived a black woman named Cora Smith. She had to be a hundred years old! She lived alone and was the only black person who lived in Pittston. No one knew where she came from or if she had any family. She sat on the porch every day, watched us play, smiled, waved, and waited for the mailman. Every now and then, she would give us lemonade. It was good!

We all played baseball in the alley and, one day, I walked up on Cora's porch and two boards cracked under my foot. We asked Mr. Johnson if he had any boards to fix Cora's porch. He gave us enough tongue-and-groove boards (the good stuff) and nails to replace the front porch. He showed us how to remove the old boards and how to install the new boards. Once we caught on, he set us free. We were carpenters!

One of the butcher shops prepared live chickens in the alley under the store. When a customer wanted to buy a chicken, one of the employees took a chicken from a cage and killed it. He drained the blood, gutted the chicken, and removed the feathers. Although we didn't participate in this process, it was very impressive. Ted couldn't watch since he thought it was "sickening" and couldn't understand why we liked going there.

Edelstein's, the junk yard, bought scrap paper, scrap metal, and sold cloth to make things such as bedspreads, drapes, and clothing. Any time we were short on spending money, we would scour the neighborhood to collect newspapers, cardboard, and scrap metals to sell to the junk yard. We could always count on Edelstein's for extra spending money.

One time Sal found a manikin in the alley behind a clothing store and started to carry it toward his house.

I asked, "What are you going to do with that?"

He said, "You never know when you'll need a manikin. Something will come up."

We also saved pieces of lumber, bolts, nails, and stuff like that—we knew they would come in handy someday.

Everything we needed was within a few blocks: family, school, church, grocery stores, a movie theater, doctors, and dentists. We didn't need lawyers back then—no one needed lawyers at that time—because we never would have thought to sue anyone.

In 1951, Ted and his family (Parents Louis and Ann and younger sisters Lois and Joan) bought a television. They invited Sal to watch the I Love Lucy show. He didn't have a television and, up to that time, he and other kids walked to Barton's Furniture Store, down the street, to watch TV. Barton's had a TV in the front window facing the street. They left the television on with an outside speaker. As long as the weather was good, everyone had a good time.

The next year, Sal had a crush on Ted's sister, Lois. He got a Valentine card from his mother's store and some candy and brought them over to her apartment across the street. He knocked on the door and Ted's mother, Ann, answered.

Ann said, "Well, hello Sal. How are you?"

Sal's voice trembled as he asked, "Is Lois home?"

Ann smiled as she saw the things in Sal's hand and said, "Yes."

"Can I talk with her?"

"Yes, I'll get her."

When Lois came to the door, Sal said, "Happy Valentine's Day."

He gave her the card, the candy, and a quick kiss on the cheek.

Then he did what any normal nine-year old would do ...he ran home. Well, everyone got a kick out of that—Sal's first crush, his first valentine, his first kiss, and his first embarrassing moment with the opposite sex. And to think, he and Ted are still friends!

During our summers, we went to Harvey's Lake to swim and to Atlantic City for our yearly vacations.

Each year, school got a little more complicated. In addition to reading, math and writing, there were several plays a year and weekly singing, both of which were mandatory. During "recess," the boys and girls separated and played in the lot behind the school.

Playtime occurred daily throughout the school year—rain, shine, or snow. Academically, the instruction that separated Saint Rocco's from the public schools was Catechism--lessons in theology. So, academically, we learned what other kids learned and we learned about Catholicism. School wasn't that complicated.

During the summer of 1955, I went with Sal and Ted to Atlantic City for vacation. We were lying on the beach and noticed something new. There were college-aged guys carrying boxes over their shoulders. The box was about 12" x 24" x 24".

They were walking around shouting, "Ice cream and ice; get your chick a lick on a stick."

When I heard "ice cream," I stopped listening. Sal, on the other hand, heard the "Get your chick a lick on a stick" and asked what we thought that meant. We thought they were selling popsicles. He thought there was a hidden meaning. We couldn't ask his mother since that would have been embarrassing. We waited until we got home to ask Mike.

At home, we asked Mike about our observation and he thought they were just selling ice cream. End of story. Mike was smart and knew lots of things. We trusted him.

The cub scouts had activities such as hiking, fishing, camping, and play-acting. We also had fundraising once a year to offset the costs of the Den.

Hiking was our favorite pastime. We met at the church and rode to a location from which we hiked. Once at our destination, we grilled hamburgers or ate sandwiches our mother's made and packed for us. After lunch, we fished or hiked again. We had activities to instill Cub Scout values such as Fun and Adventure,

Character Development, Respect, Personal Achievement, and Spirituality. It must have worked since we were all good kids!

One time our Den put on a "Hawaiian Night" event. Our mothers prepared Hawaiian food. Ted, Sal, and I went on stage and performed a Hula dance. There we were with long grass skirts trying to dance the Hula. Talk about embarrassing! We each received a set of pictures. Sal and I still have ours.

Another time, we hiked along the railroad tracks until we got to Suscon Lake. We sat on a rock wall to have lunch. As we were eating lunch, we looked down. There were snakes everywhere with their heads sticking out between the rocks. We all screamed and jumped off the wall. Good thing they were black snakes. It could have been disastrous if they were poisonous!

I have some vivid memories of my years at Saint Rocco's school. Probably, what I remember mostly is the strict discipline imposed by the nuns. They freely used the ruler to slap your hands if they believed you misbehaved. One time, in the sixth grade, Sister Mary Alice hit Sal with a ruler for starting to sing before it was time. He grabbed the ruler out of her hand. I suppose he had enough of her type of discipline. The principal called his mother to the office but his mother defended him. The following year, Sal left Saint Rocco's to go to Pittston Junior high School.

Several nuns over the years at Saint Rocco's had chastised me for not paying attention in class because I was "doodling." I often drew pictures of my classmates or my teachers. The nuns believed the drawings were doodles. Mike, Ted, and Sal thought the sketches I did were good pictures.

I sketched Sister Anna Marie, our sixth grade teacher. It was an amazing likeness of her in her little nun's outfit. I added "horns" to the sketch. As I was showing it to Sal, I felt someone behind me. It was Sister Anna Marie behind me. She had a different opinion of my artwork.

She said, "Well, well, well. And, what do we have here?"

"It's just a drawing of my favorite teacher."

"And, the 'horns?'"

"Those are horns?"

"They look like horns to me."

"No, sister, they're part of your hat."

"I don't think so. I'm taking this 'chicken scratch' to the principal."

Instead of seeing my drawing for the artwork it was, she was irritated. The next day, I showed up with a new drawing—this time I added horns and a pitchfork. Sister Anna Marie never saw this one. I told Ted and Sal I would keep this sketch hidden at home since I liked to keep a record of important moments in my life.

At the end of eighth grade, Ted left to go to Saint John's Catholic School where he graduated. I went to Wyoming Seminary, a high school prep school famous for producing doctors, dentists, lawyers, politicians, and other high-profile careers. Mike went to Pittston public schools during his entire elementary education.

***

History of Railroad Street

THE CITY RENAMED Railroad Street, the street on which Sal grew up. The story goes like this, there were so many murders on Railroad Street it was getting a bad name. One time, someone murdered a Mafia boss in cold blood. The man pointed the gun at him pointblank and pulled the trigger.

The Mafioso was so mean to everyone, all the people who lived on second floor apartments above the stores came down to the street to spit on him. After everyone spit on him, they stood there and clapped because he was dead.

Railroad Street was renamed Columbus Avenue in an attempt to give it some class. I don't know. Maybe it worked, maybe not.

Pittston was nicknamed "Pistol City" for obvious reasons.

History of *Saint Rocco's Church*

ITALIANS WANTED THEIR own Catholic Church in Pittston—just as they had in Italy.

In 1919, immigrants from southern Italy and Sicily formed "The Saint Rocco Society" in Pittston. A year later, Pittston had a new church on West Oak Street, Saint Rocco's Roman Catholic Church. Saint Rocco's was an Italian Church with Reverend John DePietro, a member of the Oblates of Saint Joseph and a native of Italy, as its first priest.

Many communities had clusters of immigrants from Italy, Poland, Ireland, Germany, and other European countries. Most of these communities started a church and a school for their ethnic groups—they wanted to be in America but didn't want to give up everything they had in the old country.

Italian, Irish, and Polish Societies and other similar groups supported their churches and schools. The respective church congregations, likewise, became predominantly Italian, Irish, Polish, and so forth.

These churches filled a niche providing comfort and support for newly arriving immigrants who lived within a few blocks of the church. These proud immigrants didn't ask the government for support--food stamps and Medicaid didn't exist. They were happy for the opportunity to work for a living. Every Sunday at Saint Rocco's Church, the priest gave one sermon in Italian and the rest were in English.

In 1945, the Religious Sisters of Saint Lucy Filippini arrived in Pittston to create a school, known as Saint Rocco's Parochial School, which officially opened in 1946 and remained opened for 25 years. Parents expected private, Catholic schools to provide an academic education as well as a religious education. They also accepted other nationalities.

Music was important to us. We listened to Elvis Presley, Danny and the Juniors, the Platters, the Everly Brothers, and Ricky Nelson...

Chapter 4

Junior High School

1955-1957

We were scattered around town in different neighborhoods and in different schools but we managed to stay close friends. Mike and Sal were having fun at Cleveland School; Ted and I continued to endure the torture from the nuns at Saint Rocco's Catholic School. My mother was motivated to keep me in Saint Rocco's School since that was my link to Catholicism. She may have been afraid I would lose that connection. Sal missed poking fun at the nuns but he had new targets for his antics.

Sal's mother was busy in her store. She opened at 7 a.m. and closed at 6 p.m. His parents worked hard saving for things they wanted—a car, a house, and vacations.

The formula by which our families lived was:

1. Live below your means,
2. Save as much money as you can, and
3. Pay cash for what you want once you saved enough money.

Our parents saved for their first cars, paid cash for them, and then started to save for houses. They didn't have credit cards.

In 1955, Sal's grandfather, Salvatore Greco, died. Sal was upset, as were his aunts, and uncles. Losing such a patriarch was difficult for everyone. Uncle Joe Greco stepped in to replace him as the head of the family.

At the funeral, Aunt Lena Greco told us a story of when she was in ninth grade walking home from school one day and encountered a bully...

One of the older boys, an Irish boy, standing in front of the poolroom with his friends, told her:

"Hey 'Dago,' get off the sidewalk and walk in the street. You're not good enough to walk on our sidewalk!"

She walked along the gutter until she was safely away from the boys. When she walked into the house with tears in her eyes, Sal's grandfather asked her why she was crying.

"Lena, what's wrong?"

"A boy who goes to my school called me names and made me walk in the gutter in front of the poolroom. He said I wasn't good enough to walk on the sidewalk."

"Do you know this boy?"

"Yes, it was Johnnie McNulty, a boy a year older than me in school. He's in the tenth grade."

The Greco family was quiet and peaceful. They never invited confrontation. However, this incident exceeded the patience of even Sal's grandfather.

Salvatore Greco was only five foot, six inches tall, but because he walked proud, the impression he gave was of being six feet tall. He had thick, brown hair, olive skin, and a handlebar mustache. He grabbed his shotgun in one hand and Lena in the other hand and proceeded to take her back three blocks in his bare feet, long johns, and suspendered pants to speak with this "boy." Sal's grandmother, Maria, grabbed the rosary beads to pray that no one would be killed.

When they arrived at the poolroom, there was Johnny McNulty standing with his friends and smoking a cigarette.

"Lena, which of these boys called you names?"

"It was the boy in the gray plaid shirt."

"Are you Johnny McNulty?"

"Yes," said Johnny, with a frightened, crackling voice. He

wasn't the arrogant bully he was earlier when Lena Greco was walking home by herself. Of course, when you're fifteen and someone is talking to you with a shotgun, scared is a normal response.

"Did you call my Lena names?"

"Yes, Mr. Greco but I didn't mean it. I was only kidding. You know how us kids like to tease!"

"Did you make her walk in the gutter?"

"Yes, Mr. Greco but I was only playing."

"Playing? I don't think so. You need to apologize to her right now."

"Yes sir."

Johnny looked at Lena and said, "I'm sorry I called you names and made you walk in the street. It will never happen again."

Sal's grandfather said, "You're right, Johnny. It will never happen again because I'm holding you responsible for anything that happens like this again. If anything happens to **any** of my children, I'm going to come after you. Do you understand?"

"Yes, Mr. Greco, nothing will happen again. You can count on me."

There were no future incidents in the Greco family and Lena never had to walk in the street again.

Mike, Ted, Sal, and I graduated from Cub Scouts, Den 303, and moved onto the Boy Scouts, Troup 303. We all continued to go to Harvey's Lake on Sundays and to Atlantic City one week during the summer.

During High School, we spent most of our time listening to music--record hops with disc jockeys and dances with live bands. Elvis became a phenomenon and changed the world—at least our world. For our parents, Elvis represented the kid from the proverbial other side of the tracks—, the kid our parents wanted us to avoid.

His music and persona, however, were so overwhelming that our parents were powerless to stem the tide. The rock and roll explosion ushered in singers such as Neil Diamond, Bobby Darin, Ray Charles, Tony Bennett, Bob Dylan, and Paul Anka to name a few. Some of these artists still perform today; others died tragically. WARM radio (590 on your dial), Scranton, Pennsylvania, expanded to round the clock music.

Rocky Glen Amusement Park in Moosic, Pennsylvania, hosted many musicians. It was an escape from reality for teenagers from Northeastern Pennsylvania, the Pocono Mountains, Philadelphia, and New York. Live, outdoor concerts drew as many as 100,000 people. Teenagers swarmed upon Rocky Glen Park like bees to a hive to listen to some of their favorite artists--Chubby Checker, Bobby Rydell, Bobby Vinton, Neil Diamond, and Fabian.

We saw Neil Diamond live.

When we weren't listening to music, we watched TV shows--"I Love Lucy," "Have Gun Will Travel," "Bonanza," "The Honeymooners," "Dragnet," "Twilight Zone," "Perry Mason," "Alfred Hitchcock," and Dennis the Menace."

Walter Cronkite reported the news.

Albert Sabin developed an oral polio vaccine.

Chapter 5

High School

1957-1961

HIGH SCHOOL ISOLATED us geographically but it didn't isolate us emotionally. Our new schools gave us opportunities to interact with other kids and we learned a new set of academic and social skills. Through this upheaval, we stayed best friends.

After school, we met at the "Music Box" on Main Street in Pittston to listen to records. On Monday nights, we met at Saint Rocco's Church dances to hear live music. "Mel Wynn and the Rhythm Aces" and "Joe Nardone's All Stars" performed live. We followed the bands to wherever they played. Occasionally, with our older friends, we snuck to San Souci Park dances in Hanover Township—not the place we could tell our parents about.

It was a great time to grow up--The dawn of Rock and Roll, lighthearted, funny TV shows, the world relatively at peace, significant advances in health, and many inventions to make life easier and more efficient. Although we knew this was a great time to grow up, our parents thought differently--the devil himself (Elvis) was taking over their children!

Our circle of friends expanded to include kids from each of our respective high schools. Although there were others who came in and out of our group, the four of us constituted the core group of close friends. After all, we had a lot of stuff going on—dances, dating, and sports. Although I went to Wyoming Seminary, I cheered for the Pittston teams as did Mike and Sal. Of course, Ted cheered for Pittston except when Pittston High School played Saint John's High School.

My father encouraged me to choose non-denominational, hundred-year-old Wyoming Seminary high school. There, he believed I would have the best chance at a good education.

My "doodling" had advanced since my days at Saint Rocco's and my drawings evolved into pen-and-ink sketches. My grandfather, Dominic, gave me a fountain pen for confirmation and I used it for many of my sketches. Although I sketched historic sites around Scranton, Wilkes-Barre, and the Pocono Mountains in Pennsylvania, my real passion was drawing people.

"People have character; they have emotions, I can get into their souls with my sketches."

Popular people around Wyoming Valley became my subjects, some of whom I met when they ate at my grandfather's restaurant, Coccina Italiano, in West Pittston.

My parents were outgoing and they constantly put me in situations that encouraged social interaction—at school, at the clothing store, and at the restaurant. I waited on tables at the restaurant and waited on customers in the store.

Wyoming Seminary differed from Saint Rocco's grade school. My classmates were children of successful businessmen--doctors, dentists, lawyers, and educators. Saint Rocco's had a few professional parents, second generation Italians, but most were first generation immigrants who struggled to make a living.

Although I was among affluent students at Wyoming Seminary, I stayed grounded. This environment didn't negatively affect my personality or my friendship with my real friends. Unlike Saint Rocco's grade school, which had mostly Italian, Catholic students, Wyoming Seminary had a large proportion of Jewish students, most of whom, like my father, were progressive

Jews.

Two Jewish students in my class asked me to join a study group. My new friends, David Silverman and Alan Miller, lived in Kingston. David's father was a dentist and Alan's father owned a car dealership. We studied together in the library, which was convenient for all of us since I lived in Pittston, 20 minutes away from Kingston.

During study group, we often discussed careers, religion, and girls. I told them about my pen-and-ink sketches and my dream of becoming an artist. David wanted to be a dentist like his father and Alan was going to take over his father's car business. David and Alan were curious about growing up Catholic. I told them I was happy and made many quality friends at Saint Rocco's Catholic School. I also said I respected my parent's decision to raise me Catholic.

Although happy to be Catholic, I was curious about conversations I overheard about Jewish Holidays and bar mitzvahs. When I was a sophomore, I asked David and Alan about bar mitzvahs. Both had recently celebrated their own bar mitzvahs.

I said, "Exactly what is a bar mitzvah?"

Alan said, "Do you want the short version or the long version?"

"Just the basics, it isn't like I'm studying for a test."

David said to Alan, "Let me handle this—he'll want to hear it from the horse's mouth. First, being a Jew is complicated; history and nationality contribute to our beliefs. There are essentially two main types of Jews— Orthodox and Reform or Progressive. Albert Einstein and Sigmund Freud were progressive Jews. Most of the Jews in America are Progressive-- Ashkenazim Jews who came from Germany and Central and Eastern Europe. Alan and I are progressive and have a little different slant on what we celebrate and observe within our religion than Orthodox Jews. We're all Jews and have the same

41

beliefs but we have a different emphasis on traditions and celebrations."

Alan said, "A bar mitzvah is when boys grow up—the 'coming of age.' Bat mitzvah is the 'coming of age' for Jewish girls. Bar mitzvah is very important, bat mitzvah, not so much. Orthodox Jews don't recognize bat Mitzvah at all since they believe girls are less important than boys."

I said, "Wow. What do your mothers and sisters think about an attitude like that?"

David ignored my question, which appeared to show too much empathy for women and said, "All religions have age-related milestones. In our faith, thirteen years of age is a milestone for boys—they go from childhood to adulthood. This is a big deal because prior to this milestone, parents are responsible for everything their children do. Once a boy becomes an adult and has a bar Mitzvah, he is responsible for his actions and behavior. With girls, the age is twelve because girls mature more quickly than boys."

Alan said, "I had a big party for my bar mitzvah."

I said, "A party?"

David said, "Don't listen to him. There could be a party but not necessarily. Some people have parties. I didn't. I had dinner with family and friends—nothing extravagant. However, I did get a few gifts. I don't know if the party was for me or for my parents who were no longer responsible for me. My father thanked God I made it to adulthood without him being called in by the police or, even worse, by Rabbi Horowitz."

I asked, "Did you have to study for your bar mitzvah?"

David said, "Alan, let me take this one as well. You need some background information. There is a weekly 'holiday' called a Shabbat, which begins at sundown on Friday night and ends at sundown on Saturday night. During Shabbat and other holidays, we pray and read the Torah in the synagogue. People attending read and pray and it's considered an honor to be called to read."

"That would do me in." I said. "I hate to be in front of people and I don't like to be the center of attention. I'm really nervous at times like that."

David said, "Once a boy has a thirteenth birthday, his bar mitzvah is held on the next scheduled 'reading day,' a celebration takes place immediately following the ceremony at the synagogue. As Alan said, at times, there are parties. The tendency is to have bigger and bigger celebrations, sometimes bigger than a wedding.

"In our religion, the ceremony is more important than the celebration. During the celebration, there are gifts of religious books and gifts of money or stock, usually in multiples of eighteen. Many men will receive their first set of Tefillin, which is a black leather box containing parchment inscribed with biblical passages.

"Some of the older, unmarried women, in their twenties, come to a bar mitzvah to see if they can find eligible bachelors— you know, brothers or uncles," Alan said. "Once you become of age, some of the high school girls want to see if they can 'break you in' if you haven't had sex. It's sort of a challenge to them.

"Alan received one hundred, eighty shares of General Motors stock," David said. "Of course, what would you expect since his father sells Cadillacs?

"Rabbi Horowitz taught us to read and speak Hebrew."

I said, "Wow, you can read Hebrew? Is speaking Hebrew harder than speaking Spanish?"

"Not that hard."

"I can speak Italian," I said, "but I don't know how to write it. Anyway, I guess confirmation is similar to bar mitzvah. When boys and girls are between twelve and fifteen years old, the bishop comes to the church to perform Confirmation. We study the catechism to prepare. During the ceremony, the bishop walks around asking questions. You have to know the answers if you want to be confirmed. The nuns tried to scare us into studying so they wouldn't look bad. I suppose they were successful since no one missed any questions. We also had a little party and got some gifts. No big deal."

"Why the age range?" Alan said.

"The bishop has a busy schedule and only performs confirmations every couple of years at any particular church."

"What's the matter," Alan said, "he can't take time off from his golf?"

David said, "Some Jewish traditions are based on history. Rosh Hashanah is the Jewish New Year--a day of remembrance and judgment in which Jews cast off the sins of the previous year. Sukkoth is a seven-day festival commemorating the years Jews spent in the desert on the way to the Promised Land. Hanukkah is the 'Festival of Lights' commemorating the defeat of the Seleucid Empire that tried to prevent Israeli Jews from praying. Passover is a fast of the first born to remember the 10th plague when God killed Egyptian's first born while sparing Jewish first born children."

I asked, "What's the big deal about pork?"

Alan said, "Pigs are considered dirty animals because they carry disease. Two thousand years ago, no one knew about the spread of disease. Orthodox Jews still believe the Rabbi must kill the animal to be safely eaten."

After my conversation with David and Alan, I asked my father if I could go to synagogue with him. My father often went to both the synagogue and to Saint Rocco's Church with the family. My mother, Rose, smiled and nodded with approval since she knew it would be good for me to learn about my father's religion.

Conversations about girls increasingly distracted us from our studies. My study group was more concerned about girls than about math; Alan was more interested in studying girls than studying anything else. Ted, Mike, and Sal liked girls more than they liked school and spent more time studying them than they did learning math and science.

Ted's family moved from their apartment above his grandfather's clothing store on Main Street to Market Street a few blocks away. Once Sal's parents saved enough money to buy a house, they sold their store on Main Street and moved to Swallow Street a few blocks away in the opposite direction from Ted's new house.

Although Sal was farther away from Ted, he now lived on the same street as Mike and me. Sal brought a lot of stuff he collected around Main Street to his new house. His mother wouldn't let him take the pinball machine that he wanted for his bedroom. Well, after a bit of discussion, he agreed with his mother, his bedroom was too small for anything other than a bed, a dresser, and a desk.

He thought, "Really, who needed the desk?"

We had a good time growing up. We met and had breakfast before going to Saint Rocco's Church for 11:00 a.m. Sunday Mass. We alternated at whose house we met. After breakfast, we walked to church. Since Sal's mother, Katie, made great pancakes, we met there more often than not on Sunday mornings. Katie would go to 9 a.m. mass to get home early enough to make breakfast for us.

When we got to church, Mike always took his seat at the end of the pew. Sal always sat next to Mike, then Ted, then me. We always kept that order no matter who sat with us. People often tripped over us to get to the middle of the pew. Mike had a habit of shaking his foot up and down during mass. Sometimes he would get going and the whole bench would shake—like an earthquake. He couldn't understand why people changed their seats and nobody wanted to sit in the same pew with us.

Just up the street from where Mike, Sal, and I lived was West Park. The Pittston High School football players practiced there every day after school. Coach Feleski looked like Jackie Gleason—big and round. During practice, he stood on the

45

sidelines in his windbreaker with his hands in his pockets mumbling something about what the players were doing wrong. He always had chewing tobacco in his mouth and the timing of his "spit" had a rhythm of its own. Occasionally he would call someone's name and tell him to "take a few laps" or "take a shower." These were a bunch of kids "playing" football. They weren't athletes. Of course, he knew that.

One year a fascinating thing happened, Coach Feleski got sick just before the beginning of football season and had to take off a year. The school contracted a local businessman to coach the team.

On the first day of practice, John Savakinis, the new coach arrived. He was tall, slim, and had on a gray sweat suit. He carried a clipboard and looked like he meant business.

Coach said, "OK. Gather around. I'm Coach Savakinis."

All the players huddled around the coach.

"While Coach Feleski is on leave for a year, and I'm your coach now. Practice will start promptly at 3 p.m. I won't put up with anyone who is late for practice. We'll start with stretching and calisthenics. After that, we'll practice our routines. Make sure that you know your plays and have memorized my 'playbook.' "

"After our routines, we'll take a run or two around the field. I'll do the calisthenics and laps with you. I expect you to give me at least one-hundred percent. Sissies can quit now."

Some of the players were mumbling. A lot of players and spectators thought Coach Savakinis was "crazy." Mike, Sal, and I didn't. He was organized and had a plan. The team was very successful that year. We called it!

Around 1960, my parents moved across the Susquehanna River from Pittston to West Pittston, Pennsylvania. There were advantages to living in West Pittston. My mother would be close to her parents, to her father's restaurant, and to her brothers, Uncle Giuseppe and Uncle Anthony, who had taken over the restaurant. Her younger sisters, Aunts Josephine, Mary, and Theresa still lived in Pittston. Aunt Angella, who married an attorney, also lived in West Pittston. I could go to the restaurant more easily to see my uncles. This was a good move for my parents but not so good for me. I thought my parents snatched me away from my "family," Mike and Sal.

Once my parents moved to West Pittston, they joined Fox Hill Country Club in Exeter, Pennsylvania. My grandfather, Dominic, was already a member. My father wanted to give his family and their children a place to socialize, a place to golf, and a place to swim. I looked forward to learning to play golf. My father and I took lessons from Felix Serafin, the head golf pro.

My mother wasn't interested in playing golf. She told my father, "Why would I want to play a game I can only play on Tuesdays and weekends after 2 p.m.? I'd rather shop. You golf, I'll shop!"

As people achieve financial success, they tend to move close to others in the same socioeconomic circumstance. With this success comes the yearning for a bigger house, a nicer car, membership at the Country Club, and access to better schools for their children. People in Pittston often moved to West Pittston once they "made it." It was just a given. That's what you did. No explanation was necessary.

We were busy little beavers. The high school years had their share of demands. There were new classes--serious classes--requiring more time to study and master. We needed to learn things to help us get into college and, ultimately, to get a "good job."

Just as moving to West Pittston was a well-known status symbol, getting a "good job" was something of which to be proud. When parents ran into each other at Church, at Insalaco's Supermarket, or at the bank, the question often asked was, "How is your son (or daughter) doing?" Parents looked forward to friends inquiring about their children—it gave them the opportunity to brag. "He's doing well. He got a *good* job" was the usual response. A "good job" was a job teaching or a job with the government. Both jobs were high on the bragging list. The expectation was just that--to be a teacher or a government worker but not to be a doctor or lawyer. Becoming a professional would happen in the next generation. We took it one-step at a time, one generation at a time.

There were also work demands. We needed to learn skills for the future. Throughout high school, I worked in my grandfather's restaurant, now run mostly by my uncles. The restaurant had some banquet rooms for catering weddings, funerals, graduation parties, and anniversaries.

I worked at the restaurant whenever there was a catering job. When I worked as a waiter in the restaurant, I met and sketched many interesting people. John D. McArthur, a local philanthropist; Lou "Machine Gun" Butera, a professional pool player famous for his rapid pool shots; Charley Trippi, a professional football player born in Pittston and who dated Aunt Phyllis; Art Wall, a professional golfer; and Jimmy Cefalo, a journalist and news and sports broadcaster to name a few.

Famous politicians were customers of the restaurant. The most famous was John F. Kennedy who had dinner there during his campaign for presidency. Dan Flood, the U.S. Representative for the Wyoming Valley congressional district and frequent customer, convinced JFK to visit Wyoming Valley. When JFK came to town, Dan Flood took him for dinner at Coccina Italiano. I was helping at the restaurant and I was excited to meet a big celebrity. I asked if I could sketch them sitting at the table with my grandfather. They were happy to accommodate me.

I completed a sixteen by twenty inch pen-and-ink drawing of Dan Flood, JFK, Dominic, and my mother, who "happened" to be at the restaurant. My mother pretended not to want to sit at the table and had to be "coaxed" into it. I would cherish this drawing for the rest of my life. My mother would forever thank me for including her, always saying, "He's such a good boy, my Jeffrey!"

After all, everyone appreciates good food. At the restaurant, there were the typical Italian specialties such as pasta with marinara, Alfredo, garlic and oil, butter sauces, and pasta with vegetables such as broccoli, peas, and squash. Chicken and veal dishes such as Parmigiano, Françoise, Romano, Piccata, and Saltimbocca were a main stay. A traditional Sicilian favorite, Eggplant Parmigiano, was the house specialty.

In addition to the mob, "real Italians" gravitated to Coccina Italiano because all food was prepared from scratch, and a customer could ask Dominic to cook whatever he or she wanted to eat. An accommodating type, Dominic would cook anything his customers wanted.

"I don't care about the menu," Dominic would say. "Tell me what you want and I'll cook it."

He was never too busy to custom make any dish you wanted. He was never too busy to talk to customers when they were in the restaurant. He stopped at your table asking if everything was OK. When you have good food and are willing to please your customers, people will find you.

Wyoming Valley had its share of reputed mob figures. Many brought their families to Dominic's restaurant for dinner. The mob types were very demanding—never wanting what was on the menu but wanting something that fit their fancy. Dominic took care of them as he did everyone else who ate there. Although I waited on mobsters, I avoided interacting and sketching them for fear of getting in trouble. They would kill you as sure as look at you!

I also worked in my father's clothing store on Saturdays. I learned how to "dress" customers and, in so doing, learned how to dress myself. I helped in the store, but I really preferred working in the restaurant because I would meet interesting people to stimulate my creative side.

The summer before tenth grade, Sal worked in his uncle's restaurant in Pittston, IL Primo Ristorante. Sal's grandmother started the restaurant and his uncles, Mike and Sam Piazza, took over when she retired.

One Saturday, Il Primo Ristorante had two weddings, one in the upper catering hall and another in the lower level catering hall. Sal and I were in the upstairs kitchen. "Peaches" Tarantino, Aunt Sue Piazza's nephew, was working in the lower kitchen. The upstairs kitchen was directly above the lower kitchen and a rather primitive dumbwaiter connected them.

Someone could see from the upstairs kitchen to the lower kitchen through the opening of the dumbwaiter. At one point, Sal and I were standing next to the dumbwaiter and he looked into the lower kitchen and saw Peaches smoking a cigar. Sal and Peaches had this one-up-man-ship thing going on from grade school (Peaches started it!) and Sal just couldn't let this opportunity go by.

Sal said to me, "Watch this!"

Aunt Sue was working in the upper kitchen with two of Sal's cousins.

Sal said, "Aunt Sue, I didn't know Peaches smoked cigars."

"What cigars? He's smoking! I'll kill that son of a bitch."

Aunt Sue ran to the dumbwaiter opening and looked downstairs.

She said, "Peaches Tarantino, you little prick. Put out that goddamn cigar and get your sweet ass up here!" Aunt Sue was prone to cussing, and her language didn't surprise anyone.

Well, when Peaches got upstairs, he got the lecture of his life from Aunt Sue. Sal and I just smiled. He looked like he wanted to kick the shit out of us.

Mike worked in his Uncle Sam's tailor shop in Pittston and caddied at Fox Hill Country Club in West Pittston to earn some extra money. He became a good golfer by caddying.

Ted worked in his grandfather's clothing store in Pittston.

Because Ted's father was a social worker for the state, there wasn't much for Ted to learn at his father's work.

In addition to work demands, there were social demands, very serious social demands--learning to interact with the opposite sex—girls!

The social demands were more challenging because, after all, we were in the midst of puberty. What was once an easy interaction between boys and girls became more difficult. Before puberty, we didn't differentiate between girls and boys. We were just kids hanging out together and having fun. We just got along.

Now, for some boys, the girls were getting in the way. It was interesting to watch the social development. Some boys were shifting from an interest in sports like baseball to an interest in girls. Those who were "behind" in development and lacked interest in girls were disgusted with the boys who were more socially developed and, thus, more popular with girls. Friendships rapidly fell apart, albeit, only temporarily. This didn't affect our group—we had already developed beyond our years.

One of our favorite pastimes was going to Argento's deli around the corner and buying lunch. At Argento's we picked out a loaf of Italian bread baked that morning and asked Mr. Argento to make a sandwich for us. This was probably the beginning of the "foot long" hoagie, only we didn't know it. We would pick the cold cuts to put on the bread and Mr. Argento would cut the loaf into four sandwiches. We had a specific way we wanted our sandwich made. Not the typical way, but it was our way—it was our "Italian Hoagie." The order of stuff was important.

1. A loaf of Italian bread (about 6" x 18") cut lengthwise but not detached.

2. A thin layer of provolone cheese on the inside of both sides of the bread so when you bite into the sandwich, the provolone cheese touches the roof of your mouth.

3. A thin layer of Italian ham.
4. A thin layer of Genoa salami.
5. A thin layer of lean capicola--it had to be lean.
6. A layer of slivered black olives.
7. Torn romaine lettuce.
8. A generous sprinkling of oregano on the lettuce.
9. A little extra virgin olive oil.
10. Fold it and cut it into four sandwiches.

We sat on the porch and ate our sandwiches. During these lunches came some of the most interesting philosophical discussions about love, life, and our future.

During the summer, especially during the summer when we were bored, we liked doing pranks but not on each other. We had a "code" just as we had a "pact"--we wouldn't "prank" each other! We lived by this strict code and we would risk injury or even death before breaking it. When Sal's family moved to Swallow Street, he snuck what was left of the manikin he found in the alley behind a clothing store into his new house—the left leg. Mike came up with a good use for the leg.

On the corner across from Sal's house was a curb with a sewer under it. Mike came up with the idea to put the manikin leg in the sewer, thigh end first, and pretend we were trying to pull someone out of the sewer. So, three of us held the leg and the fourth ran back and forth as if in a panic around the other three holding the leg. The one running motioned to the others to pull the leg out of the sewer. The scenario was this: a car approached the intersection and the driver stopped and got out of the car.

Then, we would pull the leg out of the sewer and run away. We did this periodically for about a month when suddenly Lou Mantione, a Pittston policeman who went to Saint Rocco's Church, came to Sal's house and knocked on the door. Sal's mother answered the door and he was behind her with his head poking out.

Sergeant Mantione said to him, "We've had several reports about some kids playing jokes on drivers. Apparently, they have a manikin leg they put in the sewer and pull it out as a driver approached them. Do you know anything about this?"

Sal said, "I haven't seen anyone hanging around the corner."

Sergeant Mantione said, "Playing like this can cause an accident and I wouldn't want to see any of you kids get hurt."

"I'll be on the lookout and tell the rest of the "guys" about what you said. I don't think it will happen again."

The next Sunday we saw Sergeant Mantione in church and were glad he didn't ask about the manikin leg again. We wouldn't have been able to lie in church.

Other kids our age,--Jackie Adams, Chucky Grasso, Sonny Piero, and Al Pecorny--lived on Vine Street. Chucky Grasso was a major prankster. One day around July 4, Chucky Grasso had some fireworks he lit on the old wooden fence at the back of Sal's house. Afterwards, Chucky and Sal walked to West Park. When they got back, the fence had burned down. Sal's parents weren't too mad since they wanted to take down the fence anyway.

On another occasion, Chucky Grasso, Butchie Arcudi, who lived on Price Street next to Aunt Phyllis and Aunt Connie Piazza, Butchie's eight-year old nephew, and Sal went to the American Theater for a matinee. While they were in the theater, Chucky went to the men's room, lit a cherry bomb, and ran back to his seat next to where the rest of them were sitting. The firecracker went off and scared everyone.

Ten minutes later, the manager and a police officer came to their seats and escorted all of them to an awaiting squad car. The police took them to the police station and called their parents. Sal's mother was working at Il Primo Ristorante and had to leave work and walk down to the police station to get him. As he sat in one of the front offices, he saw his mother walking up the front steps.

As soon as she saw him, she started waving her fist.

She said, "Wait until I get you home!"

While they were walking back to Il Primo Ristorante, Sal explained to her that none of them knew what Chucky was going to do. She wasn't as mad because she knew Chucky was a troublemaker. However, Sal couldn't hang around with him anymore.

Mike, Ted, Sal, and my interests were changing. The heaviness of adolescence replaced the lightness of being a kid. High school sports like football, baseball, or basketball were less attractive to us. Our parents didn't push us to play sports. It just wasn't like that back then. Only a few kids were interested in playing sports, and there were only a few programs in which to participate.

We didn't have golf, t-ball, soccer, or lacrosse like schools have today. High school is more challenging now than in our day, especially after-school activities. Today, if both parents work and have a couple of children, the "rat race" begins from the moment the alarm clock sounds in the morning until bedtime.

Mike, Ted, Sal, and I accepted the social challenges. We learned to dance early by watching Dick Clark's *American Bandstand* on TV. Sal's mother could watch the dancers and teach the dances to us. In Sal's family, dressing well, looking good, interacting with his relatives seemed to have a greater significance than academics. Both Mike and Sal were good dancers and popular with the girls. Ted didn't know how to dance but was popular because he was a nice person and smiled a lot.

Wilkes-Barre had a copycat American Bandstand called TV Bandstand on channel 16, WNEP. High schools participated each weekday. A few times a year, high schools in Pittston were invited. Sal's mother drove him and Mike to the live show. A highlight of every show was the "multiplication dance" during which a couple started the dance and, periodically, when the music stopped, each person picked another partner until the end of the song. Sal's first experience was dancing to Fats Domino's *Blueberry Hill*. Since it was "Pittston Day," most people watched the program. His aunts, uncles, and friends at school who watched the program teased him-- really, really teased him.

School was easy for me—I was a quick learner and applied myself well. Attending class at Wyoming Seminary with smarter kids helped me to raise the bar. My parents were more aggressive in helping me with my studies since both were college educated. As time went on, I was more interested in studying and learning than I was in social events such as dances. Mike and Sal plugged along in school. Mike impressed more teachers than Sal did. Ted applied himself well since he was in a more demanding school and his family expected him to be a high achiever.

Sal was about to enter a new career. After his second year in high school, his father sent him to barber school since his father needed help in his barbershop on weekends. His father told him learning a trade would be a good thing to fall back on and he could always cut hair to make some spending money no matter what he did later. All the Greco men could cut hair and would often bring their sons to the barbershop. Once he became skilled enough to complete a haircut, he worked in the shop with his father on Saturdays.

We all got haircuts from Sal once he learned how to cut hair. His father had a typical barbershop including three barber chairs, a shoe-shine stand, and reading materials—Wall Street Journal, New York Times, Baron's, and US News and World Report (all of which he read daily). Between customers, his father read the financial publications. He was a successful stock investor with the information he learned from his reading. Sal said, "I always knew when the stock market was doing well because he'd smoke a "Tiparillo" cigar."

There also were Playboy magazines in the shop. His

customers were more interested in Playboy than the financial papers and magazines. One time, a man and his six-year-old son came to the shop for haircuts. While they were waiting for haircuts, the man picked up a Playboy magazine off the magazine rack. A few minutes later, Sal heard their conversation.

"Daddy, are those lungs?"

"Yes"

After that, Sal removed all the Playboy Magazines from the shop.

The major milestone in high school was turning sixteen and getting a driver's license. This was not as big a deal for the girls, but was a huge deal for the boys. We counted the days on the calendar until we could get our driver's permits. To us, driving was the milestone signifying we had "come of age." Forget confirmation and bar mitzvah. This was the defining moment for us.

We could get in the car and drive to places away from the "reporters" who would tattle tale to our parents. We could meet girls from other towns, go on dates, drive to dances, more easily sneak to the San Souci dances, and go to the Comerford drive-in movie theater and "make out." We could go to Harvey's Lake, state parks, and the Pocono Mountains by ourselves—by ourselves!--without our parents. Having a driver's license liberated us—cut the "apron strings." These were happy, carefree times. I mean, what could be more enjoyable than dating, dancing, drive-in theaters, making out, and growing up.

Once I got my driver's license during junior year, I asked Angie De La Cotti for a date since we danced together at Saint Rocco's dances and I liked her. She lived up the street from Saint Rocco's Church and was a senior. I got ready for my first "car" date, I washed the car, took a shower, put on a suit and tie, and off I went to get Angie. Her hair was styled; she had on a nice flowered dress and obviously primped for our date. We went to a movie in Wilkes-Barre and then to Boris' for hamburgers. Boris' served underage customers.

The waitress asked Angie, "What can I get you to drink?"

She said, "I'll have a Sloe Gin Fizz."

I had no idea what a "Sloe Gin Fizz" was but I wasn't about to appear inexperienced.

When the waitress asked what I wanted, I said, "I'll have the same."

We had a drink, a hamburger, and talked about dances and popular bands.

Later, when we got back to her house, I parked the car and we talked for a while. I leaned over to kiss Angie and, judging from her reaction, she was pleased I wanted to make out. We kissed for what seemed forever and, afterward, she said to me, "You make me feel so alive."

I thought, "God, what the hell does that mean?" I didn't know what to say or do so I kept kissing her. Finally, we pulled away, talked a little, and I got out of the car to walk her to the front door.

I couldn't wait to tell Mike, Ted, and Sal the next day at church about my date. I also couldn't wait to tell them what she said. Angie was older than I was; she dated mostly older guys who, obviously, were more experienced—a lot more experienced than I was. I was confused.

The next morning, when I saw Mike, Ted, and Sal at church, I told them about my date with Angie the night before and what she said.

I asked them, "What did she mean by that?"

Ted said, "I don't know."

Mike was laughing and said, "I don't know either, but it can't be good."

Sal said, "I don't think you should go out with her anymore. I didn't think you should have gone out with her in the first place."

I took Sal's advice and never asked her out again.

Driving made it easy to go to the prom. Sal went to Pittston

Prom three years in a row. When he was a sophomore, he was dating a girl who was a junior—she had her driver's license and drove her own car, a yellow Plymouth Fury convertible. His friends teased him about dating an older woman. He didn't care what they said; he was having a good time.

Going to the Music Box on Main Street and Saint Rocco's dances allowed us to meet girls from other high schools-Saint John's, West Pittston, Wyoming, Dupont, and Duryea. I went to my Wyoming Seminary Prom, West Pittston Prom, and Wyoming Prom. Mike took Ted's sister, Lois, to his prom—yes, the girl who Sal gave the Valentine's Day Card and candy. Mike must have behaved since he is still alive and he and Ted are still friends.

We could now drive to Old Forge, Pennsylvania, which had many Italian restaurants. No matter where you lived, Old Forge was the place to eat. "Mom and Pop" restaurants and pizza parlors lined Main Street. Arcaro and Genell's, Brutico's, Solano's, Revelo's, and Lombardo's were among the best. Our favorite was Brutico's in which "Momma Brutico" had a table in the back corner where she sat every night to smile and wave to everyone who came into the restaurant.

Old Forge was also famous for dancing hot spots. One such place was Rock and Roll Haven. The original name was "Rock and Roll Heaven," but the Catholic Church in Old Forge made them change the name because Rock and Roll wasn't compatible with the word "heaven." Sal and I snuck out of one of Saint Rocco's dances to go to Rock and Roll Haven with his cousin Gina. She had many friends in Old Forge. One of her friends, Steve Russo, was an Elvis look-a-like.

Steve Russo came to the Saint Rocco's dances and to San Souci dances. He was an excellent dancer and quite a showman. When he danced, kids would make a circle around him and his partner and watch them dance. Steve loved to dance with Ann Gallino since she was also a great dancer. Steve really looked the part—long hair, combed over in a pompadour, long, thick sideburns, and baggy pants tightened at the ankle.

He always had a comb sticking out of his pocket. He combed his hair constantly and had a "thing" he did with his eyebrows to smooth them over. He would wet his index and pinky fingers of his right hand on his tongue and, then, would touch them to his eyebrows starting near the bridge of his nose and work outwardly toward the end, all in one motion. I never knew guys primped like this.

Becoming a senior in high school was like no other experience. We were about to reach the pinnacle of our lives. Seniors! Wow! Something was happening to us but we didn't know what.

Just when you thought, you could relax and enjoy yourself; the prospect of college comes knocking at your door. OK, if we were to go to college, we needed to look into taking college prep courses, taking the SATs, getting college brochures, and applying to college. College was just around the corner!

Mike liked business and wanted to stay in Northeastern Pennsylvania so he focused on getting into Lackawanna Junior College to get an associate degree in business. From there he could get a job as a buyer in a department store and work his way up the ladder. Mike was smart, studied a lot, and was a hard worker, so this was an easy fit for him.

Ted wanted to be a teacher and looked into East Stroudsburg State Teacher's College as his main school. Ted was also smart and would not have any obstacles in this pursuit.

I wanted to go to Wilkes College to get a degree in liberal arts. Bucknell Junior College, where my parents went to school, had become Wilkes College in 1947. At Wilkes, I would study arts, humanities, social sciences, and languages. I also wanted to continue studying my passion for pen-and-ink sketches. I had no problem getting into Wilkes.

Sal, on the other hand, had some issues when his mother

brought up the subject of college. He told her he didn't want to go to college but wanted to open a pizza parlor. He liked the restaurant business and he liked making pizza having worked in his uncle's restaurant, Il Primo Ristorante, for a couple of years. He told his mother he didn't like to study because learning was actually painful--painful but not the kind of hurt caused by a cut or bruise. It was a different kind of pain. Well, that didn't go well.

Her response was, "This is my *first* disappointment. You're the oldest of the Greco grandchildren and will be a poor example for the rest of your cousins. Your father and I always expected you go to college."

If this is your first experience with the "Italian-mother, guilt-trip phenomenon," let me explain it--Italian mothers get what they want by invoking the "guilt trip." A wife or a husband, brother or sister, boss or friend can easily summon the guilt trip. Actually, anybody interested in getting you to do what he or she wants you to do can summon a guilt trip. Children do this to their parents all the time—"But Mommy, all the kids are doing it!"

The guilt trip isn't very complicated, and we deal with it every day. ***The only difference is Italian mothers, over centuries, have fine-tuned this phenomenon to a work of art.*** Some Italian mothers get so good at this all they have to do is to give you the "look."

There are benign circumstances when the guilt trip is useful. When your mother wants you to eat your vegetables ("You want to grow up strong and healthy, don't you?"). Well, who wants to grow up weak and sickly?

Other times, your mother may want you to eat more at dinner ("I slaved over the stove for hours and you're only going to eat *one* spoonful?"). The implication is, "What good son or daughter would want his or her mother to have wasted her time over the stove?"

There are times when your parents are genuinely concerned

about your friends. ("Didn't his brother get arrested last year?") Who wants to pal around with the brother of a criminal?

Sometimes your wife wants you to put your shirt in the hamper. You know, the one you were about to throw on the floor. In this case, just a "look" will get her what she wants.

The guilt trip works effectively within close relationships— the closer the relationship, the more effective is the guilt trip. Some guilt-trips are beneficial as it was for Sal—he went to college and was happy he did.

Years later, Sal mentioned to one of his Jewish friends, "Growing up with an Italian mother was terrible with all the guilt trips." His friend said to him, "That's because you haven't grown up with a Jewish mother!" Guilt-trips are universal. Some are beneficial and others result in resentment. You need to have the correct attitude to survive.

Since Sal was dating a nurse from Pittston during his senior year in high school, he applied to two local colleges: King's and The University of Scranton. King's College was an all-male Catholic College run by the Holy Cross Fathers. The University of Scranton was also a male Catholic college run by the Jesuit fathers. Each gave an entrance test. Remember, Sal was not a good student and didn't do well on the entry test. King's College accepted him as a biology major and The University of Scranton would accept him only if he took liberal arts. Because he wanted to study medicine, he chose King's College.

So, we were moving along our path toward our goals. We got serious about school and that would help us get our "big deal" job.

After all our interaction with the opposite sex, we were no closer to knowing what type was our type. Instead of getting clearer, relationships were getting more complicated and confusing. The only thing we knew was that we wanted a "goddess." Where is she?

As far as families, we weren't ready to think about that yet.

John F. Kennedy's inauguration speech was eloquent, his confidence was high, his symbolism was dramatic, and his question, "Ask not what your country could do for you; ask what you can do for your country," was inspirational.

A peaceful world was beginning to fall apart. The United States committed money and troops to Vietnam and Russia sent missiles to Cuba.

For those of us not yet interested in the foreign policy, we listened to music and danced to the Shirelles' "Will You Love Me Tomorrow" and the Marcel's "Blue Moon."

We watched "Bonanza," "Gunsmoke," "Perry Mason," "Red Skelton," "Andy Griffith," "Candid Camera"—probably the precursor of "reality TV,"—and the reissued version of the movie, "Gone with the Wind."

Chapter 6

Transition from High School

Summer, 1961

WE DISCOVERED "FAST FOOD" at a Stop and Go restaurant in Wilkes-Barre, Pennsylvania. For fifteen-cents, we could get fries and a hamburger the size of a quarter.

Really—and why did we need fast food?

Were we in a hurry?

To get where?

Our self-imposed undertaking for the next few months was to reflect on our accomplishments, to ponder our lives, and to imagine our future. When we weren't thinking about our lives, we were working hard to save money for college. In the middle of this important time, we went to Harvey's Lake to sunbathe and to San Souci Park to dance and have fun.

We were happy to have graduated from high school. We all could share in that accomplishment. I was on the honor roll during my entire high school career, missing valedictorian by a half-point. At one point, my friends thought I was campaigning to be valedictorian—I wasn't! I was happy to have missed it since I hated giving speeches and absolutely didn't want to give a speech in front of 500 people. Anyway, who would've wanted to follow President Kennedy's speech?

I was more of a behind-the-scenes type, an artist not a performer. I didn't like being the center of attention. Sal, Mike, and Ted described me as "a quiet and confident presence." But, what did they know?

They didn't have to worry about giving a speech because of high grades. They just eeked by, graduated, and now wanted to have some fun before college.

For a short period, we bragged about our accomplishments. We learned how to dance, get along with girls, and interact with adults. We finished high school, we got into college, and we learned how to manage money—the little that we had.

We hadn't achieved any of our goals—"big deal career," goddess, or a family but that was OK since we were working on a career and learning about girls. The rest would come in time.

During the summer, I worked at my grandfather's restaurant and my father's store. When I started high school, my father, Levi, set up an account with Bache, a securities firm. For birthdays, holidays, and when I worked in the store, I received a few shares of stock—mostly General Dynamics and International Business Machines. When I worked at Coccina Italiano, my grandfather, Dominic, paid me in cash. Obviously, I preferred to work in the restaurant. Did I mention "in cash!"

Mike caddied at Fox Hill Country Club in West Pittston and continued to caddy during the summer, sometimes four to five days a week. Occasionally he carried two golf bags to make more money. He was a very popular caddy since he had the talent to suggest the correct club for the distance to the green. His suggestions earned him big tips. Periodically, since he was a good golfer, some of the members would invite him to play giving him additional opportunities to learn the game. Mike saved enough money to pay for his first year at Lackawanna Junior College.

During high school, in addition to working at Slocum Dress Company and his uncle's Il Primo Ristorante in Pittston, Sal had a car detailing business. In the 1950s, polishing cars, a full day job, involved a two-step process and special chrome cleaner for the grills and wheels. He charged twenty dollars; his expenses were about two dollars. That was a good profit margin by any standard, but he worked hard.

Unlike my father and grandfather, Sal's mother started a bank account for him. He put half the money he earned into his bank account and the other half he could spend, however he wanted. His mother believed this would teach him how to budget his money.

Sal's Uncle, Ed Leonardi, Aunt Mary Piazza's husband, had a house at Harvey's Lake, Pennsylvania. Sal's aunts and uncles took their children to the lake on Sundays for a feast. Each brought food--baked spaghetti, ravioli, sausage, meatballs, Italian bread, cake, and Italian cookies--and sat around, teased each other, and ate lunch. Afterward, it was off to the beach, a short walk from the house. During the 1950's and 1960's, Harvey's Lake was the place to go for people from Wyoming Valley to "take in the rays."

Our "job" was to lie in the sun to tan as dark as George Hamilton. Sun worshipers would get to the beach right after church and spend the entire day rubbing sun tan oil all over each other. Once nighttime came, they would stay for the drive-in movie.

For girls, the trend was to show more skin. The new two-piece bathing suits easily accomplished this goal. We were excited to see the two-piece bathing suit replace the one piece. We were ecstatic when the "String Bikini" came along; we believed we died and went to heaven. There was a lot of skin to see—the girls were practically naked. We saw parts of the female body we had never seen before except in the magazines the older kids passed around in the men's room at school. Fortunately, we were able to keep our hands to ourselves.

Sal's cousin Johanna Leonardi and her husband, Stanley Ross, "cooked" in the sun. George Hamilton would've been envious beyond words if he stood next to them. No one knew baking in the sun was bad for you.

We were all maturing and taking on the look and personality

65

traits of our parents.

Mike was five foot, six inches, slim, dark brown hair, engaging, respectful, and friendly—like Frankie Avalon. He worked hard and had a good personality. He could really dance now and the girls appreciated that. He would never "play" someone. Not his style!

Ted was very much like his mother and her father. He was five foot, six inches, slim with dirty blond hair that he was losing sooner than he wanted. Where did he get blond hair? Wasn't he Italian? Maybe there were some northern Italian genes. Many countries invaded Sicily so, even though we think we are one-hundred-percent Sicilian, who knows? Although Ted didn't know how to dance, he was a good listener. Girls like guys who listen!

Sal was five foot, six inches, good-looking, slim with dark, curly brown hair. Because he was the best dancer of our group, he was the most popular with the girls. He treated them well.

I was lucky; I got the good genes from each of my parents. I was tall, dark, and, some of the girls thought, handsome. Often, girls said I looked like Dean Martin especially during the summer with a tan and a smile. I didn't have any difficulty getting dates.

Because we all worked hard, we looked like we worked out at the gym. Of course, there weren't any gyms at that time except for training boxers.

A concession stand at Sandy Beach served hot dogs, hamburgers, and ice cream. There were pinball machines and other games inside. Guido's, a popular family-owned pizza restaurant, had locations throughout Northeastern Pennsylvania. I never tasted pizza as good as this—not even at Coccina Italiano, Il Primo Ristorante, or in Old Forge--The Pizza Capital of the World. It was addictive--really!

The folklore surrounding Guido's pizza told of the grandfather creating the recipe for the tomato sauce. He kept it a secret from everyone including his wife and children and kept it in a safe deposit box in a bank in Pittston. Each day, he would make tomato sauce for all the restaurants and the relative in charge of individual restaurants would pick up their sauce. He didn't allow anyone in the kitchen when he made his sauce. He was the pizza sauce counterpart of Seinfeld's "The Soup Nazi."

Once he died, his son and daughter inherited the secret recipe. At one restaurant, his daughter made the tomato sauce and didn't allow her husband in the kitchen in case they ever divorced. A high school friend of ours wanted to get his hands on the formula so badly, he went through the dumpster behind one restaurant searching for empty cans and other items that would give him a clue to the recipe. He even got a sample of the dough and sent it off to be analyzed trying to find its secrets. He never succeeded!

Sal's cousins Johanna and Stanley lived on Park Avenue in New York City and often stayed at the lake for summer vacation. On one occasion, a friend of ours, Jerry Bloom, came with Sal, Mike, Ted, and me to visit them at the lake. For lunch, we brought our signature Italian Hoagies made at Argento's market. Stanley who was born and raised in Bayside, Queens, New York, was smart, well read, and easily discussed almost any topic. He liked to talk about business, politics, and religion, now considered politically incorrect topics for discussion. Stanley was a self-employed broker for Italian cloth, which he sold to manufacturers of fine men's clothing such as Brioni, Nino Cerruti, and Adrian Jules.

One important accomplishment we had was learning about relationships. We went from relationships with our buddies to relationships with girls. We hung out with girls, we dated girls, we broke up with girls, and girls broke up with us. We fell in and out of love and grew up because of this experience, but we always respected everyone with whom we interacted.

All four of us, Sal, Mike, Ted, and I, grew up in families who respected women. We always behaved around the girls we knew; we always respected them. Remember, we were the group going to dances *to dance*, from the minute we got there until the last song ended. We dated and "made out" but we didn't have a hidden agenda or concealed motives. We didn't take a girl out to dinner just to get into her pants. With us, parents only had to worry about car accidents and illnesses; they didn't have to worry about their little girls getting pregnant.

In the early 1960's, there were no birth control pills or morning after pills, only abstinence and condoms, if you were inclined to have sex. However, there were doctors who performed illegal abortions should any girl find herself in "trouble" and wish to terminate a pregnancy. None of us would have ever considered that.

Of course, none of us ever had a need for condoms. Some boys carried condoms "just in case" but the condoms usually rotted in their wallets before the "case" ever presented herself. Our biggest fear was getting a girl pregnant and ruining our lives. Pregnancy meant we would have to give up our plans for the future and prematurely take care of a wife and child. **Not to mention our mothers would kill us!**

How would we find a job paying enough to support a wife, a child, an apartment, and the expenses that came with being a father and a husband? This was very powerful motivation to keep "it" in our pants. So, you can understand, since we weren't interested in giving up our futures, we were happy to go to dances to dance and, afterward, make out a little—just a little.

We knew for sure we wanted love and we knew for sure we didn't want sex. We were happy when we thought we were in love and sad when our love went away.

At Harvey's Lake, we discussed love with Johanna and Stanley.

Of course, we looked at Johanna and Stanley as the epitome of love. They met on the New York subway and eventually married. Their meeting and entering into a relationship is a good love story.

Johanna and her sister, Justine, rode the subway from Flushing, Queens, to their jobs at a bank in Manhattan. They were in their early 20s. One day Johanna noticed a nice looking, well-dressed man on the subway. They smiled at each other. A couple of days later, he got on the subway again and they smiled at each other. A few encounters later, Stanley said hello. They talked until Johanna and Justine arrived at their stop. Conversations continued whenever they saw each other--almost every day. Finally, Stanley asked Johanna out on a date. He was divorced with two children; she had never been married. They dated and married within a couple of years. Johanna and Stanley were the experts on love and relationships--a happy, fifty-year-old marriage lasting until he died would authenticate their expertise.

The conversation among Johanna, Stanley, Sal, Mike, Ted, and I went like this.

Stanley said, let's brainstorm about what loves means to us:

"Love is when you care more for the other person than you do for yourself."

"Love is an attraction, like a magnet; you can't do anything about it. If you fall in love, you are powerless to stop it."

"Love is a big commitment to another person."

"It just happens."

"Love is unconditional."

"It means giving yourself to someone."

"Love is something we can't demand from someone. It's there or it isn't there."

"Love is free."

"It can't be given if it doesn't come freely from the heart."

"Love has its own timing."

After the exchange of ideas, Stanley said, "I think love is when you're willing to do for the other person something inconvenient for you because it's what they need physically, spiritually, or emotionally. Love is a state of your soul-- something that feels good when it's there and makes you feel bad when it isn't there."

Johanna said, "Love is feeling you can't be without someone."

I said, "I agree with what everyone said but I don't agree that in love you are powerless and you don't have a choice whether or not to go on with it. I think you always have a choice even if you fall in love. I think if someone is abusive, you can walk away and stop loving that person.

So, why does it hurt so much when you lose love?

"Love only hurts when it's deep. If love is superficial, you get over it quickly. If love is deep, it takes a long time to recover the loss. The deeper the love, the more pain it causes when you lose it. So, if you lose love and it hurts really badly, appreciate that you had a deep love to begin with and are a better person for having had love in your life."

Stanley said, "Another important characteristic of love is it can't be withheld. Someone can't say, 'If you want me to love you, you must do what I want or agree with me all the time.' You can't use love as a currency."

Sal said, "You need to be comfortable with the person to whom you're married. All my uncles are comfortable with their wives. One day as I was thinking about love and marriage, I thought my father and his four married brothers (first generation Sicilians) married the 'same person'--people with the same characteristics. Their wives were Sicilian, quiet, and nurturing. They cooked and cleaned and they were good cooks and good homemakers. All their wives were low maintenance, waited on their husbands, and respected their husbands. Their full time job was to raise children and care for their families. Their husbands respected them and their marriages were great. These women were clones. See what I mean, 'the same person.' "

One of our favorite pastimes during the summer was to go to the "Flame," a bar with live bands located in the Midway Shopping Center in Exeter, which was half way between West Pittston and Kingston. The Flame looked the other way if customers were underage. No one carded us. It didn't matter if we were underage since we were going to dance and not to drink. We knew most of the people there, many of whom were from Pittston and West Pittston. We danced to the music of Mel Wynn and the Rhythm Aces and Joe Nardone's All Stars.

Another hot spot was "Vispi's," a bar in Kingston. Vispi's was a long, narrow bar, maybe 22 feet wide and 80 feet long. It had booths along the wall large enough for eight people and a bar that went at least half-way to the back. There were a few smaller booths in the back across from the restrooms. When Vispi's was busy, the booths were full and there was "standing room only" in the aisles. Vispi's was just a bar—no attraction other than drinking and talking. We ran into many of our friends from high school there, especially the older kids.

On the eve of Ted's twenty-first birthday, we went to the Flame. There were probably undercover police there because they were carding everyone. Ted handed his driver's license to the host.

The host looked at his driver's license and said, "You're too young son!"

Ted said, "I'm going to be 21 in two hours."

"Come back in two hours. I can't let you in because you're too young."

So, how have we fared with our lives so far?

We--academic students, business students, and athletes--learned the skills we needed to move forward with our lives. We learned how to set goals, how to work toward those goals, and about the satisfaction achieving those goals. We learned lessons when we succeeded and we learned lessons when we failed. We were OK with failure as long as we succeeded more often than

71

we failed.

Some of the kids were riding high; others had delayed gratification. For academic students, we were proud we studied and passed tests and completed classes to graduate; we had the personal satisfaction of learning many things; we had an inner peace knowing we could solve problems.

Although most of our classmates knew which students were the sports heroes, very few knew which students were the academic heroes. Football players were the high-school heroes. After all, who was higher on the totem pole than the football players? Our high school football team gave us excitement, pride, and bragging rights. The star football player who went on to college usually continued his hero status. For the star football player who went to work permanently in a dress factory, the ride seemed to be over.

However, they would have other achievements later—wife, children, grandchildren—but not like those of the star football player. There's no doubt graduation from high school is a milestone and it was a milestone in the late 1950s and early 1960s. For some kids, it was the end of the ride. They were satisfied talking about the "good old days" and their conversations were about stuff in the immediate past.

Now that we were independent and could drive, we decided to make a minor change in our Sunday schedule. Instead of meeting at someone's house to have breakfast and go to church afterward, we went to church and then to a diner to have breakfast. We went to 11 a.m. mass at Saint Rocco's Church and then went to the Skyliner Diner in Dupont, Pennsylvania. I'm sure Sal's mother was happy she no longer had to cook breakfast for her six to eight "children."

During high school, we hung out with a larger group of friends mostly classmates at Pittston High School. Mike and Sal walked from Swallow Street to Pittston High School. Along the way, they picked up others and, by the time they got to school, twenty minutes later, they were a crowd. The group, who mostly hung out together, went to church, and to the diner, were Sal, Mike, Ted, Romaine Falco, Patricia (Patti) Bianchi, Peter Marino, and me.

On the way home from dances, we liked the Main Diner in Exeter, because they had good hamburgers and we ran into a different group of friends. One night after going to a San Souci dance in Hanover Township, we went to eat at the Main Diner in Exeter. The Main Diner had become our favorite place to eat after a night of dancing. They were opened all night and, at that time, made hamburgers better than we could get anywhere in Luzerne County. At the diner, we talked about our life plans. We had many questions.

"When did we expect to get married?"

"What type of girl would we marry?"

"Would she be from Pittston or even from Wyoming Valley?"

"Would she be college educated?"

"Would she have attended Misericordia College, Marywood College, or Wilkes College?"

"What nationality would she have?"

"How many children would we have?"

"Would our wives stay home and raise children like our mothers?"

"If our wives worked, what type of job would they have?"

"Would it be OK if our wives made more money than we did?"

"What if her parents were more well-to-do than our parents? What if they lived in West Pittston?"

"What type of job would we need to support a family with our wives staying at home?"

"Just how important is money anyway?"

"Does anyone have a plan or a timeline for this?"

Ted said, "Unlike girls who have an age when they want to

get married and an age when they want children, I don't have a timeline. It's a girl thing, not a guy thing. My sister, Lois, wants to get married when she's twenty-five and finish having children by the time she's twenty-eight."

"I think we should get to our career goal or, at least, have the end of our education in sight before we think of getting married. If I go to medical school that would be four years of college, four years of medical school and then an internship. I think nothing sooner than the last year of medical school, perhaps, late twenties would be appropriate." Sal said.

"My parents got married a little later than my grandparents and I'll probably get married later than they did. I have four years of college and then graduate school. Art school will delay me a couple of years." I said.

Mike said, "My aunts and uncles got married mid to late twenties. That sounds like a good age. Mike said. I believe I'll be finished with school sooner than Jeffrey, Sal, and Ted, so I guess mid-twenties would be my number."

"Well it sounds to me like we **do** have a timeline, not as much an age timeline as a career timeline." I said.

Sal said, "OK. What type of girl is in the plan? My cousin Stanley is Jewish and my cousin Johanna is Catholic. Do we have a religious requirement?"

I said, "My father is Jewish and my mother is Catholic, but I don't have a preference. She could be Jewish or Catholic. She just has to believe is some higher power!"

Mike, Ted, and Sal said they didn't have a religious requirement but everyone seemed to hedge a little on this question.

"Does she have to be from Northeastern Pennsylvania?" I asked.

None of us thought it was important. Some of us dated girls from New York, New Jersey, and Florida. They were all more assertive than Pittston Girls.

"Does she have to be college educated?

Mike and Ted said no but agreed she had to be smart.

"I prefer someone who is educated since my parents are educated and seem to get along very well. They are comfortable discussing a wide range of topics at dinner. I think there are fewer misunderstandings when the two people are at the same education level and are as smart as each other." I said.

Sal said, "I need someone who is smart. I want a woman who can take the bus to New York City, go shopping, and get back to Pittston without calling the police or calling me to come and get her."

I said, "So, she has to be able to read a map?"

"Or, at least read a bus schedule or call a cab?" Mike said.

Sal said, "Don't be a smart ass. We're looking for the same thing—Pretty, smart, and big breasts."

"Wait a second, when did the big breasts come in?" Mike said.

"When did the map and bus schedule come in?" Sal said.

"OK, let's put this to rest: she has to be good looking, smart, big breasts, willing to have children, and willing to stay home to raise them." I said.

Sal said, "My God! Let's change the subject. On the question of whether she would have to be from around here or from Marywood, from Misericordia or from Wilkes, how would you know if 'The One' for you lives next door or lives a thousand miles away? It's too restrictive to say she needs to live around here. There's a whole other world out there. I'm not saying I need to date every girl in the universe, but I need to meet girls with different perspectives. She doesn't have to be Italian or Catholic."

Mike said to Sal, "What's your mother going to think of that statement since she wants you to marry a nice little Italian girl from Pittston?"

"I don't know about that. Aunt Phyllis and Aunt Connie

picked your cousin, Christina, for me when I was in kindergarten. Over time, Italian women get shorter and wider. I don't think I want to marry someone who will end up as wide as she is tall. Another thing with Italian women, once someone in the family dies, they wear black for the rest of their lives. Who wants to live with someone whose closet is filled with black dresses?"

Sal told us a story about his cousin in Buffalo. He said, "Michael Donato's friends in Buffalo had a business plan related to Italian women. They wanted to hire a group of Old Italian women who always wore black. They would, for a fee, say $5, worry for you. He called them the Sicilian Worriers. You would pay $5, write down what you're worried about, and give it to them.

"It sounds like a good business plan to me. Everyone benefits, you get rid of your worry, and some little Old Italian Lady makes a living doing what she loves to do—worry! She won't pay social security taxes or anything. She wouldn't be harmed since she would be emotionally detached."

I said, "OK. OK. We're getting off the subject. Do we want children? I would like to have four children. My parents had three and I would like to have four. I absolutely want children. What's life for if don't have children? Any future wife would have to agree to have children or I won't marry her. That's my requirement. I don't care if she works or stays home, but she must want children."

Ted said, "It would be easier financially to have a wife who worked. I don't have that requirement but I would like to have children. I liked growing up with two sisters, especially since they were younger and didn't mess with me."

"I'm an only child, but if I'm going to have children, I want to have more than one," Mike said, "Sometimes it was lonely and I think children grow up better if they have brothers and sisters. It would be nice to have a wife who made some money."

Sal said, "I'm an only child as well. Having eighteen aunts and uncles with lots of kids, I wasn't lonely at all. I want children. How many, I don't know--just some."

"Having children is important; having a wife with whom you get along is more important. But, if you are going to have children, you need to have a wife who stays home to raise them." Mike said.

"OK. I have one more question. How important is money anyway? I remember Stanley saying, 'Money wasn't important. You can't take it with you!' " I said.

That's easy for him to say coming from someone who would ultimately be so successful he would own an apartment on Park Avenue in New York City, a home in Aruba, a home in Tuscany, and a lake-house at Harvey's Lake.

"It's important but not the most important thing," Ted said.

So what was our biggest fear?

You would think our biggest fear was not finding the love of our lives.

All our activities seemed focused on this end--going to school, going to dances, going to church, going to weddings, going to other social events--all were to find the "one." Finding the love of our lives was so important to all of us. Yes, you would think finding THE girl would be our primary goal and our biggest fear would be we wouldn't find her.

However, our biggest fear was failing to find a good career— one which would pay enough to support our families and ourselves.

I said, "Many well-to-do people in Pittston and West Pittston belong to Saint Rocco's Church, but you don't have to be well-to-do to be successful. Simply, falling in the middle of the road would be OK--a family of two schoolteachers would be perfect. Both would go to work and get home in the middle of the afternoon. They could go shopping together. They could cook together. They could get in nine holes of golf together after work. Once they had children, the children would get home when the parents got home. They could save enough to educate their children; they could save enough for retirement. They could have conversations at the same educational level."

Sal said, "My uncles married the same type. That plan worked for them, as first generation immigrants. In subsequent generations, people needed someone of the same intellect for discussions. I think the life of two teachers would appear to be very compatible."

I said, "I think it would be difficult finding someone who is well-read married to someone with a Sunday Supplement mind--someone who gets the majority of their ideas from the Sunday Supplements: Parade magazine, Reader's Digest, etc. Communication would be difficult."

"On the high end of the professional spectrum, say, a physician, surgeon, cardiologist, lawyer, or dentist, there may be additional needs." Sal said. "Physicians have to go to college for four years, medical school for four years, internship, and fellowship for three to five years, and, finally, finish after twelve to fifteen years of school. Where would they find time to meet and date potential mates? What would they talk about with, say, someone who has just a high school education? Once they found someone, there would be career demands. A surgeon may have to go to the hospital often during the night and weekends leaving his or her spouse with the responsibility of raising the children alone. What happens when two high school sweethearts date while he is in college and she is working and not going to school? They marry after college and he goes on to medical school and specializes. There could be some difficulty communicating on the same level after all that."

"People who own businesses have different demands but are still distracted from relationships, Ted Said. " There's always the fear of failure of the business. In the past, physicians, lawyers, and dentists didn't worry about failure or have the potential to fail in the business end of their practices. But, there is no guarantee for any job or a career."

Pittston High School, like many other schools, had career days. Each year the school would bring in professionals to speak about their jobs.

Sal told us his experience with one Career Day, "I went to a presentation on becoming an 'efficiency expert.' The job description was to evaluate the strength of a business and recommend changes to improve efficiency. Sounded like a perfect job to me!"

Mike reflected on another career day, "Mrs. Magnuson gave our class work applications. We filled out the application as if we were applying for a job as a clerk in a department store. Some of the questions included: name, address, phone number, sex, occupation, education, and work experience. To the question of 'occupation,' one of the girls answered 'unoccupied' since she didn't have a job yet. To the question of 'sex,' one of the boys answered 'not yet, but I hope soon.' "

The teachers and potential employers had their work cut out for them with our class.

Sal decided to go to college, as his mother wanted and go from there. Good choice!

We were proud; we finished high school, were about to start college, and put together a plan for the future. Everything was cool.

Of course, we didn't know what was in store for us in September.

President John F. Kennedy was prominent during our college years.

Kennedy was the first Catholic elected President of the United States amidst concern he would consult the Pope on matters of state. That never happened.

Liberals and the poor working class hailed Kennedy as their savior-- the one who would put them on "easy street." That never happened.

People hoped he would be the Democratic president to complete the social/welfare programs started by FDR--The liberals would have it all. That never happened.

What did happen?

Crises and scandals happened. Known as the "Bay of Pigs," Kennedy ordered the unsuccessful invasion of Cuba resulting in a Cuban Revolutionary victory and embarrassed the administration as well as our country.

The U.S. discovered Soviet missiles in Cuba. The "Cuban Missile Crisis" led to major tension between the United States and Russia.

The "cold war" with the Soviet Union was getting colder; the Vietnam War was getting hotter.

On November 22, 1963, Lee Harvey Oswald assassinated Kennedy in Dallas, Texas.

Chapter 7

The College Years

1961-1965

EVERYTHING WAS CHANGING—like a caterpillar to a butterfly--the world, our country, our friends, and our families. We were out of control! It was like white river rafting except you were standing up in the raft.

In the midst of this change, we questioned the authenticity of the "truths" as we knew them, the legitimacy of our beliefs, and the accuracy of our assumptions. We questioned the wisdom of our professors. We questioned whether our parents were as smart as we were. As we explored the meaning of life, we questioned everything! Nothing was off limits for us!

A different social change was developing but not the social change liberals expected. They expected a fight for social programs such as welfare; they got a fight for women's rights instead. Women became "activists." Blacks stepped up their fight for their civil rights.

Discontented with their standing in the family, women began to assert themselves. They left the security, reliability, and comfort of their homes to push their way toward financial independence—they joined the work force! Women struggled for equal rights at work—equal opportunity, equal pay, and equal time off. They wanted control of their lives and control of their person. They wanted a say in decisions that would affect them. What's wrong with that?

In the orchestra of life, women were no longer satisfied to play *harmony*; they wanted to play *melody*. They no longer wanted to be on a pedestal; they wanted to be on a level playing field—getting what they deserved Who could argue with that?

Gloria Steinem rallied against the unfair way in which women had to choose between a career and marriage. Why did *they* have to choose? Men didn't have to choose!

Along with some attainment of the social positives for women came some negatives. The sword, after all, cuts both ways! Although women wanted independence, some missed having their "man" take care of them. Despite the fact they achieved independence by joining the workforce, they regretted missing their children's milestones. Now in charge of their destinies, they were responsible for their decisions. They had only themselves to blame. Many felt conflicted.

A number of women ultimately would be disappointed. They discovered they couldn't "have it all." At least they couldn't have all of it all the time. Women would possess a different part of it all at different times in their lives. Was that good enough?

Wilkes-Barre

Wilkes College

WILKES COLLEGE, located in the historic area of Wilkes-Barre, consisted of mansions donated by well-to-do residents. The mansions housed learning centers, libraries, and dormitories. Although I was a day student, I spent most of my time on campus in the library and at the Art Center. I had many friends in my class and took part in several study groups.

"Our study group had five students. My two Jewish friends from Wyoming Seminary, Alan Miller and David Silverman, and two new friends, Bob Strausberg and Sonny Valente. Bob's father was an attorney in Wilkes-Barre. Sonny's father was a drug rep for a major pharmaceutical company.

Sal and I discussed how our study group approached studying, especially how we prepared for tests in my History of Western Civilization class.

We divided our reading assignments. Each of us read our designated chapters and created questions and answers we anticipated the professor would ask on a test. During our meeting, we consolidated our list of questions and answers and studied them. On test day, we would have predicted over ninety-five percent of the questions."

We thought this method was a smart way to study.

The first year was easy for me because I studied at Wyoming Seminary, the top prep school in Northeastern Pennsylvania.

Wilkes College had socials and dances on weekends and Mike and Sal joined me at some of them. I met a few girls and dated one of them. I dated Rachel Smith for most of the first year but nothing came of it. I think, like the rest of my friends, I had too much to think about—studying, career planning, and exploring religion—to get serious about anyone.

I told Alan, David, and Bob that I was frustrated dating Pittston girls who were mostly Catholic.

"Pittston girls get too serious, too quickly and want commitments to get married. Once they graduate from high school, they get into high gear about getting married and having babies." I asked, "Are Jewish girls like that?"

"Some are and some not so much," David said. "It depends on what they want—marriage or career."

Alan said, "The Jewish girls I know from some of the parties couldn't care less about getting serious. They just want to have a good time."

"What parties? Where are these parties? Why haven't I been invited to any parties?" asked Bob.

"Mostly at the girls' houses, when their parents are away" said Alan.

I asked, "What do you mean by 'good time?' "

"They just want to drink and make out. If you give them a few drinks, they'll let you feel them up. If you get them drunk, a few will sleep with you--but you have to be Jewish and circumcised. They won't sleep with you, Jeffrey, since you're only half-Jewish! The circumcised part probably leaves you out as well being Catholic and all!"

I jabbed back, "That's what you think. Jews don't have a monopoly on circumcision. David told me when Rabbi Horowitz did your circumcision, he slipped, and 'Little Alan' looks like he's making a left turn."

"Smart ass!"

I said, "You'll have to invite me to one of your parties to test your hypothesis about Jewish girls and half-Jewish guys."

David jumped back into the conversation, "Jeffrey, stay away from Alan and his party girls, otherwise you're really asking for trouble."

David knew Alan was a party boy and it was only a matter of time before he got in some sort of jam.

Bob said, "OK cut it out. Are we studying here? Are we studying? If you're going to keep this up, I'm going somewhere else to study."

The following weekend, I talked with Mike, Ted, and Sal about my conversation with Alan, David, and Bob.

"Alan knows some Jewish girls who are screwing some Jewish guys during parties at their houses. They aren't like girls we know in Pittston."

"Aren't the guys worried they'll get the girls pregnant" Ted asked.

"I don't know. Alan may not be afraid; he's a party boy and a risk taker. I think David or Bob would be afraid to take a chance. They're like us."

Mike asked, "What about the girls? Wouldn't they be afraid?"

"Apparently not! David said Jewish girls would be OK if they got pregnant with some guy whose father had a lot of money. He also believes some women marry for money instead of love."

"Why is that?"

"They're afraid if they marry for love, their husbands will control them. If they marry for money, they can control the relationship. In either case, their husband would take care of them and they would be set. Alan knows some wives who "hold out" on their husbands to get things they want. He said, "One girl's mother 'held out' until she got a fur coat.""

"That's weird. What's the difference between a prostitute taking money for sex and a wife taking a fur coat for sex?" Sal said.

"Wait a minute. Let's leave that argument for another day; it's too complicated." Mike said.

"I don't believe most girls have attitudes like that." Ted said. "They know the difference between sex for love and sex for cash. We don't know girls who play games like that. In high school, we considered girls who slept around as tramps and we avoided them. We worried about ulterior motives—like getting you to marry them or faking pregnancy to get money from you."

Mike said, "Are we saying girls will sleep with you if you have a good job? Would they try to get pregnant just to marry someone well off?"

I nodded affirmatively.

"That's scary. East Stroudsburg girls were looser than Pittston girls. However, they drew the line at sleeping with everyone. They'd only sleep with a guy if they're going steady." Ted said.

"OK. So, we agree there wasn't a lot of stuff like that going on in high school." I said.

Ted jumped into the conversation, tongue-in-cheek, and asked, "So, Jeffrey, can you get us invited to any of these parties! I can say my last name is Friedman or something like that."

"I don't think so. Sorry, but you don't look like a Friedman!"

King's College

HOLY CROSS FATHERS founded King's College, located at the eastern edge of Wilkes-Barre, Pennsylvania across from the Luzerne County Court House in 1946. They also founded Notre Dame.

In 1961, when Sal was a freshman, the college consisted of two buildings on North River Street and offered majors in the sciences and liberal arts. Most students came from Northeastern Pennsylvania, New Jersey, and New York. A few came from Puerto Rico. Students were attracted to King's College for its intellectual, moral, and spiritual education.

Sal's experience differed from my experience. He didn't do well in school. His first semester at King's College was a disaster because he never learned how to study. He had to take remedial reading and remedial English. The only thing he knew in English was outlining and organizing thanks to his class at Pittston High School taught by Miss Costello, his senior English teacher. However, he didn't know a noun from a dangling participle.

To prepare for the college entrance test, he read some "vocabulary building" and "grammar" books. His preparation for college by his teachers at Pittston High School was marginal—a continuation of his poor education at Saint Rocco's.

In fact, a group of "friends" bet on how long he would remain in school.

Sal told us," When I studied the History of Western Civilization, I read every word and took notes. I couldn't identify what was important or what was 'fluff.' Before the test, I studied the notes. The first test had questions about captions under the pictures. I didn't know anything about the pictures. The more I tried, the worse it got until I was practically copying the entire chapter. I thought that I should have opened a pizza parlor instead of going to college. Biology and chemistry were easier to study because they were 'hands on.' "

"Any other classes come easy?" I asked.

"I like philosophy courses. We always have good discussions in class. We talked about topics that reminded me of our discussions with Johanna and Stanley—topics such as:

"What's worse, failing or never trying?"

"What one thing would you change about the world?"

"How much control do you have over your life?"

"What's holding you back from being who you want to be?"

We always had deep conversations; we weren't superficial people.

Sal and I had good discussions about religion. He took classes in comparative religion in which the class discussed the various aspects of Catholicism, Protestantism, and Judaism—their history, how they were alike and how they were different.

Sal and I had the same impression about kids in our class from New York.

Sal said, "Some of my classmates appear to be more intelligent than I. New Yorkers are especially impressive. They seem beyond intelligent. They could explain practically anything and talk as if they knew everything. It took me almost a full year in college before I realized the New York kids were not all that smart, they only talked a good game. New Yorkers had the gift of "gab"—salesmen and politicians possess this same gift."

Despite his difficulty in school, Sal attended King's College dances on Friday night. Mike and Sal were regulars. I often attended. Ted, of course, came with us whenever he was home for the weekend. Marywood and Misericordia, Catholic girl's colleges, "bused" in students for our Friday night dances. Often Romaine Falco and Pat Bianchi, our friends from high school, came to King's dances.

Going to King's dances and Wilkes dances seemed like a continuation of the high school dances except we always had live bands and a larger variety of girls from all over the place—Pennsylvania, Maryland, Ohio, New York, and Connecticut. They differed from the Pittston girls--they were more assertive, more in tune with their career goals. They seemed smarter, but it could've been what Sal described as the "New York" phenomenon. Some of these girls were quite obnoxious and self-centered. They didn't care about hurting someone's feelings with what they said or did.

Mike and Sal dated girls they met but didn't get serious with any of them. They had to keep on track with their career goals.

After his first year in college, Sal started to work in his father's barbershop.

East Stroudsburg State Teachers College

EAST STROUDSBURG STATE TEACHERS COLLEGE began privately but the State of Pennsylvania assumed control. Its mission was to educate students who wanted to teach grade school and high school. Ted chose this school because he wanted to teach grade school. School was easy for him because he was a good listener and learned good study habits at Saint John's high school.

Ted was a good friend to have, a "low maintenance" friend. Whenever I called him to ask him if he wanted to do something, like go to the mall shopping or go to Harvey's Lake, he would say "sure." He seldom initiated things to do but always went along with what we wanted to do—go to a dance, play baseball, play basketball, etc. We anticipated if Ted were to marry, the girl would do the asking.

Lackawanna Junior College

LACKAWANNA JUNIOR COLLEGE, Scranton, Pennsylvania, provided education for students who wanted to go into business. Since Mike wanted to work in retail, this was a good choice for him. He also didn't have any problem with school.

Wyoming Valley

WE ALL WENT TO WORK during the summer after our first year of college. I worked at my father's store and my grandfather's restaurant. Ted worked in his grandparents' store. Mike got a job at Mount Airy Lodge in the Pocono Mountains working as a waiter. Sal worked in his father's barbershop and at his uncle's restaurant.

We were happy about Mike's job because he often invited us to visit him on his off days. We swam and carried on as if we were resort guests. We could continue our "guest" status as long as we behaved and didn't get Mike fired. Sometimes there were parties, and even though we didn't want to go, we went anyway—you know, for Mike's sake.

Around the middle of the summer, Mike started dating Brittany, a New Jersey girl working at an adjacent resort in the Poconos. As he increased his frequency of dates with Brittany, he decreased his invitations to us to visit him on his days off. What happened to loyalty among friends? What about our pact?

Did our pact end with the first girlfriend?

We were happy he had a girlfriend even though neither of them seemed interested in a long-term relationship. By the end of the summer, Mike realized his high school goal of losing his virginity. A little late but, nonetheless, realized. After the summer, Brittany went back to New Jersey, Mike came home, and they never saw each other again. Our pact was renewed. Whew, close call!

In June, Sal, with his new barber license, was ready to make some serious money. Phillip Grandanetti, a barber supply rep from Scranton had an innovative idea. He shared his idea with Sal and his father.

Phil said, "In Wilkes-Barre, a few one-owner barbers want to hire a barber to substitute for them when they go on vacation. This is a good opportunity to get some business experience and to make some money."

Phil asked Sal, "Are you interested?"

Sal said, "Sure. How would it work?"

"When they take vacation, you would work in their barbershop. They would keep thirty-percent of the income and you would keep seventy-percent."

Sal said, "OK. I'm interested. How do we handle it?"

Phil said, "I'll contact the barbers and make the arrangements. Afterward, you can go by the barbershop and introduce yourself and discuss the arrangement."

Phil knew of Sal's experience and knew he would do a good job in this role. Neither Sal nor his father would have created a job opportunity like this. Phil, however, pieced it together.

Sal began his first year substituting for vacationing barbers. This was a good deal for him, and a good deal for the barber. He worked two weeks during the first summer and made a net $300. This was huge income for a college student in 1962.

During the second year, the four of us were getting in high gear! Classes went quickly for me. I was on the Dean's list three of the last four semesters. Ted was moving along. Mike finished his Associate Degree in Business and got a job as a buyer for Pomeroy's Department Store in Wilkes-Barre. He was making real money now. We often met for lunch in Wilkes-Barre during the week. Now that Mike was finished with his education, his new mission was to find "the love of his life."

During his second year at Kings, Sal learned how to study. His grades and GPA improved. He was still interested in medical school. The following summer, he continued to work in barbershops substituting for vacationing barbers. This was becoming a big deal for him. He worked in four different barbershops the second year.

The third year brought some new challenges. If we were to continue with our education, we had to apply to graduate school. I wanted to get a master's degree in fine art so I applied to Pratt Institute in New York.

As the number and type of girls to date expanded, Mike, Ted, Sal, and I observed and discussed distinct differences between the girls who went to college and girls who went to work in offices as secretaries, restaurants as waitresses, or in factories as seamstresses.

"I'm under the impression girls who finish high school and start to work, have an urgency to get out of the house, to get married, and to have babies. Our conversations with them are about this progression. When we talk with college girls, we talk about philosophy, politics, and career choices." I said.

"I agree, they want to get married and they want to have children but there seems no urgency to get there. Family goals are weaved into career goals." Sal said.

"That may be the case, but they all want to get married and have babies." Ted said.

We finally made it to our senior year in college. Although Mike had been working for a year now, we noticed he was maturing a little faster than we were and getting more serious about life. Whereas Sal, Ted, and I knew that we would get serious about life, we were content to let life flow along for a little bit longer while we scurried around on the sidelines.

Once boys and girls reached the marrying age, they were prime "take over" targets. In Northeastern Pennsylvania, ethnic families--Italian, Polish, Irish, and German—were predisposed to arrange marriages. A friend or relative always had someone in the wings who would be perfect for you!

Mike's family didn't interfere with his choices in women— they behaved. Good for them!

Ted's parents also took a back seat in this process. One of Ted's aunts did try to influence him but he wouldn't listen. He didn't think his aunt had good taste in women. Anyway, he wasn't interested in getting serious with anyone.

My parents didn't interfere with my dating or with my search to find the love of my life. I was surprised since my mother was Sicilian, and you would think would have had someone ready for me. I dated girls of all different types, Catholic, Jewish, slightly educated, and well educated as if looking for a piece to fit my puzzle.

Sal was different. His mother was one of eight children—two brothers and six sisters. Two of her sisters never married. His father was one of ten children—six brothers and three sisters. Two of his brothers and two of his sisters never married. Those who did marry had between three and five children, although not as many as the preceding generation. As you would expect, practically everyone had someone he or she thought was perfect for him. Sal's maternal grandmother always had a cousin who would be just right for one of her grandchildren to marry. I guess it was a carryover from the old country.

Some of the old timers believed, "You should marry your own kind." Aunt Phyllis Piazza dated an Irish man after high school and Sal's grandmother did not approve. She eventually broke up with him and she never married.

Attitudes about nationality ruined many lives. I guess his grandmother's reaction to Aunt Phyllis' boyfriend discouraged her younger sister, Connie Piazza, from dating anyone. Aunt Connie was good looking and would have easily found someone. She was smart, had a nice body, dressed well, and had a yellow Plymouth convertible. Hot stuff!

Aunt Phyllis and Aunt Connie had someone picked out for Sal as early as kindergarten. A friend of theirs, Maria Belli, a first generation Sicilian, had a daughter, Christina, who Aunt Phyllis and Aunt Connie thought would be perfect for Sal. We're talking kindergarten here!

He dated Christina many times over the years, not because of family pressure but because he liked her. She liked to dance and they had a lot in common. After all, they were the "same kind." She was also Mike's cousin! Sal thought he would eventually get serious about dating her and they would end up together once he finished school. They went to the Victory Dance junior year in high school, birthday parties, to the prom, and to a few college functions.

Was she his "goddess?" At different times over twelve years, Sal dated her to see if there was the spark he needed to have a permanent relationship. Every time they dated, they would get along really well, but their relationship was more friendship. They didn't talk about important things like philosophy or politics. Christina graduated high school and went to work as a bookkeeper in a factory; Sal went on to eleven years of college and graduate school and, at one point, realized they truly had little in common. Nothing anyone could do about it; it just wasn't meant to be. Marrying her would have been a repeat of what Sal's father and his brothers did. He would have married the same woman they had married. It was OK in his father's generation but wasn't OK for his generation.

As I did, Sal dated Italian girls, Irish girls, Polish girls, Catholics, Protestants, and Jewish girls—albeit only a couple of

Jewish girls. If Jewish girls wouldn't date me who was half-Jewish, they certainly weren't going to give Sal the time of day. During all this dating, Sal didn't know what he was looking for; he only knew that he wasn't ready to find it.

We were in our last semester of college. Pratt Institute accepted me and I was excited to finish my last semester at Wilkes College. One of my art classmates, Joseph Cusano, who acted in plays at the Little Theater and the Showcase Theater in Wilkes-Barre, was also going to study at Pratt Institute. We both would study for a Master of Fine Art. Joe and I wanted to share an apartment. Occasionally, Joe hung out with us at dances. We had a lot in common since his family was also from Serradifalco, Sicily. Mike, Ted, Sal, Joe, and I were all descendants of immigrants from Serradifalco.

Another classmate of Sal's at King's College, Santo "Sandy" Loquasto, had a similar background to ours. He was an English Lit major and very active in designing sets for King's College plays. He went on to get an MFA from Yale and started his career as a Costume Designer. He progressed to Set Designer and ultimately to Production Designer for many Woody Allen Movies and Broadway plays. He won several Tony awards. Sandy may be the most famous King's College alumnus.

By our senior year, Sal's interest in medical school was a dead end. Because he liked teaching, he went to speak with one of the professors in the Education Department, Mr. Becky, to discuss his options and create a plan.

Early during the last semester of college, on a Friday night, Mike, Ted, Sal, and I were at a Wilkes College dance. With twenty-minutes remaining, all four of us were standing inside the entrance to the dance hall--bored and with no prospects to ask to dance. A slow dance began to play and I felt a tap on my shoulder. When I turned, I saw a short, pretty girl with black hair. She had to get on her toes to reach my shoulder since I'm 5'10". She had a smile as big as a billboard.

"Hi, I'm Paula. May I have this dance?" she asked.

"Absolutely. I'm Jeffrey."

We walked to the dance floor and began dancing.

Paula dressed in a white tailored shirt and a cute little navy blue skirt was a wave of energy. She looked like a "free spirit," but in a good way—fun loving and carefree.

We stayed on the dance floor for a few more dances.

I asked her, "Would you like to go to Kearney's and get something to eat?"

"Yes, I'd like that."

On the way out, I introduced her to Mike, Ted, and Sal, "This is Paula Cohen. We're going to get a bite to eat." That being said, we left.

Wow, your life could turn around in an instant. Mike, Ted, and Sal looked at each other and smiled. They were surprised Paula mesmerized me but were happy for me. We weren't accustomed to women approaching us—we were the ones who initiated contact. In the 1960s, men asked women to dance not the other way around--except for those dances designated 'ladies' choice."

That Sunday, we met at Saint Rocco's church and went to the Skyliner Diner for breakfast. I told everyone a little about Paula. She was Jewish from outside San Francisco and she's majoring in music. She said she was an "oops" baby since she was the younger of two girls and there was a ten-year difference between her and her older sister. She concentrated in string instruments and her favorite instrument was the violin. I'm going out with her next weekend.

The following Saturday night, I took Paula to Arcaro and Genell's Restaurant in Old Forge. We talked about Wilkes College and talked about how we met. After we ordered dinner, we had an edgy conversation.

I said, "That was pretty gutsy of you to ask me to dance. What will you do for an encore?"

Paula smiled and said, "I don't think I'll give you any more surprises for a while. Girls ask guys to dance all the time in San Francisco. Do you mean to tell me I'm the first girl to ask you to dance?"

"No! Well.., actually, yes. I don't know, girls never ask me to dance. I'm the one in pursuit most of the time. I was just surprised."

"Why wouldn't girls ask you to dance? You're good looking and quite a good dancer, especially slow dancing. I like the way you slow dance; I liked the way you held me. You made me feel safe and secure. I like a man to hold me tightly when we dance."

After a pause, Paula said, "I assume you know that all the girls think you're good looking."

"No, I don't know that. I haven't noticed how girls look at me. Mostly, I'm too busy to see that. I've been studying, painting, and working too much to pay much attention to the vibes girls send."

"I've seen you before in the library. You didn't notice me, but I noticed you. You always had your head buried in a book reading and taking notes. Why don't you look around to see who's looking at you?"

"I don't know. At which library did you see me?"

"The Osterhaut on South Franklin Street."

"That's where I research my term papers. Why didn't you say hello before?"

"You didn't seem very approachable, but I had my eye on you. When I saw you at the dance, I reckoned it was my last chance to meet you since I'm finishing this semester. What did I have to lose?"

"Reckoned? They use that word in San Francisco?"

"No. I thought, since Wilkes-Barre was in the middle of the "sticks," that would be a word to which you could relate."

"We're not in the "sticks." This is Wilkes-Barre, Pennsylvania, not Amarillo, Texas."

Feeling a little off my game, I thought I would change the subject. I asked, "So, now that you are almost finished with school, what's the plan?"

"My parents are into real estate in the Bay Area and own commercial real estate, apartments, and condos. I thought I would hang out there and get a job with a band or an orchestra. They're giving me a condo for graduation. I like the city and like the excitement of being in the middle of the action.

"What are your plans?"

"I'm going to art school in New York. I've been doing pen-and-ink sketches for as long as I can remember. I got into a lot of trouble at Saint Rocco's Grade School with my teachers accusing me of doodling and wasting time. I didn't care what they thought, I liked it, and that's what I was going to do. Sometimes nuns can be a real pain in the rear end. People just need to leave you alone."

"You went to Catholic school? How did that happen?"

"My father is Jewish and my mother is Catholic. Before they got married, they agreed to raise their children Catholic."

"You're Catholic! Rosenbloom... I thought you were Jewish. Rosenbloom!"

"I'm half-Jewish. For the past two years, I've been going to synagogue with my father and learning about Judaism."

"Good, you're converting. You are converting, aren't you?"

"No, I just want to learn about my heritage."

"I really thought you were Jewish with a name like Rosenbloom!"

"Are you disappointed?"

"Well, maybe a little... I assumed."

I was so enamored with Paula I played up the Jewish heritage thing since she was Jewish and I wanted to keep seeing her. I was worried she now didn't like me as much. I also didn't know if she was right for me or if we had potential for a future together. I liked her playful personality, her quirkiness, and her energy. I was really torn—I really liked her and I really didn't like her. I preferred girls who were reserved.

Paula was like a cheetah after a gazelle--in hot pursuit. She obviously liked me. We made a date to go to the movies to see Our Man Flint. Paula wanted to see the movie about a secret agent, Derek Flint (James Coburn), called in from retirement to fight a global criminal organization that flexed its power over the weather and the structure of the earth. Flint trekked through Europe in hot pursuit of a female spy named Gila Golan.

Paula's choice for a movie didn't surprise me. I don't think anyone else would have expected her to pick the biblical movie "The Greatest Story Ever Told" which was also playing at the same time! We had a good time at the movies.

The following weekend, we went skiing in the Poconos. I picked up Paula at her dorm around 8 a.m. and drove to Jack Frost Ski Resort for a day of skiing. We had a quick breakfast when we got there and skied for the rest of the morning. After lunch, we skied for the rest of the afternoon. We had a great time--laughing and clowning around. I don't think I've had this much fun in my life! I felt a real chemistry with her. Each of us forgot about why our relationship wouldn't work.

There we were--in a dilemma! Pittston girls were too serious about settling down, getting married, and having babies. College girls were too serious about their careers. Then, there was Paula, who just wanted to have fun. Paula was very refreshing for someone like me—I needed some humor in my life; needed some lightness to my being.

The following Saturday, we went to the movies and had a great time. After the movies, we went to Kearney's Drive-In Restaurant. We got something to eat and then talked for a while. I took Paula back to her dorm and parked outside for a while.

We kissed a few times. I was very impressed at what a good a kisser she was. She seemed pleased with my kisses as well. We made out for a while before I took her to the door. I wondered,

"Is this going to be a repeat of my parent's instant attraction to each other at Bucknell Junior College?"

Before Paula and I knew it, we had been dating for a few months and April was almost over. We went on many movie dates, dinner dates, and to a few dances together. I went to some of Paula's recitals. Paula went to some of my art class exhibitions. The semester was about finished and the weather was warming up.

Although Paula and I were not planning to carry our relationship beyond our time at Wilkes College, we were having a good time and enjoying each other's company. I sketched an eight by ten, pen-and-ink inch portrait of her, had it framed, and gave it to her as a going away present. She thanked me for my gift, and she said she would cherish it forever.

One night at the end of the last week of school, Paula and I went to an apartment of one of her friends. We had some wine— maybe a little too much wine--and started making out.

"Make love to me." Paula said.

We had talked about sex before and we admitted to each other that we never made love. This is a big step for her—to want me as her first lover. We both had done some heavy petting--unusual stuff for college seniors. None of my life-long friends had ever made love before.

I said, "I don't have any 'protection'."

"Don't you want to make love?"

"Yes, I want to."

"What are you waiting for?"

"I don't know."

"What would we do if you got pregnant?"

"I won't get pregnant, I have it covered."

"I don't know, Paula."

Paula said, "Don't worry, I won't get pregnant."

She must have seen a troubled look on my face and said, "If you're worried, just pull out when the time comes!"

We worked our way into the bedroom—kissing, rubbing, and grasping while we undressed each other. There was no going slowly with the excitement of the first time. Not for us!

We got on the bed and, before I knew it, I was inside her.

As I stroked her and our excitement rocketed, Paula whispered in my ear, "I want you to stay inside me."

Thoughts were going through my mind at light speed. At the height of passion, I had mixed feelings; I wanted to finish inside her but I feared the consequences.

Then my mother's voice popped into my mind: "Jeffrey, you son of a bitch, don't you dare get this girl pregnant!"

At that moment, I felt myself beginning to ejaculate and I pulled out.

Paula, looking visibly distressed, wrapped herself around my leg, and in a voice I didn't recognize said, "Why did you do that? You ruined it!"

Our passion was over. In more ways than one!

"I'm sorry; I don't know what came over me. I didn't want to get you pregnant."

We lay tightly embraced on the bed and she began to cry. She said, "I wanted it to be perfect! I wanted our love to be perfect."

We hugged for about thirty minutes and then we got out of bed, put on our clothes, and I took Paula to her dorm.

I knew I had ruined it for Paula. Our lovemaking was supposed to be a beautiful thing. Your first time should be beautiful. I knew I would never see her again. I knew I could never make it right.

For the next few days, I was down in the dumps. It was obvious my mother, Rose, did her job well. Even without her presence, I started acting out a guilt trip. I was worried I ruined my life for a moment of pleasure.

The next day, I told Mike and Sal what had happened. I was so happy to have made love to someone I liked, but I was so sad

I ruined it for Paula.

I sketched a larger portrait of Paula--similar to the small one I gave her--to remind me of our relationship.

Overseas, we were fully involved in the War in Vietnam.

Stateside, Selma, Alabama became the focus of a civil rights movement when activists worked to register black voters. In the Watts section of Los Angeles, five days of riots broke out, the most severe in the series of riots during the Sixties.

We liked to listen to The Temptations, The Four Tops, The Supremes, and Martha and the Vandellas.

We listened to their love songs, "My Girl," "Since I Lost You Baby," "I Can't Help Myself," "Stop in the Name of Love," "Back in My Arms Again," and "No Where To Run."

Chapter 8

The Post-College Years

The Search Begins

1965

Wyoming Valley

WE REFUSED TO ALLOW the world to dictate how we lived our lives. However, no matter what good news or good prospects there were, something or someone attempted to ruin our party. The most worrisome "black cloud" in 1965 was the Vietnam War and the probability of a letter from "Uncle Sam" ordering us to report for duty before we had arrived at our career destination.

In response to the threat of the letter, Mike joined the Army Reserve in Wilkes-Barre. I was still in school and wasn't a draft risk. Ted and Sal were teaching, and were temporarily exempt from military service as well.

During Mike's two-year career, he received two promotions. Mike continued to live on Swallow Street and commute every day to his job in Wilkes-Barre with his new Chevy convertible, purchased when he traded the 1953 Plymouth he bought from my mother. He now was on the fast track for his "dream career."

Mike, Sal, and I each had the "Life of Reilly." Our parents catered to us—we had a place to sleep, fresh cooked meals every day, and laundry washed and ironed. We often talked about the poor women who someday would fall in love with us and have to deal with three of the most spoiled people we knew.

Ted was ready to move to Binghamton, New York, to teach elementary school. Although he didn't know anyone there and it was less than an hour away from Wyoming Valley, he could come home anytime. He got an apartment there during the summer and was making new friends. He spent most of the summer in Wyoming Valley because he just couldn't stand to be without his buddies. After he moved to Binghamton, he still came home every weekend.

Sal continued to work as a "fill-in" barber as he did the previous year. He enjoyed interacting with customers and learned a great deal from this experience not to mention the money he was making.

New York City

I ENROLLED AT PRATT Institute in Manhattan, a section of New York City. I found a three-bedroom, third floor, walk-up apartment on 13th street in Greenwich Village with fellow Wilkes College art student, Joseph Cusano. Joe, one of four children, had two older brothers and a younger sister. His family was Sicilian from Bayside and he knew his way around the city. We planned to look for a third roommate once we started school.

After a week in my apartment, I invited Mike and Sal to see it and to show off Greenwich Village and Pratt Institute. Mike and Sal took the Greyhound bus to New York to visit that weekend. Although New York City apartments were not a good value for their size, Mike and Sal were impressed with it and its location. The rent, for a garage to store your car some eight blocks away, was obscene.

I cooked dinner for us--Ziti with marinara sauce and meatballs.

Sal said, "Wow, you learned to cook!"

"Yes I did. How did you like the food?"

"Dinner was great."

Of course, my uncles, Giuseppe and Anthony taught me how to cook when I worked in the restaurant but I didn't take it seriously until I was on my own.

Dotted around my Greenwich Village neighborhood were parks, bookstores, theaters, and comedy shops. My apartment was a few blocks away from some impressive clubs. We were living in the middle of history but didn't know it.

The Village Gate on Bleecker Street had an unbelievable history. During its thirty years in business, notables such as Billie Holiday, Duke Ellington, Dizzy Gillespie, and Dave Brubeck performed there. Aretha Franklin made her first appearance at the Village Gate.

Multitalented Mike Porco ran another club, Gerde's Folk City, on West Fourth Street at the corner of Mercer. Mike, an Italian who was an expert in hand made sandwiches, was able to hand pick talent such as Joan Baez, Phil Ochs, Judy Collins, and Bob Dylan. Mike described Dylan as a cross between a choirboy and a beatnik. Monday nights were Hootenanny night--wouldn't have missed it for the world!

Peter, Paul and Mary, Arlo Guthrie, Pete Seeger, Isley Brothers, and Tommy James and the Shondells recorded their music at The Bitter End.

Down the street, at the corner of Broadway, was the Bleecker Street Cinema that showed many independent and foreign films. It showed the works of directors such as Kubrick, Eisenstein, and Truffaut. Years later, after it stopped showing independent films, it had a brief stretch as a porno palace before closing.

Wyoming Valley

MIKE AND SAL RAN into Jimmy Walsh at Vispi's on Saturday

night. Jimmy, now an engineer, was a year ahead of us at Pittston High School. Jimmy was athletic and was a good golfer; he played to a ten handicap.

Since I was mostly in New York City, Mike, Ted, Jim, and Sal started golfing at Hollenback Golf Course, a public golf course in Wilkes-Barre, Pennsylvania. With low greens fees, Hollenback was affordable. Private Country clubs such as Fox Hill, Wyoming Valley, and Irem Temple were too expensive. They played other public golf courses such as Scranton Municipal, Happy Valley, and Shadowbrook. At times Jerry Bloom, with whom Mike and Sal graduated High School, joined them. Jimmy Walsh was clearly the best golfer among all of us.

In September, Sal began education classes at King's College. Some good came from his experience—he became a better student by learning how to break down information to teach it to others. He told me if he had been in this environment growing up, he would've had more choices in his life.

During the first semester, Sal planned to teach high school biology and chemistry but started thinking about alternative careers as well. Bob Martinelli, a guidance counselor at King's College, discussed his career options. As far as Sal was concerned, the pizza parlor was still on the table. Bob suggested the *Strong Vocational Blank*, an interest inventory test that compares your interests with interests of people in specific careers. Mr. Martinelli told him the test results would show him careers for which he was most compatible based on his interests.

His top three most compatible careers were chemistry teacher, dentist, and carpenter and the two least compatible careers were army officer and government worker. That's funny since many people from Pittston looked favorably on government workers.

Sal always liked doing things with his hands—carpentry, auto repair, and handyman stuff. He thought he would give dentistry a chance. So, he continued with his education program and planned to take the *Dental School Admission Test*.

He told Uncle Joe Greco, a dentist in Pittston, about the interest inventories test.

Uncle Joe said, "Why don't you come to the office the week during semester break and see what I do every day."

On the second day, toward the end of the morning, Uncle Joe extracted a front tooth from a patient and put it in alcohol. He told Sal, "Let's see how much talent you have. I'll give you the tooth, a small block of wax, and some carving instruments to take home. Try to carve a replica of the extracted tooth out of the wax block. Come back to the office after lunch."

Sal was excited about his "assignment." He went home, had lunch, and carved the tooth.

Around 2:30 p.m., Sal returned to Uncle Joe's office and gave him the tooth he carved. Uncle Joe looked at the carving and the tooth for a long time and asked, "Did you do this by yourself?" Of course, Sal said, "Yes."

Uncle Joe was so pleased. He couldn't believe Sal was able to carve a tooth as close to the original without any experience or instruction. He said, "I'd apply to dental school if I were you."

During the second semester, Sal did his student teaching in biology at West Wyoming High School. He was familiar with West Wyoming since he had gone to their senior prom a few years earlier. Mrs. Phillipini taught a biology class to tenth graders. Students liked her. Sal was to teach her class as his student teaching project.

His student-teaching supervisor, Mr. Finnegan, was a happy little old man with gray hair and wire-rimmed glasses. He always wore a brown suit, a white shirt, and a tan, bow tie. He often walked into class, unannounced and unexpected and sat in the back row, prompting a global sweat response by all the student teachers. He sat there and took notes and didn't say a word or make any jester. He was a very nice man and was very nurturing but intimidating just the same. He was a good mentor!

Binghamton

TED STARTED TEACHING in Binghamton. He was not the only newly graduated teacher at his school—about twenty percent of his fellow teachers were fresh out of college. Both new and seasoned teachers shared a difficult task—how to keep the kids motivated to learn. Ted was a likable sort and I knew the kids liked him.

New York City

AFTER A FEW WEEKS in class, Joe and I were at the cafeteria where we usually had lunch and I noticed, in front of us in line, a young, attractive lady, about mid-twenties, short, 5'2," with long blonde hair. Although she wasn't my type, I wanted to meet her. I preferred women who were tall and thin-- brunettes with legs that went all the way to the sky. Although I always said I liked that type, I never dated anyone who looked like that.

"My name is Jeffrey."

She smiled and said, "I'm Brandi."

"Do you work here or are you a student?"

She answered somewhat guardedly, "I work here."

"Where do you work?"

"I'm an executive secretary for one of the graduate professors."

"Are you from New York?"

"Yes, from Queens."

"Is that a long way to travel to work every day?"

"No. It wouldn't be far to commute but I have a studio

apartment on Emerson Place in Brooklyn, up the street from here."

We exchanged some small talk and it was time for her to get her lunch.

I asked, "Would you like to get together some time?"

"Sure. Why not?"

"If you give me your phone number, I'll call you."

Brandi gave me her phone number. Her "work" phone number.

I thought, "That's usually a "yellow" flag when a girl gives you her work number and not her home number."

I promised to call her once I completely moved into my apartment.

The next week, I ran into Brandi again and said, "Would you like to sit together?"

"I better introduce myself completely, my name is Jeffrey Rosenbloom."

"I'm Brandi Walker."

We both giggled. After a short time talking, the conversation went on effortlessly and we discovered we had many things in common--Italian food, theater, dancing, and hiking. I told Brandi I liked golf but hadn't played much during school. She told me golf seemed boring.

Since the conversation was going well, I asked her, "Would you like to go for dinner next Saturday?"

"Dinner would be great."

"Would you like to add dancing to dinner?"

"Sure, dinner and dancing would be nice."

"How does Villa Penza on Grand Street in Little Italy sound?"

"I love Villa Penza. I know a club up the street where we could go dancing afterward. Why don't we meet at the restaurant at 6 p.m.?

I was happy to have a date since Joe had been going home on

weekends leaving me alone in the apartment.

On Saturday, I took a cab to Villa Penza to meet Brandi for dinner. I wanted to be sure that I got there before she did so I could select a cozy little booth in the corner. Brandi arrived shortly after. When Brandi approached the table, I stood up and hugged her. I gave her a firm hug; she gave me a restrained hug. Neither of us knew what to expect.

Brandi said, "Nice hug. Do you always hug like that?"

"Yeah, pretty much, I'm half-Italian. You know how Italians are—a hug and a kiss when they see you, a hug or two during 'together' time, and several hugs and kisses when you're departing. The Italian half is a huge hugger."

"I like that. My family hardly ever hugged. In fact, they rarely expressed emotion about anything. I thought you might be Jewish with a name like Rosenbloom; I didn't realize you were part Italian. I can see that now. The Italian part of you softened the Jewish angles in your face. Neat!

"I'm half Jewish and half-Italian but I was raised Catholic."

"I was raised Episcopalian and go to the church around the corner from the school, Saint Mary's."

In our conversation, I downplayed the Jewish part and emphasized the Catholic part since Catholics and Episcopalians are similar.

"Did anyone ever tell you that you look like Dean Martin?" she said.

"Yes, a few times. I don't see it."

Villa Penza, known for its excellent homemade Italian food, was crowded. Their specialty was fish and calamari marinara. When the waitress came with the menu, she took the drink order and suggested the calamari. We each ordered a glass of wine and ordered a calamari marinara appetizer to share.

While we waited for our drinks, we engaged in some small talk about Pratt Institute and Brandi's job there and some small talk about my interest in art and pen-and-ink sketches. When the waitress served the drinks and calamari, we were ready to order dinner.

Brandi ordered chicken Piccata and I ordered trout, one of my favorite fish dishes. While we waited for dinner, we talked about New York attractions. Brandi liked going to fashion shows, not surprising since every time I saw her she was so well dressed.

A short time later, dinner arrived. During dinner, the conversation was different from that of the girls I knew in Pittston and at Wilkes College. Brandi was mature and not especially interested in talking about getting married or having children. She didn't appear to be "on the clock." The conversation was easy. I didn't feel Brandi was interviewing me for the job of *husband.*

I was quite happy with our conversation and was becoming more and more infatuated with Brandi. She seemed to be having a good time.

When we had about finished our dinners, Joe Favale, the owner of Villa Penza, stopped by our table and asked if we enjoyed dinner. We both quickly said yes. I started a conversation with Joe about Italian restaurants and told him about my grandfather's Italian restaurant in West Pittston.

Joe Favale asked me, "How did your grandfather get started?"

I said, "My grandfather, Dominic Agostino, came from Sicily, opened a restaurant, and named it Coccina Italiano. It seats about eighty people and has a few banquet rooms for special events. Food is freshly prepared and the restaurant is very popular with local politicians and professionals. When I worked there during high school and college, I sketched interesting people who dined there; it was a hobby of mine. I have a drawing of JFK when he ate there while campaigning for president.

"It sounds like my place here. We have a lot in common. I'm happy to meet you and invite you to come back soon."

111

Brandi and I left the restaurant and walked to a club up the street stopping at a few stores to window-shop on the way. They were relaxed and not in any hurry. The club was not as crowded since it was early. In an hour or two, there would be wall-to-wall people. Brandi had been there a few times and liked the music. The club had a more mature look than my typical "hideouts." Other patrons looked maybe early to mid-thirties. We danced for almost an hour—some fast dances and a few slow dances.

During one slow dance, Brandi whispered to me, "I like how you hold me tight when we're dancing; it's sexy. None of the men I've known dance like you. Of course, I've never been out with an Italian before."

I thanked her for her compliments.

The band started to play another slow dance and Brandi said to me, "I have a favor to ask."

"Sure, anything you want."

"I left my keys in my apartment and it's too late to call my landlord. Do you think I could stay with you tonight?"

I thought, "Whoa!" My neurons started firing full speed and the velocity of my thoughts was numbing. "This is a first."

Then the dialogue began in my head. "Now be cool. Don't appear too anxious! Be cool! Take your time. Don't blow it."

In what probably seemed too long for Brandi to wait for my answer, I said, "Sure. You can live at my place."

The rapid thoughts continued, "Live? Where did that come from? Live at my place. God, she'll think I've never been on a date before."

I had only made love once a few months ago but wanted Brandi to think I was a "man about town" especially since she was older and probably had more experience."

I continued talking and attempted to correct my mistake, "Brandi, I'd love to have you stay over. My roommate, Joe, is at his parent's house on the island. He goes home every weekend. Why don't we grab a cab and go to my place. "

About 30 minutes later, Brandi and I got to my apartment building. We walked up three flights of stairs to my apartment. I poured two glasses of wine and showed Brandi around the apartment. I showed her sketches I had done: Sister Anna Marie with the horns and the pitchfork, JFK sitting at one of the tables in my grandfather's restaurant, Daniel Flood sitting at another table, Bobby Vinton, and one of Paula who I said was a "relative."

After the tour, I put on a Johnny Mathis album. Brandi and I danced for a while. I held Brandi firmly against me as she said she liked and she put her right leg between my legs as we danced.

"You feel good against me." Brandi said.

"We're a good fit." I said.

We started to make out. Brandi was an aggressive kisser. We didn't know each other for more than a couple of hours and she was pushing her tongue deep down my throat.

I thought, "The woman knows what she wants! Either she's hot after me or very horny. Let's leave it at 'she's hot after me.' "

In a highly excited state, Brandi told me she wanted to use the bathroom to get ready for bed and she would meet me in the bedroom. She used my bathroom and I used the guest bathroom to get ready. Then, I went to my bedroom, undressed, turned down the sheets, got in bed, and waited in bed for Brandi. It seemed like she was taking an eternity to get ready. I thought, "What can she be doing in there?"

When Brandi came in the bedroom, she was naked except for a pair of black, lace, bikini panties.

"Wow," I thought. "I don't think it gets better than this. To think, I almost didn't introduce myself to her."

Brandi slipped into bed. We hugged and kissed. As we kissed, I rubbed her back; she ran her fingers through my hair. We kissed some more and then made love. Afterward, we laid there for a while—I was on my back and Brandi had her head on my chest.

Lying there, I thought about how nervous I was during the whole process. I had never *slept* with anyone before. This was only my second time making love and the circumstances surrounding Paula's reaction to our lovemaking marred our experience.

On the other hand, Brandi was comfortable coming to my apartment, getting naked, and making love to me. Like most men under circumstances like this, I began wondering, "What type of woman is she? Is this her routine? Does she really like me? Does she really feel comfortable with me?" Well, I wasn't about to overanalyze what happened. I resolved to enjoy the evening with someone I liked and with someone toward whom I had a strong attraction.

Interestingly enough, Rose was absent from this encounter.

Around 7 a.m., Brandi woke up first and started playing around with me. She tickled me and started hugging me. We played around with each other for a while and made love again.

We both expressed how much we enjoyed the evening with dinner and dancing and how much we liked making love. I asked Brandi if she would like to see me again and she said, "Yes." We got up and made breakfast.

After breakfast, Brandi took a shower and got dressed to go to her apartment. She told me she wanted to take the subway back to her apartment, but wanted company walking to the subway station.

I was happy about last night. I thought, overall, it was a fantastic evening. "I don't think I've had as much fun in my entire life." When Brandi was ready to go home, I walked her to the subway. I couldn't wait to see her again.

Over the next two months, Brandi and I went out almost every weekend. Often I met Brandi at a restaurant for dinner and dancing before going back to my apartment. Other times Brandi came over to my apartment and we cooked dinner. Sometimes, we went to the Pocono Mountains for a day trip.

Wyoming Valley

THE FIRST TIME WE all got together again was for Thanksgiving. Ted had been going home almost weekly, I hadn't been home since starting school in New York. Mike and Sal were doing their thing. Johanna and Stanley were in town and staying at Sal's house.

Thanksgiving morning, Mike, Ted, and I went to Sal's house. It was like old times, Sal's mother was ecstatic with her little "chickens" back to the roost. Johanna and Stanley had just awakened and Katie made breakfast for everyone. Of course, Johanna helped with breakfast.

I told Johanna and Stanley about my apartment in Greenwich Village and my classes. Stanley invited me to call them within the next couple of weeks so we could get together for dinner. I said I would. Johanna asked me if I was seeing anyone. I said I had gone out with a couple of girls but nothing serious. Johanna told Stanley, "Maybe some of our friends in the City know someone for Jeffrey."

My God, you just can't take the Sicilian out of the girl!

In Wilkes-Barre, Sal had a meeting with Mr. Finnegan, his King's College student-teaching supervisor. During their meeting, Mr. Finnegan told Sal, "Now that you're ready to begin teaching, you'll attend teacher staff meetings. I suggest you sit back and listen to what everyone has to say and, afterward, ask questions or give your opinion. This is the approach of an intelligent professional. Let the others speak first. Learn from them. If you speak first, you may appear to have less potential than you actually have."

Sal believed this advice was the best advice he ever got

during his college years.

New York City

I CALLED JOHANNA and Stanley about a week after Thanksgiving to arrange dinner. Johanna said she would make reservations at Sardi's on 44th Street for dinner on December 6.

When we arrived at Sardi's, I was impressed. I saw caricatures of famous people hanging on the walls. This was a dream come true for me especially since my sketches and drawings lined my grandfather's restaurant. While we were eating, we saw Arthur Treacher, Phyllis Diller, her husband, and Rodney Dangerfield walking from the upstairs dining room. The waiter told us they were appearing on the Merv Griffith Show.

Wyoming Valley

MR. FINNEGAN CALLED Sal to his office. With a month remaining for the semester, he truly believed he was in trouble. Mr. Finnegan never called anyone into his office unrelated to his class observation, and he hadn't observed any of Sal's classes for a while.

Mr. Finnegan said, "Hanover Township School District (west of Wilkes-Barre) has an opening for a chemistry teacher. Some of the students in the industrial chemistry class were unruly and their teacher had a nervous breakdown and quit. The job consists of teaching three chemistry classes, one of which is to industrial students. I'm recommending you for the job. If you take it, classes would count toward your student teaching credits."

Sal couldn't believe what he heard. He was very flattered by

Mr. Finnegan's offer. However, he was concerned about the class discipline in the industrial chemistry class.

"I'm not sure that I can handle a problem like this being so young and inexperienced."

"I wouldn't have asked you if I didn't think you could do it. You have a confident way about you and I don't believe students would attempt to take advantage of you. You just need to decide what you want to do in class and stick to your plan."

"OK. Do I have to interview?"

"Yes, only to see the school and talk with the principal. The job is yours if you want it."

Sal interviewed and the principal offered the job to him.

Sal was always reading about the stock market and discussing it with his father, Sam. Sal took the Wall Street Journal to school every day during college and had it with him on the first day of class at Hanover Township High School. When he went to the Industrial Chemistry classroom, the students, as expected, were acting up and talking. He put his briefcase on the desk, sat down in the teacher's chair, opened the Wall Street Journal, and started reading.

Curiosity got the best of the students when they didn't get the response they expected. Everyone stopped talking. Once they stopped talking, Sal stood up, turned around, and wrote his name on the chalkboard.

"Why are you reading the Wall Street Journal? One student asked.

"I'm interested in business and investing and was just reading about U.S. Steel. Knowing what's happening helps me make good investment decisions."

Sal knew the students would interested in U.S. Steel because of their program.

Bingo! Sal hit upon something that got their interest. He thought, "There are only a few weeks of school remaining, why not tie in their learning chemistry to something in which they were interested."

Every day, the class discussed the stock market for ten to fifteen minutes before discussing chemistry. Sal didn't come up with the idea. The idea fell upon him. Lucky him!

Christmas, 1965

I WAS VISITING PITTSTON again and went to meet Mike and Ted at Sal's house. I told everyone about Sardi's and about the pictures on the wall. I also told them about the good time I had with Johanna and Stanley.
Mike asked him, "What did you eat?"
"I can't remember. I was too excited to pay attention to my food."

On Becoming Us

President Lyndon Johnson declared war on crime and created the Bureau of Narcotics and Dangerous Drugs (now DEA).

Liberals and conservatives differed in their view of crime.

Liberals believed social conditions (racial inequality and limited opportunities for young people) were the cause of crime, poverty, and addiction. They believed they could decrease crime by addressing these social conditions.

Conservatives argued that irresponsible or bad choices caused crime. It wasn't social pressures such as racism, low employment, lack of desirable housing, and poor education. The choices people made created poverty, criminal behavior, or drug addiction. Social programs only enabled these choices. Programs fostering good decision-making would lead to less crime.

The war on crime intensified in 1968 when President Richard Nixon and his administration rejected the social explanation of crime in favor of leniency in the criminal justice system. Nixon insisted the "solution to crime lies in more convictions and not more government spending."

In the mid-sixties, crime in New York City was at an all time high—riding the subway was risky. Transit authority "police" rode crowded cars to discourage crime—there was a cop on every train and a cop in every station during the nighttime hours.

In the financial markets, the rise in stock prices gave new life to the theory that the Dow-Jones Industrial Average is inversely proportional to women's hemlines. The DOW hit all time highs while the miniskirt and hot pants became very popular.

Chapter 9

The Post-College Years

The Search Continues

1966

HAYATO KATO NEEDED an apartment. He was a classmate of Joe Cusano.

Hayato asked Joe, "Do you know of anyone who wants to share an apartment?"

"Why? Are you looking?"

"Yes. My girlfriend, Natsumi, and I live together in an apartment in Queens. We've been dating since high school and went to NYU together. I need an apartment to share because, whenever her parents or my parents visit from Tokyo, I have to scramble to find a place to stay."

"Has she finished school or is she working?"

"She's in law school at Columbia. A permanent address and a place to crash occasionally when family visits would be helpful. We don't want our parents to know we're living together. In Japan, it's improper for us to have the same address without marriage."

Joe said, "Jeffrey Rosenbloom and I have a three-bedroom apartment and we want to get another roommate. I'll ask him if he's ready to add another person. An 'absentee' roommate to share the rent would be great."

Joe told me about Hayato's proposal, "A classmate in my speech class asked me about sharing our apartment. He lives with his girlfriend but needs a permanent address so their parents won't know they're living together. He's willing to pay a third of the rent but none of the utilities since he really won't be living here."

I said to Joe, "Brandi stays with me most weekends since I met her at the beginning of last semester. This has worked out well since you're away most weekends. I'm OK with Hayato's proposal especially since he will be at his girlfriend's apartment most of the time."

Joe said, "OK. Let's have lunch so you can meet him."

Joe stood there about to turn away but looking as if he had more to say.

I said, "Joe, you look like you have a question."

"I do. Can I ask you a question about Brandi?"

"Sure, what do you want to know?

Joe said, "Does Brandi always stay here?"

"Yes. For some reason, after we go out, we always end up here."

"You never stay at her apartment?"

"No. She always stays here."

"But, you've been to her apartment?"

"No. Actually, I've never been to her apartment. We always meet at a restaurant or a dance club on Friday or Saturday night and then come back here to spend the weekend. Sometimes, we'll meet here, take a cab to my car, and leave the city to go to the Poconos."

"You never date during the week?"

"No. Whenever I ask her to do something during the week, she either is working late or has a commitment. I guess she wants to be a "weekend girlfriend.' "

"Well, she's good looking, has a great body, and is happy to screw your brains out. I assumed that's what you wanted. You don't seem like the settling down type."

"Well, it wasn't what I wanted but it's what I got. Sometimes relationships don't go the way of your intention."

"I wouldn't be concerned unless you're serious about her and want to marry her. If not, just keep on truckin!"

I thought, "Apparently, Joe doesn't know me very well. We were at Wilkes together and hung out at school periodically. He knew about Paula and he knows about Brandi. Maybe Joe thinks I'm a 'player' and just want to screw every chick in a skirt."

I said to Joe, "I'm not serious about her. Actually, I don't know what I am about her. I've been too busy to think about it. Let's get back to Hayato. What type of guy is he?"

Joe said, "He's a nice guy...quiet...respectful...serious. His father is an executive for a car company. He went to NYU and wants to get on Broadway."

"OK. Let's meet and see how it goes."

A few days later, Joe, Hayato, and I had lunch. All went well and we invited Hayato to "move in."

For the last week, I've been agitated about the questions Joe asked me. He brought up a few important issues about which I should be concerned. My biggest problem: "Why have I not been concerned? Has my head been in the sand?"

In all fairness, at times, taking a break from goal-related activities is necessary because the break gives you a chance to step back and evaluate what you are doing. Dating without the goal of finding the love of your life, taking classes not related to career, having sex just for fun could be a good thing.

My father once remarked about one of his grandchildren who, at two years of age, was feverously playing with her toys, "Playing is her *job* right now." I wouldn't have described child's play as her "work."

I thought, "I need to figure this out now. Over the past five-months, I haven't been to Brandi's apartment and we've never been on a date during the week. Never, not even once. We've seen each other three to four weekends a month during this time. Every time we go out, we end up in bed, my bed, making love—sometimes two or three times over the weekend. On Sunday, she leaves to go to her apartment. She has never talked about settling down, getting married, or having a family like the Pittston girls. Maybe she's married! Am I an idiot? I liked not having pressure to commit to a relationship at first, but I am concerned about it now.

"After five months in an "intimate" relationship, I don't feel any closer to Brandi now than I did when we first started dating. We have a great time when we're together—dinner, dancing, and making love. I don't believe what we have is only a sexual thing, but I'm not sure what a sexual thing feels like.

"Even though I'm not seeing anyone else, we never talked about going steady. I do feel committed to see Brandi every weekend and would feel guilty if I saw someone else during the week.

"I'm not even sure what I'm doing is dating.

"Is *she* seeing someone else—we never talked about it? She could be seeing someone during the week.

"I'm surprised I hadn't thought about this issue before—I've been too busy studying and too busy painting. In fact, the only time I saw Brandi was during the week in the cafeteria.

"I'm not ready to get married, and, if I were ready, I don't believe Brandi is the one I would choose. Maybe it *is* only a sexual relationship. How could I be physically inside her while making love and not feel close to her? It seems like there should be some sort of connection. Maybe Joe is right—I'm a player!

"Life is surely complicated.

"The big question is, "Why, all of a sudden, am I concerned?

"As Joe said, she's good looking, has a nice body, and is hungry for sex with me. Although I couldn't come up with a solid reason to investigate the basis of my relationship with Brandi, I now want to know more. I don't want to be in a 'relationship' when the right one comes along. I wouldn't be available when the 'right one' comes along. The one with whom I could spend the rest of my life."

The only presents Brandi and I gave each other were Christmas presents before I went home to Pennsylvania for Christmas break. I gave her a framed eight by ten pen-and-ink drawing of her looking out over a valley at the Delaware Water Gap. She gave me a silver money clip with my initial.

On Monday, February 14, I brought a dozen red roses to Brandi's office. When I walked into the department office, Brandi was standing at the end of a hallway with her back to the door, talking with an older man.

I thought, "That must be her boss."

The man had his hand on her waist—actually a little below her waist—and was looking at her, somewhat intimately. The man turned and walked away and Brandi turned toward where I was standing. When she saw me, her face turned red--deep red.

I knew!

There are things a man knows about a woman and a woman knows about a man at times like this. The "look" can fill volumes of books. Brandi attempted a smile as she walked toward me, but she couldn't hide her upset. Even the best movie actress can't hide feelings at times like this. When feelings are there, they're there.

We lightly hugged and I gave Brandi the roses.

"Happy Valentine's Day."

Brandi said, "Thank you so much for the roses. I didn't expect to see you. I have a gift I was going to give you next weekend. Will we see each other Saturday?"

"Sure, let's stay in and I'll cook a Valentine dinner for you... In fact, why don't you come over about 2 p.m. and we'll cook together. Don't forget to put the flowers in water."

"OK. See you soon."

That night, I had dinner with Joe and told him what

happened. I gave Joe the blow-by-blow account of our meeting. Joe listened to the whole story without saying a word—exactly what you would expect from a good friend.

After I finished my story, I looked at Joe and asked, "What do you think?

"I have a few questions. First of all, just how low was his hand?"

"It was pretty low! It was practically on her ass. You know how, when Sicilians hug, they like to do the 'reach around' to squeeze a girl's ass?"

"*That* low!"

"Yes!"

Joe asked, "What do you think is going on with Brandi?"

"I've thought about it all afternoon. I think she's involved with her boss and sees him at her apartment during the week. He's probably married. That would explain why she only wants to see me on weekends."

Joe said, "I would ask her directly what's going on. Assumptions never reveal the whole truth."

"I intend to. She's coming to dinner on Saturday and we'll talk then."

"Does she know you're suspicious of her and her relationship with her boss?"

"Well, she may be suspicious now. I don't think I was able to hide my reaction. She must have seen something in my face because she asked if we would be seeing each other on Saturday. She asked in a way that told me she thought there was the possibility we wouldn't see each other."

The next weekend, Brandi took the subway to my apartment. She arrived just after 2 p.m. I had gone shopping for groceries to make tomato sauce and lasagna. Brandi gave me a bottle of wine. As I put the wine on the table, she started playing around with me. She liked to reach around from the back, tickle me, and massage my "stuff." This was her typical foreplay whenever we returned from a date or when she came to my apartment. I almost dropped the bottle of wine. We hugged, kissed, and made love."

Later, Brandi and I got out of bed and started cooking. This wasn't the first time I cooked for her but it was the most effort I put into it. Usually, I cooked spaghetti and meatballs or baked ziti.

I made tomato sauce like my grandfather taught me. We had a good dinner and curled on the couch to watch a movie on TV.

After the movie, I "casually" asked Brandi, "Who was the man in your office with the rolled up shirt sleeves?"

"He's my boss, Herschel Freeman. I would have introduced you but he was busy and I was surprised to see you."

"He looks old... Well, he looks old enough to be your boss. Does he have a wife and kids," I asked.

"Yes, he has two young children. They live in Greenwich, Connecticut and he commutes back and forth every day."

"He seemed pretty friendly toward you."

"He is very friendly. I like him a lot."

"What's his wife like?"

"I don't know. I've never met her."

"Where does he stay when the weather is bad and he can't make it home?"

"Jeffrey, you're acting like a prosecutor with the rapid fire questions. I know where you're going with this. I want to be honest with you so you can stop asking questions."

"You're a nice man, respectful, and kind. We get along well and have fun when we're together. I enjoy weekends with you but I have someone else I see during the week. I assumed you had someone during the week as well."

"I don't have anyone else; I don't have anyone I see during the week."

"Herschel and I are involved. Our affair started about two years ago, a year after I started working for him, during a time when he was having problems at home. He and his wife

127

separated, he moved out of their house, and he rented a flat near the school.

"Sometime after that, he asked me if I would have dinner with him. He said he needed a friend with to whom to talk. He told me that he respected me--how mature I was and how I always made sensible choices. I felt sorry for him and I said OK. We ate at a restaurant and he told me about his wife. She had an affair with the rabbi at their synagogue and wanted to be with him. After dinner, he went to his apartment and I went home.

"Over the following month, we had dinner about a half-dozen times. One night I had a little too much to drink, and we ended up in his apartment. We fell asleep next to each other fully dressed. We didn't have sex. I think he was depressed and needed comforting. I didn't have anyone and being close to him filled my need for companionship. I always seem to need someone around.

"I was living at home and commuting to work. I never made it home that night. My parents were very upset until I told them a coworker's boyfriend committed suicide and I needed to stay with her. I told them it was too late to call them.

"The next week, Herschel and I went for dinner. After dinner, we went to his apartment, laid on the bed and fell asleep. I stayed over that night, but, again, it was platonic.

"Later that week, we went for dinner and to his apartment. As we sat on the couch, he started rubbing my shoulder. After a few minutes, he kissed me. That was the first time we had sex. It was like a friendship that turned into a relationship. It was an accident. However, after that, I started staying over and having sex a few times a week. How often can two healthy people lie next to each other and not engage? We 'dated' for about five months.

"Six months later, he and his wife reconciled and he moved back to Connecticut. His apartment had ten months remaining on the lease and he offered his apartment to me. He told me he would pay for balance of the lease, and I didn't have to be concerned about him coming over now that he and his wife were back together. I agreed."

"We worked together without discussing his home life. A few months went by, and, one day, New York City had a blackout, and he was unable to get home. He asked if he could stay with me and I agreed to let him stay. How could I say *no* since he was paying the rent. We had dinner and made love.

"After that, he started to come over once a week, usually on Wednesday. As time went on, he started to come over twice a week, on Monday and Wednesday and sometimes on Thursday. Each time he picked up dinner, we ate in the apartment, and made love. He usually went home after making love. When the lease was up, he asked if I wanted to extend the lease for another year, and I said yes.

"I never wanted to be the 'other woman,' but that's what I had become. I thought, 'I must be a whore to be doing this—sleeping with a married man.' Then, I did what I always had done—I rationalized. I thought our relationship was just two friends in need of comfort. I neither expected him to divorce his wife nor expected us to be together."

"How long has this been going on?" Jeffrey asked.

"About a year and a half."

"That's a long time to be involved with a married man without any resolution with his marriage."

"Jeffrey, when we met in the cafeteria, I wanted to see you and end it with Herschel. I wanted it to be different with you. I'm attracted to you and I like you. You excite me just by being near me. I'm excited when we touch, when we hold hands, and when we're together, even without sex.

"I'm completely satisfied when I'm with you and when you are inside me, and, at that time, I can't think of anything else or anyone else. When you have an orgasm inside me, your warmth lasts the whole night. Certainly you know I love you and I'm not in love with Herschel or anyone else."

Brandi put her arms around me, we snuggled on the couch for a while, and she fell asleep.

I thought to myself, "I need to be able to think with my head and not with my dick. Exactly, what is going on here? Is she a psycho? Is she the 'new woman' Cosmopolitan Magazine described?

"What do I know about this woman?

"She's attractive, sexy, and fun. My God, the sex—the sex is unbelievable! That's a good thing and that's probably why I didn't question our relationship before.

"We went out on our first date and she asked to stay with me that night, probably lying about forgetting her keys.

"She was comfortable sleeping with me, someone who she only knew marginally.

"She continued seeing Herschel and sleeping with him during the week. I don't know if she told him about me—she must have deceived him as well.

"She didn't break it off with Herschel like she said she intended, perhaps another lie.

"She never gave Herschel a clue she was seeing someone else, more deception.

"The bottom line is I think she's a liar and is now attempting to manipulate me. That won't work for me. I can never trust her again."

Brandi woke up and wanted to go to bed.

The next morning, Brandi got dressed to go to the subway.

I told her, "I can't see you anymore."

"Why? I told you everything, and I thought you were OK with our relationship."

She started to cry and held him so tight he could hardly breathe.

"Please reconsider. I'll break up with Herschel and move in with you."

There is no way I am going to be OK with this. Brandi held on for a long time. She began rubbing herself against me. She started kissing me and continued rubbing her breasts and pelvis against me. I guess she thought she could convince me stay with her.

I began to get excited. I thought, "I can't give in."

Resisting her was too difficult. We started to make out and had sex again. We both cried the whole time. We knew this would be our last time together; we knew this would be the last time we would have sex. We were so excited we had simultaneous orgasms. This was the first time we had synchronized organisms since we met. We knew how good it felt being together all these months, how good the intimacy felt. This was the best sex I had ever had.

I don't know why first-time sex, break-up sex, make-up sex, and vacation-sex feel so much better than just regular sex.

I have to be strong. I can't prolong breaking up. I knew if we stayed together, each time we finished having sex and I was able to think sensibly, I would want our relationship to end. It was the right thing to do. It was the only thing to do.

Brandi got dressed again, I walked her to the subway; we both said goodbye.

When I got back to my apartment, I remembered a time when Brandi looked through the living room window. She had moved the curtain aside to watch the snowfall. She stood there barefooted in a short, red robe, her hair covering her shoulders, steam coming off her mug of hot coffee she held in her left hand. I remembered the look in her eyes while watching the snowfall. Her look was like that of an eagle studying his prey. Her stare was so intense; I was reluctant to say anything to her. Finally, I said "a penny for your thoughts." She smiled, walked over to me, and gave me a peck on my cheek. She never did tell me what was going through her mind.

I sat down and took a long time to detail every part of the

expression on Brandi's face, every aspect of her body language, and every thread of emotion. After the details were in my mind, I began to sketch her on a sixteen by twenty sheet of drawing paper. Unlike my typical sketches, which started in the main area of focus and worked away from there, I outlined the scene with my pen and then filled in the details after that. After I finished the sketch, I colored the robe red. It was fantastic. Everything was black and white except the red robe. I was so proud of my sketch, I forgot about my loss.

Wyoming Valley

I SHOWED MY SKETCH of Brandi to Mike and Sal in Pittston. They were speechless.

Mike said, "The man has talent!"

Sal said to Mike, "Jeffrey is accumulating quite a collection of pen-and-ink sketches of girls with whom he has had a connection--a sexual connection."

Mike said, "This is like 'kiss and tell!' "

After we talked about Brandi, Sal said, "I've taken the Dental School Admission Test and have applied to several dental schools in Pennsylvania."

I asked, "What are you going to do about teaching?"

"I'll continue teaching in case dental school doesn't work out."

After teaching the last month of the year at Hanover High School, he decided to look for a different job. West Pittston High School had a job opening for a Biology and Chemistry teacher, which paid $4,500 per year plus benefits. Saint Ann's Academy, a prep school for girls, in Wilkes-Barre, had a job opening for a Biology and Chemistry teacher also at $4,500 per year plus benefits. Saint Ann's Academy offered the teaching job to Sal and gave him a couple of days to think about it.

Uncle Leo Greco, a politician, knew about the job in West Pittston. His friend called Sal and Sal told us of the conversation.

The politician said, "You can have the job in West Pittston. You'll pay a $200 "finder's fee" and we'll raise the salary $200, to $4,700—'a wash.'"

Although he didn't expect a call like this, Sal was offended someone was asking him to pay for a job.

Sal said, "I'm a good teacher and I don't have to have to pay for a job."

The politician said, "You're not paying for the job. You're paying a 'finder's fee.' "

Sal said, "I'm not interested."

He immediately hung up on the caller.

Sal thought, "What kind of cockamamie reasoning is that?"

About 20 minutes later, Uncle Leo called Sal and said, "What the hell's the matter with you? He's giving you the job!"

Sal told him, "I'm not paying for a job. It's against my principles. Anyway, I believe it's against the law."

At that time, Sal still lived with his parents and had no financial responsibilities.

I asked Sal what decision he would have made if he had a wife and children to support.

Would he have thrown out his principles for the benefit of his family, take the job, and stand firm. Would he have stuck to his principles and looked for another job?

Fortunately, he didn't have to weigh his principles; he took the job teaching at Saint Ann's Academy. He was excited to work there since his cousin, Diane Augello, was starting ninth grade, and they could ride to school together.

I asked Sal, "Why are you willing to work for a Catholic school with nuns in charge rather than work in public school?"

He said, "Although I had a negative experience at Saint Rocco's Grade School, I thought it would be easier to work for nuns than to work for politicians."

Now that Sal had a real job, he needed a real car. He always liked sports cars. My father gave me a British Racing Green Austin Healey 3000 for college graduation and Sal loved it. He liked Triumphs and bought a 1966 Triumph TR4a--Fire-engine red! We wouldn't have expected any other color.

Things were looking good for Sal, he had a contract to teach high school, he bought a new car, and he had applied to dental school. He planned to pay off his car in one year. He didn't want the burden of a car loan while he was in school.

Ted and I were home for summer break. Of course, Sal never left home, and Mike was still plugging away at work. None of us had a girlfriend. Actually, it was downright irritating that we didn't have any love interests! Mike had been working three years, and Ted had been working one year.

We were all looking for the love of our lives, "the goddess that would love us more than life itself"; some of us were looking more seriously than the others. We had hit a dry spell. We were no longer among numerous college girls providing an assortment of potential dates. We dated less frequently than before. One night as we discussed the lack of potential women from whom to choose to date, Mike was disgusted and said, "Good girls are hard to find, you can always find the other kind...except when you need them." Well, that was revealing. Were we running out of prospects?

Atlantic City, New Jersey

A FEW DAYS BEFORE Labor Day Weekend, Mike, Ted, Sal, Barry Warren, and I went to Atlantic City. Barry lived on Swallow Street. He was a senior at University of Pittsburgh Dental School.

We got the last two rooms in a hotel on Michigan Avenue, a street we liked because it was half way between the Steel Pier and the Million Dollar Pier where most of the action occurred. On the afternoon of our last day, Ted and Sal walked out of a bar where we were hanging out and sat on a bench outside the bar. We weren't "bar" types but went to pass the time.

A girl came out of the bar and sat next to Sal.

"Hi, my name is Ginny. How are y'all doing?"

Sal said, "I'm Sal and this is Ted. We're doing well."

"You look bored. Aren't y'all having a good time?"

"Yes, we've been going to the beach and taking in the 'rays.' "

"What have you been doing?"

"My girlfriends and I have been here for a week and I have to carry them back Atlanta tomorrow. We rode to Margate the other night. What a view! Lights coming at ya from all over the place."

"You don't talk like you're from around here."

"Golly no! We're from the south!"

She looked at Sal and said, "Would you like to come see the lights with me?"

Sal was dumbfounded and said, "Yes, I'd love to, but I don't have a car."

Ginny said, "Honey, I *have* a car, I'll drive."

Sal thought, "Wow, this was like when Paula picked up Jeffrey at the dance." We weren't accustomed to women approaching us. Things "were a-changin."

Sal and Ginny met outside the hotel, walked to Ginny's Red Mustang Convertible, and drove to get something to eat. Afterward, they drove to Margate and parked on the beach to watch the lights. They kissed a few times and began to make out. Kissing progressed to heavy petting and Sal wanted to stop. He hadn't made love and wanted to wait until he was in a relationship for his first time.

Ginny said, "Darlin, you can't stop now and leave me under

135

this condition. I won't be able to sleep or nothing."

Sal felt guilty since he was responsible for Ginny's condition—"all hot and bothered"--and needed to fix it. He thought about the lessons his mother taught him about responsibility and the guilt trips he experienced growing up but didn't think his mother intended for her "lessons" to apply in situations such as this.

So, lesson learned--finish what you start!

During their drive, back to Atlantic City, Sal told Ginny, "This was my first time."

Ginny said to Sal, "Honey, if had known that, we could of gone to my hotel room and took our good old time. I could have made it exciting for you."

Sal said, "Doing it in the car was exciting."

Ginny said, "I enjoyed our sex--you made me feel alive."

On the way back to Pittston the next day, Sal was quiet.

"Sal, you're not saying much. What's going on?" Mike said.

"Nothing's wrong. I'm just thinking that we aren't kids any more—we're growing up."

"He got laid last night and who knows where his brain is," Ted said.

"It must have been good. Was it the girl from the bar?" I said.

Ted said, "Yes, that's the one."

Sal was quietly reflecting on his first sexual experience.

He said, "It seems that attitudes about love and marriage have changed without my knowing. Where had I been? Did I have my head in the sand?

"I don't know what's going on anymore. In the past, we listened to songs about love and talked about falling in love. We listened to songs about marriage and talked about getting married. We listened to songs about families and talked about having children. We all wanted to meet the 'right one,' fall in love, get married, and have a family.

"Last night, I 'had sex!' It had nothing to do with love. It wasn't love! I wonder if she remembers my name!

"What happened to the things Elvis sang about in 'Love Me Tender and the things the Temptations sang about in 'Sunshine on a Cloudy Day?'

"I suppose attitudes are changing. Would we ever be the same again? We appreciate things more when they come slowly—like friendship and love, than we do for things that come quickly--like one-night-stands.

"Were customs and attitudes changing or were they remaining the same and our outlook was changing as we grew up?

"I don't like the way I feel!"

Barry said, "You'll get over it. The first time is delicate for everyone. As soon as you get your 'kielbasa' in a few more chicks, you'll stop questioning the meaning of life! My advice is to enjoy it while you can."

Wyoming Valley

LABOR DAY CAME AND WENT and we were moving on. Mike went to work on Tuesday as he had for the past three years. Ted drove to his apartment in Binghamton to start his second year teaching. Sal drove to Saint Ann's Academy to begin his first year teaching. I drove to my apartment in New York City to start my second year at Pratt Institute.

Saint Ann's Academy, Wilkes-Barre, founded in 1878 by the Sisters of Christian Charity was in the old Mallinckrodt Convent. Faculty and administration included the principal, Sister Agnese, eighteen nuns who were teachers, and three lay teachers-- Mrs. Callahan, Mrs. Mulderig, and Sal.

The science lab on the second floor was for chemistry

students to conduct experiments. Students made appointments with Sal to discuss academic issues and they met in his office, which was in the corner of the lab.

Students, mostly from Northeastern Pennsylvania and a few from surrounding states were daughters of physicians, dentists, lawyers, politicians, and prominent businessmen. Although academic standards were very high, not all students were highly intelligent or intelligent enough to gain acceptance into Ivy League Colleges. However, all students graduated and some became physicians, lawyers, educators, and prominent citizens. A few became homemakers.

Sal taught Biology to sophomores, Chemistry to juniors, and advanced Biology to seniors.

He was a good teacher. His tests always included a philosophical question. The answer to the philosophical question was worth five points (5%) which he gave students if they thoughtfully attempted to answer the question. There was no right or wrong answer to these questions. One time the question was, "What would you eliminate in the world if you had the power to do so?" Typical answers were "money," "sickness," "lying," and "cheating."

Sal told us the questions he was going to ask and then shared some of the answers students gave. We discussed the question and potential answers. We loved doing this. We discussed philosophy since we were in grade school.

Sandi Slovenski was one of Sal's chemistry students who always gave interesting answers to his philosophical questions. He looked first for her test paper to correct. She was attractive and he liked her. She had a sister, Loretta, in Diane Piazza's class. Although Sal talked with Diane about Sandi often on the way back and forth to school, he didn't let anyone know he liked her because of his position at the school. Keeping a secret from Mrs. Callahan and Mrs. Mulderig was difficult, but they never suspected.

Sal enjoyed driving to school with his cousin Diane. She constantly told Sal she would be happy when some conditional thing happened.

She said, "I'll be happy when this semester is over," "I'll be happy when I finish this project," or "I'll be happy when I finish high school."

One day Sal told her, "You'll never be happier than you are right now."

It took a while for that to sink in and she said to him, "So, I have to make my own happiness." She was always "happy" after that discussion.

Sal was in the middle of giving final exams before Christmas break when he received an acceptance letter from the University of Pittsburgh Dental School. That was fantastic news for him and he shared it with Sister Agnese, the faculty, and students. He did this as soon as he heard since they had to look for his replacement.

New York City

IN SEPTEMBER, I BEGAN my second year of graduate school. I was excited about two externships I would do this year: Crime Illustration and Courtroom Illustration. During the first semester, I spent time in court with a courtroom sketch artist to learn the methods of sketching individuals in the courtroom—the accused, the lawyers, the judge, and the jury. I knew, because of my ability to sketch people and tell a story with my sketches, I could put my talents to work in the courtroom. I also knew, with the detail and intensity of my sketches, I could contribute to solving crime.

The Mafia Crime families in New York City were increasingly coming under the "gun." The five families were undergoing "thinning out" due to a power grab and photographs and sketches of them were in the paper daily. I fondly remembered my time at my grandfather's restaurant when reputed crime bosses from northeastern Pennsylvania came for dinner. My experience and exercises all came together.

On Becoming Us

In the 1960s, the term "Race Riots" implied "whites attacking blacks."

The "party line" was that race riots erupted from perceived grievances—poor living conditions, poor working conditions, government oppression, and conflicts between races and/or religion. The blacks had all that going against them, especially in Los Angeles.

Southern blacks relocated to Los Angeles for work. The migration happened more rapidly than could be integrated. High paying jobs, affordable housing, and politics excluded blacks. It was difficult, if not impossible, for them to find housing in the suburbs or in urban areas. Additionally, discrimination against blacks by the Los Angeles Police was commonplace.

The pivotal moment in Los Angeles was when police stopped Marquette Frye, an African American, for reckless driving. His brother, a passenger in the car, ran to get their mother, Rena Price. A scuffle occurred, and a mob formed leading to a riot known as the Watts Riots of 1965. By 1967, riots or unrest occurred in Newark, Plainfield, Detroit, and Minneapolis-Saint Paul. A year later, the riots spread to Chicago, Washington, D.C., Baltimore, and Cleveland.

Chapter 10

The Post-College Years

The Search Widens

1967

Wyoming Valley

JERRY BLOOM, NOW A chemistry teacher in Scranton, arrived home after work and found his apartment completely empty,—no wife, no furniture, and no dog. His wife of one year ran off with a black dude she met at work. She cleaned out their bank account as well. And, she took his dog!

Last month, Jerry Bloom was a happy camper. He celebrated a one-year wedding anniversary to a girl he knew for years at synagogue. He also celebrated his second year teaching chemistry. To celebrate, he bought a black MGB sports car, which he had wanted since high school.

During the week following his wife's departure, Jerry bought a new set of Michelin tires for his car. In racing circles, everyone knew Michelin tires came with square edges, which had to be "rounded" before entering any competitive rallies. Jerry picked up Sal the next day after supper to deal with the tires. They drove on a backcountry road in Suscon Township, southeast of Pittston to round out the edges of the tires.

Their adventure did not turn out as they planned. As Jerry

attempted to go around a corner, he lost control of the car and hit another car almost head on. Jerry died on the way to Pittston Hospital. The hospital admitted Sal.

Mike, Ted, and I went to the hospital to see Sal. He told us what happened and that he woke up in a field near the accident. He said he remembered lying in the ambulance going down Swallow Street thinking his mother was going to kill him.

That was the least of his worries. He was in the hospital for almost a week. We were all very sad because we had been friends with Jerry since high school. We never got over it.

Sal had not yet corrected final exams at Saint Ann's Academy. Grades for final exams were due so graduating seniors would have final grades. Two of the nuns went to Sal's house to help him correct papers. Within the next two weeks, he completed his teaching assignments. Sal was able to work in the barbershop later that summer and was able to save some money before starting dental school.

New York City

HAYATO, THE ABSENTEE roommate, asked Natsumi to marry him and she accepted. They planned a small wedding sometime during the summer and Hayato would "move into" her apartment after the wedding. Their families were coming to New York City for the festivities. Hayato invited Joe and me to the wedding. Everyone was looking forward to this event.

I completed my graduate education at Pratt Institute with a Masters of Fine Arts Degree. I learned pen-and-ink, acrylic, watercolor, and oil media to use in my illustrations and paintings. Through two externships, I learned courtroom and crime illustration and was very interested in forensic sketching.

I applied for several jobs in advertising. One job was with

Dolye, Dane, and Bernbach. In the late 1950s and early 1960s, Jews had difficulty finding jobs in advertising because many clients refused to have Jews work on their projects. At that time Bill Bernbach took several staffers from Grey Advertising and began a new firm—Dolye, Dane, and Bernbach—which was predominately a Jewish firm. Although I interviewed with them, they told me they weren't hiring at the time.

I took a job with a smaller advertising agency, Adams, Brooke, and Ziegfeld. I liked the sound of the agency and I liked their motto, "At Adams, Brooke, and Ziegfeld, we got you covered from A to Z." I thought, "You have to start somewhere. I'll get my foot in the door and begin to build my resume." I also began to freelance in painting and sketching.

Joe and I decided to continue renting our apartment without any additional roommates.

Joe told me, "My girlfriend, Rene Elise, and I are getting serious and we are planning our wedding for next June. You can count on me as a roommate for only another year."

Our apartment was centrally located and was nicer than we could find anywhere else for the same rent. With both of us working, the financial burden of rent was small. We asked the landlord to update the apartment with a fresh coat of paint. The landlord agreed if we would pay for the paint. We did.

Once the painters finished the apartment, Joe and I wanted to replace the "student" furniture with "grown-up" furniture. After all, we were now professionals and wanted our apartment to reflect that. Joe and I went to West Pittston to visit and look for furniture at Kurlancheek's in Duryea. My father went to synagogue with Mr. Kurlancheek and knew he could buy the furniture wholesale. We spent the better part of the day shopping and even longer haggling about the price of the furniture—there are several levels of "wholesale!" Kurlancheek's would deliver the furniture the next weekend.

Two weeks later, Mike, Ted, and Sal came to New York for

the weekend to visit me.

Mike said, "Your apartment looks great. I like how you decorated it with your sketches."

I displayed sketches I did when I lived in Pittston, when I was at Wilkes College, and when I was in Art School. My bedroom had a portrait of Paula and one of Brandi.

Sal said, "If you don't get married soon, you're going to run out of wall space for your 'conquests.' "

I enjoyed my work at *ABZ*. I went out of my safety zone and tried to get involved with forensics, perhaps in Yonkers, New Rochelle, or White Plains."

None of the cities I visited had a full-time sketch artist. The police chiefs told me they would call me if they needed someone with my expertise. I was discouraged, not because there weren't any jobs available, but since the police officers with whom I spoke seemed to believe that forensic artistry wasn't important. I completed an application in hopes someone would call me.

I thought forensic artistry was an important discipline because of the involvement of a forensic artist with the recent capture and arrest of Richard Speck, who after entering the residence of nine student nurses with a gun and knife, systematically raped and murdered eight of them. One of the nurses, who injured him during the crime, hid in a closet and provided information to a sketch artist. The police circulated the sketch and an ER doctor recognized him.

Pittsburgh

IN AUGUST 1967, PITTSBURGH was quiet and had no obvious racial unrest. However, selecting an apartment was important should racial "calm" turn the other way. The dental school was located on Terrace Street near Robinson Street on the border of a high-crime neighborhood.

Sal went to Pittsburgh to look for an apartment. He took Ted with him since he had experience with apartments. They found Sal a studio apartment above Baum Boulevard Realty on Baum Boulevard. The owner of the realty company was a "big game" hunter and displayed his stuffed animals in a large storefront behind which were the realty offices. He had an elephant, a tiger, and other various creatures. There were six apartments over the realty company, four studio apartments, and two one-bedroom apartments. It was cool living over a jungle.

Sal's apartment on Baum Boulevard was a short bus ride from school. He continued cutting hair to pay for his apartment and enjoyed having some spending money left over.

The University of Pittsburgh Dental School was on Terrace Street and surrounding it were the schools of medicine, nursing, pharmacy, dental assisting, and dental hygiene. Salk Hall contained classrooms for these schools and had a cafeteria. It was a busy place with an enormous student population, secretary pool, and assorted staff, all converging on the cafeteria for lunch. The dating pool was huge. Because most of the dental and medical students were married, single dental students were popular with the other students and staff.

Many of Sal's single classmates dated dental assistant and dental hygiene students. Some of them married girls they met at school. Others dated nurses who were plentiful in and around the medical and dental schools, adjacent to Presbyterian Hospital nurse's residence. It occurred to him that if someone didn't have a girlfriend, he certainly could find one here.

Sal loved dental school because there were just enough hands-on tasks to do and just enough thinking and memorization tasks to do. There were six students in his section--Cliff Evans, Sam Farina, Jerry Felenchak, Jeff Frand, Bill Garrison, and Sal.

Bill Garrison had an interesting story. His father worked in the steel mill and Bill worked with him each summer throughout college. He met his wife, Sherri, while driving home from work one summer. Sherri was driving down the street and he was driving in the opposite direction. Once he saw her, he couldn't help himself. He made a U-turn and followed her until she pulled into her parent's driveway. Bill pulled in behind her. He got out of the car, introduced himself, and asked her out. A year later, they married. Love at first site!

They had a good group of people—quiet, personable, and talented. They enjoyed interacting with each other while they learned the skills they needed to become good dentists.

In addition to taking courses in basic sciences and dental sciences, dental students took labs to learn how to prepare fillings, crowns, and dentures. One of the labs was Dental Anatomy taught by two black professors: Doctor Wallace and Doctor Thomas. Both professors were in private practice and worked in the dental school two days a week teaching this class. They had a good sense of humor and made class fun.

One day, to evaluate student's knowledge of dental anatomy and manual dexterity, Dr. Wallace and Dr. Thomas assigned the task of carving a tooth out of wax. He was confident he could do this easily. The class had ninety-minutes to complete the exercise.

Our requirements were to carve the *mirror image* of a central incisor (upper front tooth) and polish it. The wax tooth had to be exactly the same size (length, width, thickness, and proportion) as the original. The students used nylon stockings to polish the wax. The married students brought in one of their wife's nylon stockings. The three female students had their own nylons. The single guys went to the department store to buy a pair. Can you imagine the look on the sales clerk's face when we bought our nylons?

After twenty-minutes, Sal completed the exercise and brought the wax tooth to Dr. Wallace. He looked at the tooth and then looked at his watch.

Dr. Wallace said, as Sal stood next to him, "Dr. Thomas, you need to come over here and take a look at this. Dr. Greco, here, thinks he was able to finish carving his tooth in twenty minutes! You need to take a look see."

Sal thought, "Christ, I'm in trouble now. What's the matter with you? Doctor Wallace thinks I'm showing off. I didn't think I was showing off! I wasn't thinking about going slowly, just about doing a good job."

In front of the class where everyone could hear, Doctor Thomas said, "Well, let me take a look... hmmm...I don't know... It looks too small to me. The original tooth is bigger. Let me get my calipers."

As he was measuring he said, "Yep, too small."

Dr. Wallace asked Dr. Thomas, "Do you think Dr. Greco, here, needs to do it over again?"

"Yes sir, I think he needs to do it over again. We can't be setting a bad example for the rest of the students, and we can't be letting him slide. If we let them slide, what kind of dentists will we be putting out there?"

Sal thought, "Well, there's nothing wrong with the carving. I measured it, and I knew it was correct. However, I can't argue with my professor. I need to learn how to play the game."

Dr. Wallace handed the tooth back to Sal with a new block of wax. He had to do it over again. Now, only about thirty-minutes remained to complete the project. He finished carving the tooth in time and it passed inspection. He never handed in anything early again. Lesson learned! Check!

Pittsburgh was a great town in which to live—big enough to be interesting, but not so big it was overwhelming. It had everything—restaurants, parks, sports, colleges, museums, and zoos.

Many of the single students in his class were Jewish. He was comfortable around them since he always had Jewish friends growing up. They hung out together and studied together. Sal was amazed how many classmates were married; he was further amazed how many had children. Dental school was difficult enough for Sal without the responsibilities of a wife and children.

Since this was his first time away from home, he had to make many executive decisions without input from relatives and friends. The first decision was his apartment. There would be many more decisions to make—some went well, others, not so well. He figured if he got ninety-percent right he'd be OK.

Wyoming Valley

ALL FOUR OF US WERE happy to see each other again for Thanksgiving. We went to the Flame to dance and afterward to the Midway Diner for something to eat. We talked about all the things that had happened since we last saw each other last August. We still hadn't gotten over Jerry Bloom's death and we talked about how sad we all felt.

In New York, I was working and had a lot to tell my friends about my experiences. Mike told us what was happening in his job. Ted told us about how things were going in Binghamton.

Time ran away from us and, when Sal got home at 3 a.m., both his parents were sitting in the living room waiting for him. When he walked into the house, his mother hollered at him for staying out late. Don't forget, he was twenty-four years old, living away, and he didn't think he had to explain himself.

However, his mother had a different take on this and asked him where he had been. He told her, in his typical smart-ass way, "I met a girl, we went to a motel, and time got away from me."

She never again asked where he'd been when he was late coming home.

We talked about growing up in Pittston. The main vice for

teenagers was underage drinking—mostly beer. Of course, most Italians had homemade wine on the dinner table every night. Hard liquor seldom played a role in our environment. Marijuana, drugs, and hard liquor were risk factors in New York and Pittsburgh but not in Pittston.

Sal talked about Walnut Street in Shadyside and the live bands at some of the clubs. He liked to have a date over for dinner on the weekend. Because of the great Italian food at Groceria Italiano, an Italian Grocery store up the street, he didn't have to cook much to have a dinner prepared.

He expanded his dating options to neighboring schools— Carnegie-Mellon University and Chatham college. Carnegie-Mellon girls were the most interesting—short skirts or hot pants with pastel tights--very colorful! Chatham girls were prim and proper--like Ivy League girls. Think of Smith College or Mount Holyoke College.

With the girls he met, Sal was convinced that feminism was alive and well in Pittsburgh. Betty Freidan's book, The Feminine Mystique, was very influential and caused women to reconsider their traditional roles and to voice their disapproval of old stereotypes such as being housewives and mothers. Many women wanted to free themselves of the bonds of chauvinism and to seek professional careers. They symbolized this by burning (throwing away) their bras and walking around braless. Certainly, we all favored this symbolism but it did confuse us. We knew how to act and react with women the old way, but we were puzzled about how to act the new way.

The emergence of the birth control pill gave women the freedom to do what they wanted. The pill gave them more liberation than the Declaration of Independence. Women believed they couldn't exercise their personal liberty or enjoy their pursuit of happiness if they weren't free to decide for themselves, free to express themselves, and free to control their procreation. If they were able to control their bodies and reproductive choices, they were able to control their economic, political, and sexual destiny. They would be "free at last!"

In Pittston, girls waited for guys to signal what was going to happen in relationships. Everyone knew the rules and everyone followed them. None of us knew the rules anymore.

When Sal met a girl from Carnegie-Mellon University and asked her on a date, she showed up with a large purse (He said, "Almost like a shopping bag"). That struck Sal as unusual, but CMU girls were unusual. They went to Squirrel Hill for dinner. Afterward, they drove to Shadyside and spent some time at the Fox Cafe listening to rhythm and blues.

Sal and his date went to his apartment and, when they got there, she opened her purse and took out some toiletries and a negligee. "My God, was she moving in?" So much for the woman waiting for the man to give the signal!

Two of Sal's best friends in dental school were Bob Weisner and Phil Sutterman. Phil had an identical twin brother, Mike, who went to optometry school. If they were triplets, the third would have been Richard Harris, the actor. The resemblance was scary. Phil had a first floor apartment in Oakland near the dental school.

Their parents gave each of them a new Corvette as an "acceptance" gift to professional school. Phil had a burgundy convertible, which had an alarm. A curious type, Sal had to learn about the alarm.

Sal said, "I've never seen an alarm on a car before. Tell me how it works."

Phil said, "The alarm is turned on and off from a key behind the front wheel-well on the driver's side of the car. Once "armed," the siren sounds if someone opens a door, the trunk, or the hood. The siren also sounds if anyone tries to start the car or tow it."

Really, can you see what's coming next?

Bob and Sal absolutely could not let this go by without a

prank.

Remember, Mike, Ted, Sal, and I had a code of ethics--we would never prank each other. Sal didn't have a code of ethics with anyone in dental school; they were just classmates, not friends from as far back as Cub Scouts. One night after going to Shadyside, Sal and Bob went to Phil's apartment and found his car parked in front. They lifted the front end of the car and the alarm went off. They ran and hid behind another car and watched Phil as he ran from house to inspect the car and re-set the alarm.

They didn't tell him they set off the alarm.

A few weeks later on Friday night, they knew Phil and his girlfriend were in the house. They waited for the lights to go out and, about fifteen minutes later, lifted the front end of the car. This time, when the alarm went off, Phil ran out of his apartment in his boxer shorts and a baseball bat in his hand. He inspected the car and re-set the alarm. They waited another fifteen minutes and repeated their prank. Phil ran out, again in his underwear, baseball bat in tow. After he re-set the alarm, they called out to him and identified ourselves.

Sal and Bob couldn't understand why Phil was so mad--it was just a prank. They also didn't know why his girlfriend, Elaine, wanted him to take her back to *her* apartment. If they really were malicious, they would have gone to her apartment and repeated their prank. They didn't! After all, they were friends. By Monday, Phil had forgiven them.

The second semester, Bob and Phil got an apartment together. The movie, *The Odd Couple,* with Jack Lemmon and Walter Matthau was playing in theaters. The theme of this movie was about two people sharing an apartment each with different ideas of lifestyle and housekeeping. The movie later became a TV program by the same name and starred Tony Randall and Jack Klugman. The writers must have been flies on the wall in Bob and Phil's apartment. Bob was the Felix Unger (neat-niek) and Phil was the Oscar Madison (slob). When Phil drank orange juice from the carton, Bob would holler at him. When Phil didn't pick up after himself, Bob would chastise him.

Sometime later, Bob, Phil, and Sal got together at their apartment to study for an anatomy test. Phil had a cold and Bob was upset with Phil since his hygiene wasn't as Bob expected. Of course, he didn't want to catch Phil's cold. Over the last two days, Bob was extra diligent about Phil's housekeeping routines. Bob labeled one orange juice carton with his name so Phil wouldn't drink from it and pass on his germs to Bob. While they were studying, the phone rang and Phil answered it. It was Elaine, Phil's girlfriend. They talked for a couple minutes and Phil hung up.

After a big pause, Bob said to Phil, Aren't you going to spray it?"

"Spray what?"

"Spray the phone!"

"Why would I spray the phone?"

"I want you to spray the phone so you don't give me your cold!"

"Don't be ridiculous! I'm not spraying the phone!"

Bob got up, went to the kitchen to get a can of Lysol, and sprayed both the phone and Phil.

By this point, Phil was madder than a hornet, grabbed the Lysol can, and sprayed Bob.

The next year, Bob and Phil had different roommates.

By the second semester, Sal and a few of his classmates went on a group date. Jeff Frand suggested the Casbah in Shadyside.

They met at the Casbah for dinner at 6 p.m. with the band playing shortly after. When they were finishing dinner, the owner, Eddie Edelstein, came over to their table and asked if everything was OK. They told him the food was excellent and they were enjoying the music. He asked Jeff if he wanted to sing a song or two. Jeff shook his head to say no. Fred Grillo, Phil Sutterman, and Sal looked at each other puzzled by Eddie's question to Jeff. Jeff was always so quiet. What would he sing in front of all these people? Eddie persisted and asked Jeff again. Jeff nodded his head "no" again. They talked a minute more and Jeff agreed to sing a couple of songs.

Sal whispered to Fred, "Can he sing?"

"I don't think so. He never said anything about singing; he's always so quiet. I never even heard him whistle a tune."

"I don't know about this. I hope he can sing."

"I hope he doesn't embarrass himself."

While Jeff was walking to the bandstand, they all nervously waited to see what was going to happen. Sal remembered saying to himself, "Please God, let this be good for him."

Sal glanced at Jeff's wife and she sat there expressionless! He had no clue! Eddie jumped on stage, grabbed the microphone, and he announced he had a surprise guest who would sing a few songs. Eddie announced Jeff like a master of ceremony in a three-ring circus.

Ladies and Gentlemen, "Let me present Pittsburgh's best singing talent, Jeff Frand, the 'Singing Dentist.' " Almost instantly, Jeff ran onto the stage singing "Mack the Knife." They were beyond shock. On stage was the guy who sat next to them for a year hardly speaking a word. If they had closed their eyes, they would've sworn it was Bobby Darin. Jeff's second song was "Splish Splash." Wow! The joke was on them.

Mike, Ted, and I visited Sal and went to Shadyside to see some of the sights. The central street running though Shadyside was Walnut Street, a five-block shopping district. There was standing room only at clubs such as the Encore, The Razzberry Rhino, Lou's, and the Fox Cafe.

Young, well-dressed people were all over Walnut Street waiting to get into the clubs. Rhythm and Blues bands were standard fare with a few folk and rock acts. If you had the time, you could take in several acts in one night just by walking across Walnut Street. On weekends, cars and motorcycles cruised up and down Walnut Street.

While we were at the Fox, Ted said, "I'm dating another teacher at my school."

I said, "You are? How long has this been going on?"

"A few months. She's hot after me."

Now, Ted never said anything about his life unless you asked him about it. Even then, he didn't say much.

Sal said, "Tell us more about this 'chick.' "

"She teaches at my school. We've been dating for two months and she wants to marry me."

I said, "Holy shit, she wants marry you? Where did this come from?"

Sal said, "We want to know more, lots more about her!"

"Yeah, spill the beans!" Mike said.

"She's tall, skinny, and really good looking. She's always at my apartment."

"Has she moved in?"

"No, but she may as well have moved in—she stays over most of the time."

I said, "OK, How do you know she wants to get married?"

"She asked me to marry her."

"Wow! Does she want children?" I asked.

"I don't know, I haven't asked her that."

"We're getting married in a couple of months."

Mike said, "Wait a minute, this is the first we are hearing about her and you are getting married in a couple of months? When are we going to meet her?"

"Soon" Ted said, and that was the end of the conversation.

Sal found dental school easy because of his education at King's College. Courses like histology and embryology were almost like repeat courses for him. Even though he didn't make an "A" in those classes in college, he remembered everything he learned. Classmates who graduated from prestigious colleges, asked him to identify liver cells, heart cells, and brain cells.

On Becoming Us

The war on crime escalated in 1968 when Richard Nixon and his predecessors rejected the "social" explanation of crime in favor of leniency in the criminal justice system. Nixon insisted the "solution to crime lies in more convictions and not more government spending." Amen.

Chapter 11

The Growth Years

The Search for a Good Career

1968

New York City

THE *NEW YORK DAILY NEWS* headline read, "*Sexpot Trial Tale: Crimmins custody fight in 1960s ends in death.*" The trial of Alice Crimmins, a woman accused of killing her two children, was about begin. I had been working in advertising for about six months, and I knew I belonged in the courtroom--not because of the implied sex but because I couldn't possibly believe that a woman could kill her two children. Her own flesh and blood! No way!

Alice Crimmins and her husband, Edmund, were separated and living apart. On July 14, 1965, at 10 in the morning, Edmund called the police to report his two children, Missy, age four, and Eddie, age five, missing from their apartment at Kew Gardens Hills, Queens, New York.

When the police arrived at the Crimmins apartment, Alice (aka "Rusty" because of her red hair) opened the door and greeted them in a tight flowery blouse and provocative, attention-getting, white toreador pants showing off her sultry and shapely figure. Her makeup was perfect and every strand of teased red hair was in place.

A detective asked Alice, "What happened here?"

Alice said, "I went to the children's bedroom and unlocked the door."

"You unlocked the door?"

"Yes, I unlocked the door and found the room empty."

"Why was the door locked?

"I lock them in their room every night."

"What time was this when you locked them in their room?"

"Just before 9 p.m., like I do every night."

"So, you locked them in their room at 9 p.m. and unlocked the door this morning."

"Yes. I checked on them around midnight and they were sound asleep."

"What happened when you went to their room this morning?"

"When I opened the door, they were gone."

"What did you do next?"

"I called my husband, Edmund, to see if he had taken them."

"What did he say?"

"He told me he didn't take them."

"Why do you lock the children in their room every night?"

"To keep chubby little Eddie from raiding the refrigerator. He's too fat, you know."

At the time of questioning, police thought she was too calm for a mother "facing her worst nightmare." What could be worse than losing your children to kidnappers?

One police officer whispered to another, "Rusty is some cold bitch!"

Later that morning, when Alice saw the body of Missy, found strangled in an empty lot across the street, she didn't react as would be expected. She didn't shed a single tear. Five days

160

later, police found Eddie's body alongside the expressway.

Alice Crimmins had quite a bit of baggage. When eighteen, Alice, essentially from the other side of the tracks, married Edmund, a well-paid airline mechanic who worked nights. She quickly tired of him. To offset her boredom, she found excitement in the beds of numerous lovers. Her philandering infuriated her husband, Edmund, who moved out of their apartment.

Edmund told the police, "Before I moved out, I bugged her bedroom to monitor her. I hid in the basement and listened to her loud, moaning lovemaking. After I heard what was going on in the bedroom, I sued for custody of my kids."

For the eighteen months following the death of her children, the police had Alice under a fine microscope and scrutinized her every move.

"She couldn't pee without us knowing! We couldn't foresee the subsequent peep show." One detective said.

After the death of her children, Alice began working as a cocktail waitress and cultivated her art of bed hopping. She was with a different man every night and a different place every week.

I was very interested to learn more about the case and went to the police station to find out when and where the trial would begin. I was told it would start sometime in May.

I asked, "Can I sit in the courtroom during trial?"

A police officer gruffly said, "Suit yourself, kid."

The "Sexpot" trial began on May 6, 1968. Although there was no real evidence of Alice's guilt, the prosecutors played up her promiscuity. After all, they reasoned, "how could a woman with so many lovers be innocent?"

On the first day of trial, I went to the courthouse. There I met the sketching artist, Colleen Smyth.

"How long have you worked in forensic art?" I asked her.

"About five years."

"I'm in graduate school and am interested in forensics."

"What school?"

"Pratt."

"Would it be OK if I hung around and watched you work?"

"Sure, stay near me and the judicial staff will treat you well."

Colleen and I talked about her craft.

"I try to illustrate the essential nature of the trial, usually with one or two sketches. I focus on the main drama. It isn't about the witnesses or the lawyers; it's about recording the pivotal person in the trial—the one who makes a difference. The main drama could be the accused, the prosecutor, the judge, the jury, or a witness."

I felt like a sponge soaking up information from Colleen. She seemed knowledgeable and I respected her opinion.

The trial lasted thirteen days. Each day, before court went into session, I met with Colleen to discuss the previous day's events and what she thought was important. We also reviewed each other's sketches from the day before. Several times Colleen and I caught got a quick bite to eat after the court session to discuss the trial.

Midway through the trial, Alice Crimmins was on the stand and I sketched her.

"I told Colleen that I believed Crimmins was the pivotal person in the trial. After all, she was on trial for murder."

Coleen said, "I believe the prosecutor is the pivotal person since he had practically no evidence but made his case based on her sex life. He tried her because she was having sex with everyone."

I thought, "I have a lot to learn."

I sketched Colleen sketching the prosecutor.

Each time we got a bite to eat, I observed Colleen taking several vitamins and her birth control pill after the meal. I didn't think much about the birth control pills and chocked it up to the comfort Colleen felt around me.

An all male jury found Alice guilty of manslaughter and sentenced her to five-twenty years.

As you would expect from her name, Colleen, was Irish and she, like Alice, had long red hair. Colleen was five-foot, eight-inches, slim, and striking.

She asked, "Would you like to get dinner?"

I said, "Yes, I'd love to."

During dinner, Colleen said, "I'm about to have a milestone—my thirtieth birthday. Divorced and thirty."

"I hadn't thought about your age. I did notice that you never wear a wedding band, but many men and women don't wear their wedding bands at work."

She smiled and took her vitamins and her birth control pill, as she had done in the past. This time she left the blister pack of birth control pills on the table longer than usual—long enough to be certain I noticed. I observed the birth control pills before, but didn't acknowledge them.

I thought, "What's going on here? Is she teasing me or does she want to sleep with me? Is 'Mrs. Robinson' coming after me like in the movie, 'The Graduate?' Maybe, I'm getting way ahead of myself."

She fumbled around her purse and returned the pills and vitamins.

I thought, "I don't know what to do. If she wants to sleep with me, I certainly don't want to pass up the opportunity even though I don't think it's a good idea to sleep with a colleague. Should I keep it professional?

"She's looking at me in a way she hasn't looked at me before. I don't have enough experience to know what she wants. I'm going to look like a fool if I'm reading her wrong. Maybe, I'll should wait and see what happens. Let her lead the way!"

All of a sudden, I'm getting excited about Colleen. As our conversation continued, Colleen ran her index finger over her lower lip and, at times, moistened her lips with her tongue.

While I was talking, she ran her eyes over my face starting with my eyes and progressing to my lips. At one point, she stared at my lips almost as if she were going to eat them.

My attitude was changing from having an eye of a "connoisseur" to having an eye of a "hunter."

I told myself, "I'm going to go with whatever she wants to do."

The sexy details presented in the trial—the description of Alice's outfits and description of Alice's sex with various men was a turn on--like foreplay. Perhaps Colleen had a buildup of emotions during the trial as I have had. Now that the trial is over, maybe we both want to let loose.

After dinner, Colleen said, "I'd like to see some of your sketches. Can we go to your apartment and take a look?"

"Absolutely, I'd love to show you my work."

With that said, we rushed to my apartment. When we got there, we walked in and immediately were all over each other as if we had taken aphrodisiacs. She didn't even stop to look at any of my artwork, the reason she asked to go to my apartment in the first place. Colleen and I released all our stored sexual energy. We wore each other out! The sex was better than with Brandi.

I dated Colleen for about a month. The sex was great, but she seemed a bit too controlling for my taste.

I also read about the surprise decision--Alice Crimmins' verdict was overturned.

Wyoming Valley

MIKE, SAL, AND I had lunch together.

Mike said, "What's going on? You don't seem happy. Did some chick dump you?"

"No. I dated someone and it ended like my relationship with

Brandi."

"OK. Let's hear it!"

"I covered a trial about a woman who was accused of killing her two children."

"Some woman killed her two kids?"

"Yes, the district attorney had only circumstantial evidence but took her to trial anyway because she was promiscuous. During the trial, I met a courtroom artist, Colleen, who I dated. We spent every day in the courtroom and had dinner after. We dated for a few weeks. I enjoyed the sex with her but she was a control freak.

"After we stopped dating, I began to wonder about myself. I wondered about the choices I make in women.

"I don't think I'm a player, but I end up in bed with women in dead-end relationships. Although the satisfaction of the chase and the triumph is real, it feels meaningless. I'm tired of sleeping around with no apparent benefit except to get 'my rocks off.' I want to meet someone with whom I could settle down and start a family."

I wonder just what makes someone a "player?" Is it five women, ten women? How many? Is it more the circumstances than the numbers? We knew of a guy in Pittston who, by his own admission, slept with two-hundred women. Although he was very proud, it wasn't what we wanted.

"I'm really down in the dumps, which is unusual for me. I don't think I'll ever find a quality woman with whom to settle down."

Mike said, "Over the past eight years, you've never had a serious relationship even though you probably dated more women than all of us put together. I hope you don't take this the wrong way, but do you or the women you date, have commitment issues?"

I said, "Before the past few years, I wasn't ready for a serious relationship. School came between a serious relationship and me. Lately, at least for the last two years, the women I meet seem only interested in having a 'fling.' They're older than I am, somewhat cynical, and prefer screwing you and spending the night to going home alone. The next morning, they can't wait to get out of my apartment. It's almost as if they're OK being alone during the day but not during the night.

"I don't believe they want to spend the time to develop a relationship. I just want to meet a nice girl who is ready to get married and have children. Maybe I'm picking wrong."

"I think it's the other way around--you're not the one picking; the women are picking. One problem with being good looking is women want to sleep with you. I don't have that problem. The women you meet don't seem like the 'settle down' type—more like the 'one-night stand' type, even if the one night extends to a month or more. They seem like the players to me.

"You're a nice guy and, because you are a nice guy, the women who are players do to you what the men who are players do to the nice girls."

I said, "Perhaps I need a break from dating. Maybe I can concentrate on my work for a while. If I ask anyone out, you know what to do!"

Mike said, "We'll give you a swift kick in the ass!"

"Maybe we need to put a lock on your pants zipper," Sal said.

Meanwhile, Sal wanted to go out with Sandi Slovenski, his student from Saint Ann's Academy. So, he called and asked her out.

They went to dinner and talked about her plans for school. She wasn't sure what she wanted to study. Sal picked the movie, *The Odd Couple*, which he believed to be a safe first date.

They had a few laughs during the movie. When they got to her house, they walked to the door and exchanged some pleasantries.

Although Sal and Sandi had a few laughs, he knew Sandi

was too young and immature for him. His experience--college, two years of teaching, and one year of dental school—put him on a different level. He subconsciously hoped she was the one but now knew she wasn't.

Sal knew he would never ask her out again. During the drive home, Bobby Vee's song, "Come Back When You Grow Up Girl," came on the radio. How appropriate was that?

Sal started a job with Chucky Serafin, a barber at the Host Motel Barber Shop, up the street from Pocono Downs Racetrack. Chucky told Sal he needed help during the summer because he was so busy with the racetrack customers, his regular customers were getting mad at him. He had two chairs and was a full service barbershop—haircuts, shampoo, shave, facials, and specialty Roffler razor cut. He also employed a shoeshine man, "Tiny"—a black man who was about 250 pounds.

The Host Motel barbershop was high-class and Sal was lucky for the opportunity to work there. Chucky paid him 80% plus tips. That was a great deal for him—10% more than he made in the other barbershops. Sal worked ten weeks until the end of the summer.

While he worked there, most customers wanted the full service. Sal's father got $1.25 for a haircut plus, maybe a 25-cent tip. The average tab at the Host Motel Barber Shop was over $25 including a shoeshine. It was routine for customers to tip $10.

Sal said the Host Motel Barber Shop was the best job he ever had. He wasn't going to have any problem paying off his car and saving some money for dental school.

New York

I WAS STILL THINKING about my conversation with Mike and Sal about my love life or the lack of it. I hadn't gone out with anyone since that time. I had sworn off women!

Joe Cusano was getting married in a month. Hayato, Natsumi, and I were invited. Joe and Rene Elise were going to have a big Italian wedding at North Hills Country Club in Bayside. Afterward they would honeymoon at Saint Thomas in the Bahamas.

During the wedding, I met Joe's two older brothers, Jim and Sam, and his sister, Mary Ann, the youngest of the four.

After meeting Mary Ann, I asked Joe, "Where have you been hiding her all this time?"

He said, "Down boy! I haven't been hiding her; she's just my kid sister. She's just a kid! Stay away from her! I thought you swore off women."

"How old is she?"

"Twenty, she'll be a senior at Columbia in September."

"Would you mind if I danced with her later?"

"Sure, but remember, she's not like Brandi and the other 'puttane' (whores) to whom you seem attracted. She's not your type."

"I'm just asking if you would mind if I danced with her."

"OK, but remember, she's not the type you play with; she's the type you marry. If you dance with her or ever take her out, remember, she has three older Sicilian brothers who'll eat you alive if you mess up. Capisce?"

"I understand. You should know me better than that! I know the difference. You know I'm looking for a girl with class; one with whom I could settle down."

Later at the reception, I asked Mary Ann to dance. She "let" me lead--leading was very important among the men of the 1960s, especially Italian men who always liked to be in charge. My friends and I believed dancing gave us a clue about relationships--if women wanted to lead, men thought the women wanted to control everything and the men would have problems with them in relationships.

Mary Ann was an excellent dancer; she made me look good. She had confidence but in a good way—like she knew where she wanted to go and could cut the path to get there.

Although I never articulated it, I always believed I was a "catch" for women—good looking, smart, and talented. However, around Mary Ann, I wasn't the confident man about town. I wasn't the "cock of the walk." I was more tentative, more cautious, and saw Mary Ann as the "catch." That's a switch! Something was happening to me. Is what I'm feeling related to feeling down or related to the way I feel about Mary Ann.

I glanced in a mirror near the dance floor, saw our reflection, and thought to myself, "We look good together."

I wanted to make a good impression on Mary Ann. I thought I might not see her again and not have another chance to get to know her.

"Has Joe told you anything about me?"

"No, why?"

"I just thought he might have mentioned me since we've been roommates for a while."

"No, I know you're roommates but he hasn't said anything else."

I thought, "Maybe that's a good thing."

"What do you think of Rene Elise?"

"I like her. She's like a big sister, like the sister I never had. Joe made a good choice!"

"How was it growing up with Joe?"

"Good and Bad. He's like most brothers—always wants to tell you what to do!"

"Really, he seems laid back, not very pushy."

"He's not pushy; my three brothers know what I should do and how I should do it. It may be a Sicilian thing or a big brother thing. I don't know for sure."

"I know about the Sicilian thing. Your brothers want to protect you. It's because they love you. It's rather nice. You

169

should appreciate how they feel about you."

"I know that but sometimes they go overboard. My mother doesn't take a back seat with knowing what I should do either."

I said to Mary Ann, "When they push too hard, stand your ground. They'll respect you."

"Oh, I won't let them get away with anything. I work hard to stay ahead of those 'boys.' "

"Joe said you're in nursing school. How do you like it?"

"I like it. I was interested in patient care but didn't want to go to medical school."

"What are your plans?"

"In September, I'll begin my last year of nursing at Columbia. The following year, I'll start a Master's program to become a family nurse practitioner."

"Wow. How long will the master's take?"

"Two years."

I thought, "One year plus two years, that'll take three years altogether. That's not bad, I can wait."

This was unlike me. Here, I just met Mary Ann and I'm planning our lives together. "What's the matter with me?"

I said, "Do you have any hobbies?"

"I like hiking, fly fishing, photography, and dancing-- combining more than one of them is always fun. Of course, it's hard to dance when you're fishing or hiking."

Mary Ann said, "What do you like?"

"I like hiking, fishing, golf, and cross-country skiing. I haven't been fishing or golfing lately. Actually, I haven't been cross-country skiing for a while either. Where do you like to hike?"

"Depends on how much time I have. I like Trail View State Park on the island since it is close to where we live, Granite Knolls up the East Side of the Hudson is good, and, if I want to make a day of it, the Delaware Water Gap or Hickory Run State Park in Pennsylvania."

"Where do you like to hike?"

"I like Hickory Run and World's End State Park. They were close to home when I lived in Pennsylvania. Maybe we saw each other at Hickory Run. Do you really like fly-fishing? I've never been."

"Yes. My father taught us how. You know three boys and me. As the only girl, I had to learn some 'rough stuff' if I wanted to be included!"

"I don't know any girl who likes fly-fishing! In fact, I don't know any girl willing to put a worm on a hook. Next, you'll tell me your favorite thing to do on Sunday afternoons is to watch football on television."

Mary Ann giggled and said, "You don't put worms on a hook to fly-fish."

"What do you put on the hooks?"

"Hand tied flies or insects. But, you know that!"

I asked, "Do you like to cook?"

"It's OK. I don't have to cook so I don't. If I did, I would never get anything done with three brothers who think the world is supposed to revolve around them. One time, I made Joe a grilled cheese sandwich and left the wrapper on so he wouldn't order me around to cook for him. Do you think the world is supposed to revolve around you?"

"No, I can take care of myself. I know how to cook, and I know how to do laundry. I even know how to sew!"

"Mary Ann, I'm having a good time talking with you. Would you like to go out with me sometime?"

"I don't know, you're my brother's age—old, you know? Even if I wanted to go out with you, I don't know if my parents would approve."

"One thing at a time. Would you like to go out with me?"

"Maybe."

"Next let's work on the 'approval.' If your brothers and your parents approved, would you want to go out with me?"

"I don't know yet. Keep talking! I'll let you know."

Jeffrey thought, "She's playing with me. I don't like this; she's taking all the power away from me. She's controlling our conversation. The last thing I need in my life is a smart-ass chick. I have to stop this right now."

I said, "Yeah, you're right. I may be too old for you. I mean, you're only a *junior* in college. You haven't even begun to experience life. If we were to go out, your brothers would want to sit in the back seat of the car! Then there's your father. There's no room for your three brothers and your father in the back seat of my car."

"I'm a *senior* in college, and I've lived enough life to handle you. Anyway, I don't need anyone's permission; I'm not a kid!"

I thought, "OK, she was playing! I had better not get her mad at me. If I get her mad, it may be the end of the line for me."

"OK. We obviously like each other; otherwise, we wouldn't be acting this way. You can relax--I like you more, so, you can be in control. If you agree to go out with me, I'll take you anywhere you want to go."

"Anywhere?" she asked as she rubbed her chin with her thumb and index finger contemplating something extravagant."

"Like I said, anywhere!"

"OK. Let's go hiking this Saturday. We'll drive to the Delaware Water Gap, go on a short hike, and take some pictures. I'll bring lunch. You have a camera, don't you?"

"Yes, I have a camera."

"Do you have a car, or do we have to use my car?"

"Yes, I have a car--a car and a Brownie. It takes good pictures most of the time. When it doesn't, it isn't the camera's fault. Maybe, we can find a scene and I can sketch you while you take pictures."

"OK. I have a Kodak Instamatic. It takes good pictures—all the time! Do you think we could leave the city about 8 a.m.? It takes two hours to get there. I know just the place for pictures."

172

"OK. I'll pick you up at 8:00 a.m."

The song ended, and the bandleader announced, "It's time for the bride to throw the bouquet. Can we have all the single girls over here, behind the bride?"

I noticed Mary Ann didn't show any sign of moving into position to catch the bouquet.

"Aren't you going to try to catch the bouquet?"

"No, I have too many things to do. I don't want to get married right now."

"Maybe *you* should try to catch the bouquet since you're the one old enough to be married."

"OK. OK. Don't be a wise guy."

After one girl caught the bouquet, everyone started to leave. I told MaryAnn I would call her on Friday to confirm our date and make sure the weather was going to cooperate.

I called Mary Ann as I said I would to confirm our date for the next day. The weather report was good. We discussed what clothing we would wear to hike and take pictures. I didn't get any feedback from Mary Ann if she was excited about our date.

Saturday morning, Mary Ann and I loaded my car for our trip.

"I like your car. What kind of car is this?"

"An Austin Healey 3000."

Once we were on their way to the Gap, I asked Mary Ann where she was taking me.

"We're going to Dunnfield Creek Trail. It's just off Route 80 in New Jersey. I would've taken you to my favorite place, Mount Tammany but I thought I would make it easy for you since this is our first date. They're next to each other but Dunnfield is easier. If our date goes well, I'll teach you how to fly-fish next time."

"So we're planning another date?"

"No."

"So you're taking me on the baby trail?"

"It's not the baby trail, it's a nice hike, and we can take some

173

pictures. We'll have fun."

"Tell me more about Dunnfield."

"It's about three miles long and goes up about a thousand feet. There are some cascades and some areas to fish but you need a New Jersey fishing license if you are going to fish. It's very relaxing. Are you OK with relaxing?"

"Sure, I'm OK as long as I'm relaxing with you."

"Wow, what a smooth operator! My brothers warned me about your type. Joe told me to remind you that I have three Sicilian brothers, but I don't know what he meant by that."

"You don't have anything to worry about, I'll be a gentleman. I know how Sicilians protect their families."

"Good, I'm glad you understand that but you have more to worry about with me than with my brothers. I don't want to have to beat you up."

"I'm shaking in my boots!"

"I packed a cooler with sandwiches and Coke. Joe told me about your special Italian hoagies. These may not be as good as yours, but I think you'll like them. How did you get interested in art?"

"I just liked to sketch people from when I was in grade school. The nuns didn't like it much—they thought I was doodling. Would you believe that?"

"Yeah, I believe it. I know nuns! They can be a pain."

"Growing up, I sketched lots of famous people in my grandfather's restaurant. It seemed like a natural progression—doodling to sketching to drawing."

"How did you get interested in nursing?"

"I don't know. I considered studying medicine but didn't think I would like it—phone calls during the night, rushing to the ER. I want to be a nurse practitioner and take care of patients."

Mary Ann and I talked non-stop during the two hours driving to the Delaware Water Gap. We talked about our careers, religion, and politics. Although religion and politics were usually taboo in the beginning of a relationship, it was a very easy conversation for us. I always seem to get into a discussion about religion—probably because I have a Jewish last name and was raised Catholic. Mary Ann and I learned a lot about each other and were happy with what we learned.

When we arrived, we had lunch, and hiked up Dunnfield Creek Trail. We stopped along the trail to take pictures and to experience nature. Dunnfield, as Mary Ann said, was relaxing—a welcomed change from the hustle bustle of the city. I sketched a few scenes and sketched Mary Ann taking pictures. Mary Ann took a picture of me sketching her taking pictures. They were acting silly. Mary Ann showed me where she liked to fly-fish.

After a few hours, we headed back to New York.

Mary Ann said, "I really like your car. Can I drive it? I can drive stick-shift you know."

"Sure, why don't you start off and I'll drive when we get closer to the city."

Mary Ann began to drive. I was impressed--she didn't grind the gears once.

When we got close to the city, we switched drivers.

I asked Mary Ann, "Did you have a good time today?"

"Yes."

"Good enough to go out with me again?"

Mary Ann hesitated as if she weren't sure she wanted to go out with me again—playing with me again. After a minute or so, she said she would like to go out—maybe for Italian food.

I asked, "What's your favorite restaurant?"

"Paolucci's."

"OK. We'll go to Paolucci's Restaurant. Is next Saturday good for you?"

"Yes."

"I'll come to get you at 6 p.m."

Pittsburgh

SAL MOVED INTO A studio apartment in University Housing, at the corner of Forbes Avenue and Craig Street, eight blocks from the dental school. He also rented space for his car in the basement. He bought and painted some unfinished furniture, some bookshelves, and a single bed that doubled as a sofa. His apartment was typical student decor--painted black with red accents. He was happy to have a less expensive apartment and one close enough to walk to school—less financial pressure.

Classes again were in Salk Hall. Everyone was in a frenzy to register, buy books, purchase dental instruments needed for clinic, and to get the all-important meal pass. The number of students changed. Some students quit, other students transferred from other dental schools. The three women in Sal's class returned for their second year. All his classmates who were in the dorm last year now had apartments with roommates—law students, medical students or graduate students. Because everyone was scattered, he wasn't sure about his barber business. He thought he would wait for people to ask him about haircuts and develop a plan.

Once some of his classmates asked about haircuts, he told them he would continue to cut hair, but if he had to drive, he needed enough customers to make it worthwhile—meaning, he wanted their roommates as customers as well. Most of the students lived in Oakland not far from the dental school and from his apartment so it wasn't a big deal, as he could walk. Their roommates were happy to get haircuts from Sal. This was a good deal, so he picked up a few more customers. The farthest he had to drive was to Al Silverman's apartment in Squirrel Hill, but he had two roommates who wanted haircuts.

Xerox, a company that had developed photocopiers, had installed a copier in the Health Science office. Copies were three

176

cents a page, and it changed our lives. Sal and his classmates copied each other's notes, old board tests, pages from books, and available old exams. Since he had the worst handwriting in the world, he copied Jerry Felenchak and Sam Farina's notes and didn't have to worry about taking notes. He could just sit there and listen to the lectures. Neat!

Bill Garrison and his wife, Sherri, lived down the hall from Sal. Bill and Sal walked to Sam Farina's apartment, and all three of them walked to school. Sam Farina married his girlfriend, Louise, and lived about two blocks away. Living so close to married classmates worked out for Sal. Sherri and Louise often invited him for Sunday lunch or dinner. Both Sherri and Louise were good cooks.

Between studying and learning motor skills needed to complete dental work, Sal filled his time cutting hair on Thursdays, going to dental fraternity parties on Fridays, going to Shadyside for rhythm and blues music on Saturdays, and having lunch with Sam and Louise on Sunday afternoons.

He went on a few dates with nursing, pharmacy, dental hygiene students, and a teacher. Louise fixed him up with a few of her fellow teachers; remember she's half Sicilian. Although there were many people with whom to have a relationship, it didn't happen for Sal. He was thinking he had the same problem as Mike and me with women. We just didn't find the right one yet.

Binghamton

TED WAS ABOUT TO marry the woman who had asked him to marry her. He asked Sal to be his best man. Ted knew Sal longer than he knew the rest of us—since before kindergarten--so Sal was the logical choice. Sal agreed to be the best man even though he had never laid eyes on Ted's fiancée. Of course, Mike said he would be the best man there regardless.

Ted's fiancée, Joan, planned the wedding for a Saturday night at her Baptist Church--a small wedding with just friends and family. Ted said she was taking care of all the arrangements. All Sal had to do was show up. OK!

On the weekend of the wedding, Sal drove from Pittsburgh to Pittston on Friday afternoon. Mike and Sal planned to drive to Binghamton the next day. The weather report called for rain and sleet on Saturday. Binghamton is an hour north of Pittston and is in the Snowbelt going from western New York to Massachusetts. Mike and Sal were worried. The wedding was at 6 p.m.

They were to leave at 4 p.m. to be sure they got there in time. At 3 p.m., the sleet had arrived. Sal called Mike, and they left fifteen minutes later. As they traveled north on Interstate 81, they encountered more sleet. They got out of the car every ten minutes to remove the ice and sleet from the windshield wipers. What a day!

Do you know about the old wives tale about rain and weddings? Rain on wedding days signifies good luck and a strong marriage. The logic is a wet knot is more difficult to untie. Snow is associated with fertility and wealth. We thought this had to be a good sign for Ted—rain, sleet, and snow—for a long wealthy marriage with lots of babies!

Finally, they arrived at the church at 5:45 p.m. with only fifteen minutes to spare. Mike and Sal were starving. Could they survive until the reception? Joan's family and friends were already at the church. Her parents seemed older than their years. Her two girlfriends were there, one tall and thin (the maid of honor) and one short and fat (no designated role). Ted's family arrived—his parents, his two sisters, and his aunt and uncle.

Ted's aunt walked into the room and gave Sal the "look." If you aren't Italian, you may not know the look--an emotional gaze somewhere between anger and despair. It has a little bit of concern, bewilderment, disbelief, disgust, and a lot of "Where the hell did we go wrong raising this kid? Was he switched at birth?" The words she wanted to say were, "You're friends for Christ's sake; you could've done something about this!"

The ceremony started at 6:02 p.m. and ended at 6:05 p.m. It had to be the shortest wedding ceremony in history. Mike went to the bathroom and missed the whole thing.

Mike and Sal ran downstairs to the food. When they arrived at the reception room, they found some cheese and crackers and a few soft drinks. That's it! That was all the food!

Mike and Sal were happy the fat friend was there because she was hungry and wanted to go somewhere to eat. The maid of honor (the tall skinny one) volunteered her apartment where she had cold cuts. We all agreed and quickly went off to her apartment. At her apartment, while she gathered things for sandwiches, she opened one of the cabinet doors in Sal's face. That really hurt! She seemed to have done it intentionally.

While she made sandwiches, Sal sat down to allow his eye to get red and swollen. Mike and Sal waited for the sandwiches. The tall skinny one said, "It's a good thing I can cook, not one of my two other husbands could cook."

Wow, she had two previous husbands and she was only twenty-five years old. Interestingly, she thought making sandwiches was cooking. Go figure! The fat one didn't say anything—she was too busy eating.

Still in shock, Mike and Sal headed back to Wyoming Valley. We considered doing an intervention but we never heard of a "love intervention." We had heard about alcohol intervention and a suicide intervention, but never heard of a love intervention?

Ted was now married and living in Binghamton, Sal returned to Pittsburgh to dental school, and Mike went back to work. I wasn't able to go to the wedding. One down, three to go.

Early December 1968

I HAD BEEN DATING Mary Ann for six months. We had gone to the Poconos, Delaware Water Gap, Hickory State Park, out for dinner, and to a few plays in which her brother Joe was involved. We double-dated with Joe and Rene Elise and with Mary Ann's other brothers and their wives. Early on, Mary Ann taught me how to fly-fish and we often went on "fly-fishing" parties together. Occasionally Joe or one of Mary Ann's other brothers went with us. It was a family affair. I thought perhaps her brothers were keeping their eyes on me, but they had worried needlessly.

The Cusano's invited Jeffrey for dinner many times and her parents, Joseph senior, and Patricia, liked him. When Jeffrey began going over to the Cusano's, he told them he worked at Coccina Italiano and how he learned to cook.

Patricia said, "Well now, let's see how good a cook you really are. Why don't you cook something for lunch Sunday?"

"OK. What would you like?"

"How about making lasagna?"

"OK."

"...from scratch!"

"Wow, I knew she would pick something simple."

I said I would make the sauce and bring it with me on Sunday before Mary Ann and I went to church.

After church, I made lasagna. Patricia and Joseph senior were very impressed with my cooking.

Patricia told me, "Now you need to teach Mary Ann to cook."

Mary Ann got mad at her mother. Being a good daughter, she let it go.

Since Thanksgiving, Mary Ann and I talked about what good

friends we had become, what good times we had when we went out, and how much we missed each other when we couldn't be together. We talked about how our friendship was evolving into a serious relationship.

Over the past few months, I told Mary Ann I loved her and she said she loved me as well. I told Mary Ann I respected her wishes to wait until marriage to get intimate. We talked about the Nurse Practitioner program. I told Mary Ann how proud I was of her and how important it was for her to continue school.

I asked Mary Ann, "Do you think you could finish school if you were married?"

"Are you asking me to marry you?"

"Well, I want to know what you think about a plan like that. Hypothetically, if we got married, you could still finish school. Many couples do that now."

"Hypothetically, if we got married, we would share household responsibilities and cut commute time so that we could see each other more, and I would have more time to study. I like your hypothetical idea."

"Of course, this discussion is hypothetical—what's important is we love each other, we want to build a life together, and we want to have a family. I also think two and a half years is a long time to wait to make love."

Mary Ann said, "I'm not sure that I can wait that long either. So, hypothetically speaking, I think your proposal is good."Christmas Eve, 1968

I ARRIVED at the Cusano's for dinner. I brought some gifts and put them under the Christmas tree. Their custom was to eat, exchange presents, and go to Midnight Mass.

After dinner, everyone went to the living room to exchange presents. I said I wanted to give Mary Ann her gift last. Everyone except Mary Ann and I exchanged gifts. Mary Ann gave me a pair of hiking boots we had seen at Bloomingdale's department store.

I gave Mary Ann a large box.

She opened it and found a smaller box. She looked at me and smiled.

She opened the smaller box and there was a ring box in it. She started crying.

I got on one knee and said, "Will you be my wife?"

She immediately said, "Yes."

We hugged and kissed.

Mary Ann's parents were cautiously happy.

I said to them, "Mary Ann and I discussed marriage and how she would finish her schooling. We talked about getting married next year after she starts her Master's program."

Joe senior said, "I'm happy you are making a sensible decision. You both are mature and I think this will work out."

On Becoming Us

Our troops began their withdrawal from Vietnam.

We listened to the music of the Temptations, "I Can't Get Next to You" and "I'm Going to Make You Love Me"; Fifth Dimension, "Wedding Bell Blues"; Elvis, "In the Ghetto"; and Credence Clearwater Revival, "Proud Mary."

We went to the movies to see: "Easy Rider," "Butch Cassidy and the Sundance Kid," and "Midnight Cowboy."

We all were becoming "free spirits."

Chapter 12

The Growth Years

The Search for a Good Career Continues...

1969

WE NOW WERE SCATTERED throughout the Northeast—New York City, Binghamton, Pittsburgh, and Wyoming Valley. Cub Scouts and the pact we made seemed like such a long time ago.

I wanted to be with Mary Ann every waking minute. During the last six months, we dated in New York, the Pocono Mountains, and the area surrounding the Delaware Water Gap. The Pocono Mountains had become our favorite place to escape the City. Early on, while the weather was warm, we hiked and fished at another favorite spot, Dunnfield Creek Trail, where we had gone on our first date. We enjoyed hiking around the quarries at Granite Knolls Park. In the winter, we liked ice-skating at Rockefeller Center and cross-country skiing at Bear Mountain State Park.

Because the Pocono Mountains were special to us, Mary Ann and I decided to get married on Saturday, October 11, 1969, Mary Ann's birthday, at The Camelback Inn in Tannersville. An October 11 wedding date would give us an extra day, Monday (Columbus Day), allowing a two-day honeymoon—the maximum vacation Mary Ann could take given her school schedule. We had been to Camelback skiing a few times and

185

loved the atmosphere and scenery. Unlike her brothers' wives, Mary Ann wanted a small, intimate wedding with family and a few friends.

Johanna and Stanley took us out to dinner a few times and had us over to their apartment for dinner. Stanley owned an investment apartment in the same building. The lease on the investment apartment was to expire next summer, and Stanley asked Mary Ann and me if we wanted to lease it. We jumped at the opportunity—the price was right and the location was perfect. The apartment was on Park Avenue and Fiftieth Street, between Columbia University and my work. The four of us had become friends and we didn't see any downside to this arrangement.

Pittsburgh

SAL AND HIS CLASSMATES were studying for dental boards. All the dental fraternities had old board tests to study. Many of the professors gave tests using old board questions. Even if they missed some questions while they were studying, they learned the information. Interestingly enough, depending on the year, the correct answers to a few questions changed. Go figure!

Binghamton

TED HAD BEEN married three months and we hadn't seen him—he and Joan didn't visit Pittston. Had the wicked witches from Binghamton kidnapped him? Really, we hadn't even heard from him—no phone call and no Christmas cards. Didn't he learn anything growing up? We learned later that his wife didn't get along with the Pittston crowd (family). We couldn't understand her attitude since his parents and two sisters were nice and easy going.

Wyoming Valley

MIKE WAS STILL plugging away at Pomeroy's Department Store. He was dating but wasn't finding anyone he liked.

New York City

MARY ANN FINISHED her last year of nursing school and was preparing to enroll at Columbia. I would keep my apartment until the wedding and we would move into Stanley's apartment as soon as we got married. Planning the wedding involved many choices—decorations, seating, and the menu. We also had to choose necessities such as dinnerware, serving ware, table linens, crystal, cookware, electric appliances, and bed and bath items as well. We would look for these things during the summer.

Pittsburgh

SAL'S SECOND YEAR of dental school was over and he chose to start the clinical phase of his education in June instead of September giving him an extra three months to complete his requirements for graduation. He liked living in Pittsburgh and continued barbering to make money.

New York City

I WAS THE COURTROOM artist for a murder trial in Brooklyn. A young Asian man shot and killed the owner of a dry cleaning store during a robbery. Witnesses said the owner, as requested by the robber, handed the money from the cash register to him.

Once the robber had the money, he said, "Don't look at me that way" and shot him. The police apprehended him as he ran out of the store. They were responding to a domestic call a few doors away and saw the robbery and murder unfold. Bad luck for the murderer!

As I was about to enter the courtroom, I ran into Colleen. We stopped to say hello.

Colleen said, "Hey good looking, I haven't seen you in a while, how are you?"

"I'm doing well, how are you?"

"I'm OK. You look good! Sexier than I remembered."

Somewhat embarrassed, I said, "Thanks, you look good as well."

"Are you covering a trial?"

"Yes, the "Dry Cleaning Murder.""

"That should be interesting."

"We'll see!"

Colleen said in a sultry voice, "I'm not seeing anyone right now. Would you care to have lunch and catch up? I miss you."

"Sorry, I can't. I'm engaged and am getting married in a couple of months."

"Well, you're not married yet!"

"Sorry, it doesn't work that way for me. It was good to see you. Bye."

Binghamton

AFTER MONTHS IN seclusion (perhaps as a "sex slave"), Ted left teaching and began working with NCR who advertised for computer teachers. NCR wanted to educate teachers about computers and to train them to teach other employees. NCR hired Ted for that position for over twice what he was making teaching grade school.

New York City

MY ADVERTISING FIRM, Adams, Brooke, and Ziegfeld, added architectural renderings and book jacket designs to its line of products. I participated in the book jacket designs; some were abstract and others were illustrative. In addition to my regular duties creating illustration copy for advertising, I continued working as a courtroom consultant submitting sketches of high profile crimes to local newspapers—The New York Times, New York Daily News, New York Post--and to several news stations. I tried to be involved in criminal forensics as much as possible.

Mary Ann started her Master's program at Columbia, which included advanced science courses-- physiology, pathology, pharmacology, and clinical studies--Diagnosis, Advanced Practice, and Health Assessment. During her education, she interned with a general practice physician since her goal was to get a Family Nurse Practitioner degree.

October 11, 1969

OUR BIG DAY HAD arrived. Mary Ann and I were getting married at 6:45 pm to coincide with the 7:01 pm sunset. We placed the "altar" so we would be facing the sunset. For the ceremony and reception, we hired two musicians—a pianist and a violinist.

Mary Ann and I spent the next two days in the Poconos on our honeymoon. I had moved my stuff into the new apartment we were leasing from Johanna and Stanley on Park Avenue.

Christmas, 1969

MARY ANN AND I visited my parents in West Pittston for Christmas. Mike and Sal came over to visit. We were excited to be married and were planning to start a family as soon as Mary Ann finished graduate school. Mike and Sal were happy to see that I was on my way to becoming a "family man."

On Becoming Us

After releasing "The Long Winding Road" and "Let It Be," the Beatles went their separate ways.

The Jackson Five happily stepped into the spotlight with "ABC" and "I'll Be There."

Rockers Jimi Hendrix and Janis Joplin both died from unrelated drug overdoses.

George C. Scott won Best Actor Oscar for "Patton" and refused it.

IBM introduced the "floppy disc."

Chapter 13

The Growth Years

The Search for a Career Widens

1970

FAMOUS AND TALENTED people discovered that walking on the edge had consequences. Some rockers, who experimented with drugs, learned they weren't invincible, only human. Others learned that they weren't immune to celebrity. Was their luck running out?

The Beatles, who grew up around the corner from each other, seemed destined to dominate the music scene forever. And, they did, for a while. However, they would no longer dominate as a group.

New York City

ON FRIDAY, APRIL 10, 1970, in Ardsley, Westchester County, New York, a "stranger" kidnapped six-month old, Zachary, from his back yard in the presence of his nanny. His father, Joshua Bitner, an investment banker, and mother, Charlotte Wembly, a corporate attorney, both worked in the financial district in Manhattan. The Bitners, married less than five years, bought a house in Ardsley just before Charlotte gave birth to Zachary.

They hired a nanny, Sophia Aliccini, to live in and to take care of Zachary when Charlotte returned to work. Sophia's mother, Gianna, lived there with Sophia in the detached guesthouse. Sophia spoke "broken" English and her mother spoke only Italian.

While Sophia and Zachary were on the back patio--Zachary was sleeping and Sophia was knitting--a short man approached Sophia from behind, pushed her to the ground turning over her chair, grabbed Zachary, and ran away. Sophia called the police immediately. The police and the FBI arrived within minutes. No one found a note related to the incident.

Sophia had not seen the person who took Zachary. However, Sophia's mother, Gianna, told Sophia she was looking out the kitchen window of the guesthouse, as she washed the dishes, and saw the whole incident. She saw the man who grabbed the baby. The authorities believed this to be a crime of opportunity.

Westchester County, an upscale New York suburb, had few crimes of this type, and, because authorities wanted to move quickly, the Chief of Police John O'Neil called me to see if I could help. Chief O'Neil knew me from my courtroom work, and, when I registered with the Westchester County Police, I indicated I spoke fluent Italian. Fortunately, I was in my Manhattan office and quickly left for Ardsley.

Chief O'Neil called Zachary's parents.

"An incident happened at your home. Your son has been kidnapped and we are canvassing the area," Chief O'Neil said to each parent.

"I'll leave as soon as possible," Mr. Bitner said.

"I'm on my way," Mrs. Bitner said.

I arrived at the Bitner's house and everyone was in a tizzy as you could imagine. I introduced myself to FBI Special Agent Thomas Martin, a recent transplant from Augusta, Georgia.

"I'm Jeffrey Rosenbloom, a forensic artist. Chief O'Neil called me. How can I help?"

"You're the one who speaks Italian?"

"Yes."

"Good. Go over yonder and talk with the old lady in the black dress, sitting on the patio. Apparently, she saw the kidnapper but can't speak 'a lick of English.' I don't know why they don't learn English before they come here!"

Although his remark offended me, I thought, "There are more important things going on here."

Sitting on the patio, Gianna clenched a pair of Rosary Beads--her lips were moving as if lip-syncing but she wasn't saying anything. I recognized the prayers she was saying to herself by reading her lips. I remembered my grandmother, Concetta, often praying the Rosary.

I sat with Gianna.

"Ciao, il mio nome è Jeffrey Rosenbloom. (Hello, my name is Jeffrey Rosenbloom)

Mia madre è siciliana e ho imparato a parlare italiano quando ero un ragazzino. (My mother is Sicilian and I learned to speak Italian when I was a little boy.)

Potete aiutarci fino tornare il bambino?" (Can you help us find the baby?)

"Sì." (Yes)

"Riesci a capire me?" (Can you understand me?)

"Sì." (Yes)

"Hai visto il rapitore?" (Did you see the kidnapper?)

"Sì." (Yes)

"Era un uomo o una donna?" (Was it a man or a woman?)

"Un uomo." (A man)

"Era l'uomo bianco o nero?" (Was the man white or black?)

"Era spagnolo." (He was Spanish.)

"Qual è stato l'uomo che indossa?" (What was the man wearing?)

"Pantaloni scuri e una camicia scura." (Dark pants and a dark shirt.)

195

"Quanto è alto era lui?" (How tall was he?)
"Short. Forse un metro e dieci centimetri." (Short, maybe five-foot, four-inches.)
"Che colore di capelli aveva?" (What color hair did he have?)
"Marrone" (Brown.)
"Che colore occhi aveva?" (What color eyes did he have?)
"Marrone." (Brown.)
"Aveva i peli del viso?" (Did he have facial hair?)
"No." (No.)
"Era il suo viso rotondo o ovale?" (Was his face round or oval?)
"Rotondo." (Round.)
"Questo sembra come lui?" (Does this look like him?)
"Sì. I suoi occhi erano più vicini." (Yes. His eyes were closer.)
"Questo sembra più simile a lui?" (Does this look more like him?)
"Sì. Il suo naso era più ampio." (Yes. His nose was wider.)
"Come funziona questo aspetto?" (How does this look?)
"Meglio. Proprio lui." (Better, that's him.)

After making the modifications according to Gianna, I finalized the sketch and gave it to the FBI, who immediately showed it to family.

Neither Joshua nor Charlotte recognized the person in the sketch. Sophia didn't recognize him either. Agent Martin and his men went house-to-house in the neighborhood with my sketch.

Finally, one of the workers, a cook, working a few houses away, said she knew the man in the sketch. "I saw him yesterday with the maid, Carmelitta Vega. He's her 'boyfriend.' She works sometimes over there." She pointed toward the Bitners' place. "The maid is in the house now, working."

The FBI went into the house to talk with Carmelitta.

"Someone who looks like your boyfriend kidnapped the baby next door." Agent Martin told Carmelitta. "Do you recognize the man in this sketch?"

Carmelitta said, "Yes, he's my ex-boyfriend, Angel Santiago. He's a bad man! He 'took advantage of me' and got me pregnant. I broke up with him months ago."

"Have you been talking with him since you broke up?"

"No! I haven't talked to him until yesterday, when he came to see me. That was the first day I saw him. I was surprised, since I didn't think he knew where I lived. As soon as I knew I was pregnant, I left Nogales to come here. Against the wishes of God and my family, I had an abortion. This is a curse on my family and me for murdering my baby. I can tell you where to find the **mofeta** (skunk)."

The FBI went to the house where Angel was staying and found little Zachary sleeping as if he was unaware of his ordeal. An FBI agent took Angel into custody. Another agent returned Zachary to his parents.

FBI agent Thomas Martin questioned language-challenged Angel Santiago. Although he spoke some English, understanding him was difficult and they had to get an interpreter. After the interview, they arrested him.

Agent Martin talked with Carmelitta.

"Where did you meet Angel?"

"In Nogales, Mexico. My family arranged a marriage to him. I didn't want to go out with such a *mala vida* (low life) and I didn't want to marry him. I was mad at my father for arranging such a thing. He forced himself on me and got me pregnant.

"My family was pushing me to marry him since our families agreed on the marriage and his parents had already paid a dowry-- in cash--to my parents, who had already spent the money.

I didn't want to marry Angel, and the last thing I wanted was to have his baby. I also thought, at eighteen years old, I was too young to have a baby.

"I came to New York to seek advice from my older sister, Juanita, who worked as a maid. Juanita agreed with me that I shouldn't have to marry Angel and shouldn't have his baby.

Somehow, Angel found out I was pregnant and told me we had to get married, and, if we didn't get married, he would "fix it" so no one would ever want to marry me.

"I was upset and moved to New York to be near my sister and to work as a maid. Angel, who remained in Nogales, assumed I would have his baby and want to marry him. Once I came to New York, I decided to have an illegal abortion in New Jersey.

"Months later, when Angel, who was unaware of the abortion, found me, he wanted to restart his relationship. Angel asked about 'his' baby. I was afraid of what Angel would do if he found out about the abortion, so I told him the baby was nearby, healthy, and safe. I told Angel to go back to Nogales where he belonged. Angel must have assumed the Bitner baby was his and later came back to take 'his' baby away from me."

The police charged Angel with kidnapping.

Pittsburgh

TOWARD THE END of second semester, Sal was waiting to go into class at Salk Hall when he saw a nursing student in the hallway. She was a young, attractive girl about five-feet, four-inches with bleached blond hair pulled back into a ponytail. He walked over to her and started a conversation.

"Hi. I haven't seen you here before. Are you new?"

"No. I've been around for a while. I'm in my last year of nursing school."

Remembering what I told him about my conversation with Mary Ann and how I teased her about being too young for me, Sal said, "That would make you about twenty."

"I'll be twenty in June."

"Oh, you're only nineteen? Hum, that's young."

"I don't think so; I'll be twenty next month."

"Yea, but you're not twenty yet."

"How old are you, Mr. Smarty-pants?"

"I'm twenty-seven... I think you might be too young for me."

"I don't think so!"

"Well, we'll see. What's your name?"

"Tammie Mills. What's yours?"

"Sal Greco"

"Are you Italian?

"Yes."

"I've never gone out with an Italian."

"Who said we're going out?"

"We're going out! You think I'm cute—I can see it in your eyes."

"You're cute but you're really... really young. I don't know where I would take you if we went out. Maybe we can go get an ice cream cone."

"Ice cream is ok."

"Have you ever been to any clubs?"

"Yes, I've been to a few but not in Pittsburgh."

"Do you get carded?"

"I usually don't go to clubs, but when I'm dressed up with makeup, I look older."

"Do you think you could handle me?"

"I can handle you!"

"OK, Tammie Mills, if you think you're old enough and think you can handle me, I'll take you out Saturday. We'll go to Shadyside and listen to some music.

"OK."

"Do you have an apartment?"

"No, I live in the nurse's residence."

"Would you like to get something to eat before we go to Shadyside?"

"Yes, I'd like that."

"How does 6 p.m. Saturday sound to you? We'll go for Italian and then to the *Fox* in *Shadyside*."

"OK, I'll see you then."

On Saturday night, Sal went to the nurse's residence to get Tammie. He almost didn't recognize her; she hadn't exaggerated about looking older when she dressed up—older and sexier.

She wore tight, burgundy, dress slacks, and a long sleeve, off-white shirt maybe one size too small. With makeup and her hair down, she looked late-twenties, certainly older than she looked in her little nurse's outfit.

Sal thought, "She has on so much makeup, she must have started getting ready at noon."

Tammie reminded Sal of one of his cousin's wives who took two hours to get ready every morning whenever they stayed with his parents.

He wasn't accustomed to dating anyone as sexy as Tammie but wanted to keep an open mind. His type was wholesome—traditional style clothing, traditional fitting clothing, conservative acting, and minimal makeup. Even though Mike's cousin, Christina, didn't dress like a college student, she was well dressed and conservative. Tammie seemed the opposite of Christina. Sal thought, "This'll be a new experience."

Sal and Tammie went to Minutello's Italian Restaurant for lasagna—the house specialty.

"How did you get interested in nursing?"

"I wanted to be a nurse from the time I was a little girl."

"Why Pittsburgh?"

"I have family in McKeesport and wanted to be near my cousin, Holly. In addition, Pittsburgh has a good nursing program. I'm thinking of staying here permanently."

"Is nursing school the end of the line or are you planning to continue your education?"

"I want some experience in patient care and, maybe, enter the nurse anesthetist program. I think it's too soon to make a decision."

On one hand, Tammie was like Pittston girls—she talked about finishing school, getting married, and having babies. Even though she talked about the same things Pittston girls talked about, Sal didn't mind it since she didn't indicate these issues were pressing. Having babies didn't seem to be her driving force. She wanted those things, but not now.

Sal was worried about getting in the Fox Cafe. Although they weren't too strict about carding people, Shadyside establishments were careful. They didn't allow customers to drink too much or to misbehave because they didn't want any problems with the police. Tammie looked old enough.

When they got there, they walked in and she gave the "bouncer" a very flirty smile, batted her eyelashes, and he waved her in. She seemed to know how to get what she wanted. After she flirted with him, he wasn't about to offend her by asking for her ID.

They each had a screwdriver and listened to Rhythm and Blues music for about an hour.

Tammie told Sal she really liked music and dancing.

Sal said, "I collect records."

"Who do you have?"

"I have mostly Motown--Smokey Robinson, Fifth Dimension, Platters, Johnny Mathis, Joni Mitchell, Supremes, Temptations, Four Tops, and Carol King."

"I like all of them. I love the Fifth Dimension."

It was about 9:30 pm.

"Would you like to go to my apartment to listen to some music?"

"I don't know. This is our first date and I don't know you very well."

"I thought you said you could handle me."

"I can but you seem too sure of yourself."

"It's an act. I'm really very nervous about our date."

"If we went to your apartment can I count on you to behave?"

"Sure, I'll behave."

They went to his apartment and listened to some music. They slow danced and kissed a couple of times. After about an hour, Tammie said it was getting late and she had to work the next morning at 7 a.m.

When they got back to the nurse's residence, she asked, "Well, am I old enough for you?"

"You're OK. Am I too old for you?"

"You're OK."

Sal said, "What are you doing after work tomorrow?"

"I don't have any plans."

"OK. I'll pick you up at 4 p.m. and we can go to the park and walk around."

The next day, Sal took Tammie to Schenley Park. She had on tight jeans and a tight, thin sweater. They sat on a bench and talked about the night before.

"I'm staying in Pittsburgh for the summer." The subtle message was that they could spend time together during the summer.

That's great," she said in a pleased voice.

Later, they went to Mimeo's Pizza in Squirrel Hill. Although she wore tight clothes and was sexy, Sal didn't get the feeling she was a loose chick.

The following Friday night, they went to a fraternity party where she met some of Sal's friends. Phil said, "Wow! Nice. Where did you find her?"

"At Salk Hall. She was waiting for class."

Bob said, "I'd like to meet any of your girlfriends that are half as good looking as you?"

Tammie just smiled and didn't say anything.

Phil said, "I think you would have a better time with me. What do you say you and I split?"

Tammie said, "I don't think so!"

Don't forget, these were Sal's "friends."

Bob asked Sal, "Can we hang out more often? Maybe we can get your 'cast offs.' "

Tammie was a good dancer so they hit it off quickly. You know how much Sal loves to dance!

The next night, Tammie went to Sal's apartment for spaghetti and meatballs. They ate dinner and listened to music. Later, they kissed, made out, and slept together.

Over the next few weeks, Sal and Tammie went to the library to study a few times during the week and dated on the weekends. She stayed over most weekends.

June 1970

TAMMIE WAS GOOD for Sal--he started studying more. In the past, he was preoccupied looking for someone to date. The search took away from "study time." He continued to cut hair on Thursday and sometimes on Saturday.

One night, after dating a month, Tammie said to Sal, "We've been seeing each other a while, and I think we should be exclusive."

He thought, "She has a point. We are spending a lot of time together--studying, cooking, going out, and sleeping together. We get along well. She makes a good argument."

He said, "OK, we can do that."

Sal and Tammie became exclusive or otherwise known as "going steady"—if that was the appropriate word to use with a twenty-seven year old and a twenty year old.

Sal still had reservations about the way Tammie dressed and interacted with guys she thought were cute. It seemed like she was saying, "Look at me; look at what you're missing." Around

203

her, men acted as if she were "on-heat." As long as she didn't want to *show* them what they were missing, Sal was OK with it. He decided to wait and see what happened.

Over the next three months, they spent a lot of time together—studying, cooking, and going to local attractions such as the zoo and the park. Because Sal didn't like the fraternity party scene and wasn't into smoking marijuana, he was happy to spend time with Tammie.

A week before Thanksgiving, Sal and Tammie were preparing to go to their respective hometowns for Thanksgiving. She was going to visit her parents in Melvindale for the week. Sal was going to Pittston to see his buddies.

Tammie told Sal, "You better behave! We're exclusive now. I expect you to keep it in your pants and not to fool around with any chicks."

"You can trust me!"

Thanksgiving, 1970

Wyoming Valley

MIKE, JIMMY WALSH, AND SAL went to Vispi's the first night he was home and to the Flame to dance the next few nights. Jimmy was dating, of all people, a nurse but wasn't going steady. What was our attraction for nurses? When Sal was a senior in high school, he "went steady" with a nursing student. Now, a senior in dental school, he's going steady with a nursing student—ten years later still dating student nurses! During his senior year in college, he went steady but it was with a secretary.

There's something about the designation, "The last year," that makes you think you need someone in your life.

Mike had dated a few girls but didn't seem to click with any of them. He and Jimmy were more ready than Sal was. I was married about a year. Ted was married almost two years--if he was still alive. Regardless, we had fun together.

I told Mike and Jim I had been seeing someone in Pittsburgh for the past six months.

Mike asked, "What's her name?"

"Tammie Mills."

Mike said, "I guess you don't like Italian girls. What does she look like?"

"She's short with blonde hair and blue eyes. She's in nursing school."

Jim said, "I already like her!"

Mike said, "Is she a good dancer?"

"Yes, she's a very good dancer."

Mike, "Is this serious?"

Sal said, "I don't know; I don't think so. She's not my type. You know how I like reserved women. Tammie is the opposite-- quiet but sexy--she wears tight clothes and appears to invite attention from guys she thinks are cute. I don't know if I can handle that for the rest of my life. I'm not sure that I can see myself with her long-term. One day last summer, we were at Schenley Park, a park across from my apartment, and she had on jeans. All of a sudden, she said, 'I'm too hot.' She then proceeded to take off her jeans. She looked great in her little red bikini panties but I was pretty embarrassed."

Mike, "She took off her jeans in front of everyone? Wow! I guess you got a big hard-on."

"Yeah, so did every other guy in sight."

"Why are you going steady if you don't think she is the right one?" Jim said.

"Well, she asked me to be 'exclusive' and I didn't want to say no because I like her. We'll see."

Jim, "Does she stay over?"

"Yes, on weekends. Sometimes she stays during the week."

Mike, "OK, now I understand, you're getting laid and don't want to end it."

"It isn't exactly like that. I'm trying to have an open mind. I don't know where this is going. We'll see what happens."

Jim said, "Open mind my ass. Rationalize all you want, but you're keeping it going just to get laid. Is she good?"

Sal tried to change the subject, He asked, "What do you hear from Jeffrey and Ted?"

Jimmy said, "She must be good if he's trying to change the subject."

"Jeffrey comes in on weekends about once or twice a month. As for Ted, who knows what's going on there. Those amazons in Binghamton probably have him in a locked basement room so they could have their way with him whenever they want.

"Jeffrey and Mary Ann seem happy. They love their apartment on Park Avenue. Jeffrey said they often get together for dinner with your cousins and he was bragging about Johanna's cooking."

Pittsburgh

SAL AND TAMMIE got together the Sunday after Thanksgiving. He missed her during the last week. They cooked dinner and, after eating, Tammie asked Sal, "Did you sleep with anyone when you were in Pittston?"

Jokingly, Sal said, "Yes, just a few. Did you?"

"Yes, I screwed one of my old boyfriends. My mother ran into him last month and told him I was coming home for Thanksgiving."

"So your mother "fixed you up?"

"She didn't fix me up; she always liked him and didn't want us to break up when I left for school. He came over my house the day after I got home and we went out."

"Where did you go?"

"We went to his apartment, smoked some marijuana, and had sex. However, I made him use condoms so it wouldn't count!"

"What do you mean, 'so it wouldn't count?' "

"We used condoms. It wasn't like he was inside me."

"How many times did you see him?"

"Every day except the last one."

"Did you have sex with him every day?"

"Yes, but he always used a condom."

"I thought we were exclusive."

"We are exclusive. It was just 'condom-sex' with an old boyfriend—it didn't count. I didn't sleep with anyone new."

Sal was upset. "I was only kidding about sleeping with a few girls. I didn't go to bed with anyone."

"You could've gone to bed with someone if you wanted... and used condoms. I made my old boyfriend use condoms."

Sal couldn't help wondering if he and Tammie were from different planets or if they were speaking a different language. Is this the new women's liberation we've been hearing about?

At the time, he didn't think much about an incident that happened when he was waiting for Tammie in the nurse's lounge, but it seemed significant in light of this new information. One of her classmates, Jackie, was engaged to one of Sal's classmates, Doug. While Sal was in the lounge waiting for Tammie, he saw Jackie going out with someone else.

When Tammie came from her room, he said to Tammie, "I thought Jackie and Doug were engaged?"

"They are. Doug had to work and Jackie didn't want to stay alone in the dorm on a Saturday night."

"This was a completely new way of thinking for Sal. It's OK for an engaged person (Jackie) to go on a date if her fiancé (Doug) is unavailable. If that's the case then a married woman whose husband is a salesman can go out and have sex with

207

someone else whenever he's out of town, especially if her lover wears condoms because he wouldn't be inside her.

"If Sal were on the fence before, this surely knocked him off."

He told Tammie, "With all that you told me, I need to think about where our relationship is going. Let me take you back to the dorm."

"But we just got together and we haven't made love in a week."

"I haven't made love in a week; you, on the other hand, had sex almost every day with someone else."

"Please don't break up with me. I thought you would be OK with it."

"I don't know if I can trust you anymore, and I can't be with someone I can't trust. I'll call you tomorrow."

This whole incident and the conversation they had reminded me of my conversation with Brandi. There seemed to be many issues at play in Sal's relationship with Tammie.

Sal told us, "One time we were at a concert and a couple in their fifties was sitting next to us. Tammie had on a mini skirt and the man kept looking down at her legs. As soon as she saw him looking at her legs, she put her foot on the armrest of the seat in front of her and exposed more of her leg--up to her pantyhose. She told me, "The man next to me is looking at my legs. I'm giving him something to look at."

Sal was no longer comfortable with her and her attitude. He told us about a dress her mother sent to her a few months ago. It was a flowered dress with a "V" neck. It had a built-in, push-up bra. When she put it on, her breasts were practically falling out. She thought she looked great and her mother obviously was encouraging her behavior.

Sal called her the next day and said, "I don't want to see you any more. I can't trust you."

Tammie said, "I like you and I'd like to continue to see you even if we aren't exclusive. Sex is great and I'd like to keep sleeping with you."

Sal said, "No, it won't work out to continue dating."

"All in the Family," was the breakout television show of the decade, a sitcom about loudmouth, uneducated, and bigoted Archie Bunker who couldn't avoid the stereotypes he detested. Other members of his family included: his wife, Edith, sweet but not smart; his daughter, Gloria, who inherited her father's loud mouth; and her husband, Mike, an unemployed student of Polish decent. Next door was George Jefferson—a successful black dry cleaner, his wife, and family.

In spite of its popularity as a sitcom, the politically incorrect sitcom became one of the most influential programs tackling issues such as homosexuality, women's liberation, menopause, religion, impotence, abortion, and the Vietnam War.

The year ended with Dan Cooper, holding a $200,000 cash ransom, parachuting from a Northwest Orient plane.

We watched the movies, "Love Story," "Summer of '42," and "Carnal Knowledge." We listened to "How Can You Mend a Broken Heart" by the Bee Gees.

Chapter 14

The Growth Years

Found: Careers

1971

Pittsburgh

SAL FINALLY FINISHED school; he graduated from dental school—the last of the four friends to achieve their goals of a "big deal" career.

After his graduation, his parents, Uncles Joe, Mike, and Jim Greco, and cousins, Guy Longo and Justine Leonardi went a Greek restaurant for lunch. The Greco men made a big appearance at his graduation because he was the oldest male and the first to graduate from professional school among the second generation of Salvatore and Mary Greco.

After graduation, he joined the Navy and moved to Great Lakes Naval Training Center, just north of Chicago.

New York City

IN JUNE, MARY ANN finished her Master's degree and began working as a nurse practitioner in the student clinic at NYU, a job giving her opportunities to practice clinical diagnosis and treatment. She was so excited.

A year before NYU hired thirty-three year old Alexandra Thomas, MD, an internist, to manage the clinic. Alexandra married an attorney in her last year of medical school. The couple, savvy in running a law practice and a medical practice, had difficulty, though, "running" their marriage. Alexandra was a perky young woman, a good clinician, and was always positive and upbeat. She welcomed Mary Ann as a colleague, and they instantly became friends.

I believed the time to discuss starting a family was now. I initiated the conversation more often than Mary Ann did. Having worked for four years, I was eager to get going. I asked her, "When do you think we can start a family?"

Mary Ann, now twenty-four years old, said, "I'd like to work a year or two before having a baby. I don't want to jeopardize my position at *NYU* by having a baby and needing time off because of family responsibilities. If I take time off it would be without pay, but more importantly, I think it's irresponsible to have a baby before establishing my career."

On the other hand, I wanted to have a baby as soon as possible—that's all I ever talked about since high school. After all, I waited a year to get married and I waited until marriage to make love. I was tired of waiting.

However, I did understand her position and I did respect her desire to wait. At twenty-four, she had time to have children.

On June 5, 1971, the trial for Angel Santiago began. First order of business was jury selection. The challenge was to find a jury of peers for Angel Santiago in an area where few Hispanics lived and few were registered voters. The jury pool, as expected, was limited. However, the prosecution and defense teams were successful in selecting four women and two men with two alternates. One alternate was a Hispanic man. The prosecutor was concerned about having a Hispanic woman on the jury and the potential for intimidation by Santiago. Fortunately, there were no female Hispanic people in the jury pool that day.

The district attorney named witnesses for the prosecution—Joshua Bitner, Charlotte Wembly, Sophia Aliccini, Gianna Aliccini, Carmelitta Vega, FBI Agent Thomas Martin, and forensic artist, Jeffrey Rosenbloom. Documents were presented to the court—statements from witnesses and police along with a sketch from the forensic artist.

Colleen Smyth was the court artist covering the trial. Colleen and I acknowledged each other but avoided speaking. It had been two years since our affair after the "Sexpot" trial and less than that time since we wanted to sleep with me while I was engaged to Mary Ann.

The trial for Angel Santiago was short and without controversy. The judge charged the jury. Within fifteen minutes, the jury came back with a guilty verdict.

Upset that the police caught him and the jury found him guilty, Santiago yelled he would get back at everyone responsible for his verdict when he got out of jail. He especially targeted his girlfriend, Carmelitta, and me, because my artwork made the trial a slam-dunk. Santiago knew, without my sketch, he would have gone free. He yelled,

"Carmelitta ucciso il mio bambino. La piccola puttana ha ucciso il mio bambino." ("Carmelitta killed my baby! The little whore killed my baby!")

Carmelitta yelled: "Sì, ho ucciso tuo figlio. Non meriti un figlio!" ("Yes, I killed your son. You don't deserve a son!")

Angel yelled again, "Quando uscirò di prigione, io verrò dopo di te." ("When I get out of jail, I'll come after you.")

"Verrò dopo il poliziotto, Thomas Martin." ("I will come after the policeman, Thomas Martin.")

"Io rompere la mano del figlio di una cagna che ha dipinto la mia immagine." ("I will break the hand of the son of a bitch who painted my picture.")

213

Great Lakes, Illinois

SAL REPORTED FOR duty at Great Lakes, after completing several rotations in the various departments, and since he had a teaching background, he headed the department of preventive dentistry. He moved out of the Bachelor's Quarters and leased an apartment in nearby Lake Forest.

Wyoming Valley

SAL WENT HOME for Christmas to visit family and friends. Mike, Jimmy, and Sal were happy to be together again. They went to their favorite places and stayed out later than we expected. Everything was the same. It seemed like none of them would ever grow up; none of them would ever get married. Although they had good careers, they believed they were destined to be single and childless for the rest of their lives. This weighed heavily on them since they wanted to be in a relationship and have a family.

New York

MARY ANN AND I spent Christmas with her family.

On Becoming Us

Terrorists attacked the Munich Olympics and killed eleven Israeli athletes. High-level security became commonplace.

Hurricane Agnes caused widespread damage on the East Coast. The Susquehanna River flooded, to a height of fifteen feet at Public Square in Wilkes-Barre, Pennsylvania.

G. Gordon Liddy and his associates burglarized and wire tapped the Democratic National Committee headquarters at the Watergate office complex.

We watched "The Godfather," "Dirty Harry," and "Fiddler on the Roof."

We listened to Don McLean's "American Pie," the Chi-Lites' "Oh Girl," and Helen Reddy's "I am Woman."

Chapter 15

The Building Years

Nose to the Grindstone

1972

Great Lakes, Illinois

SO, WHAT WAS Sal doing in the Navy as the "officer-in-charge" of preventive dentistry when the lowest rated career on his *Interest Inventory* was "Army Officer?" What was he doing as a navy lieutenant? He was head of preventive dentistry for the largest naval training base in the country.

However, all wasn't peaches and cream. He constantly butted heads with his superior officers. I suppose the Interest Inventory Test was correct.

Binghamton, New York

NCR TRAINED TED TO teach computer science to their employees and he had been doing that for a while. In March 1972, he received a promotion to Field Engineer. More responsibility and more money but he took it on straight away.

Of course, we heard it through the grapevine and not directly from Ted.

New York City

I HAD BEEN WORKING with ABZ Advertising for five years. On June 8, the partners, Michael Adams, Robert Brook, and Mel Ziegfeld, asked me to attend a meeting in the conference room.

Mel Ziegfeld, the managing partner said, "Jeffrey, are you happy working here?"

"Yes, I am. My job here is better than I expected when I applied for the job."

"We've been happy with your work at the agency over the past five years as well."

Mel said, "We want to offer you a partnership in the firm."

I said, "Thank God. I thought you were going to fire me!"

Mel said, "God, no."

"Good."

"As you know, partnership comes with a buy-in. We propose that you put 20 percent of your pay toward equity for three years at which time you will be a full equity partner. We are offering this because you have been with the firm almost since the beginning and you've earned equity partnership."

I didn't have to think very hard about their offer. "Thank you very much. I'm flattered and honored to be a partner."

The Cusano's hosted a small, intimate party for me to celebrate my partnership in the advertising firm. Over the past five years, I worked full time at the firm and did some freelance work in forensic art, which gave me some degree of notoriety in the criminal justice system. I was able to continue my work at the firm, consult with the police, and continue working out of the house one or two days a week.

Wyoming Valley

SAL WAS LOOKING forward to a week vacation in Wyoming Valley with Mike Costanzo and Jimmy Walsh. He flew from Chicago to Avoca on Wednesday, June 28 and planned to return on Tuesday, July 4. His mother met him at the airport. He was happy to see his parents. His mother cooked baked ziti and meatballs for dinner.

Sal and his parents talked a long time until everyone was up-to-date about the Navy and Pittston. His mother had received a letter in the mail a few days before and gave it to him—it had only a return address, no name.

When he opened the letter, it was from Sandi Slovenski, the Saint Ann's student he liked and went out with a few years earlier. The same one he said he wouldn't take out again because he didn't have a good time.

In the letter, Sandi wrote, I haven't been able to stop thinking about you lately and wondered what you were doing. I graduated from Lehigh University in Bethlehem, Pennsylvania, and I'm going to graduate school in Tucson, Arizona in a few weeks. I've "grown up" since we last saw each other and, perhaps, we would have a lot to discuss."

The next day, Sal drove to Sandi's house in Mountaintop, Pennsylvania. He rang the doorbell and Sandi answered the door. When Sal saw her, he was amazed. He certainly didn't expect what he saw! Whereas she looked nerdy in high school, she had blossomed into a very pretty, young woman with long, layered brown hair past her shoulders. She looked as if she walked off a page from Vogue Magazine.

Sandi's mother invited Sal to have lunch with them. After lunch, Sal and Sandi we went for a ride in her new car—a brown

Triumph TR6--which she was going to drive to Tucson. He told her she looked beautiful and she reacted as if this was the first time she heard it before.

Sal asked, "What's your plan?"

"I'm beginning a Master's program in counseling at the University of Arizona in Tucson."

"What type of counseling?"

"Alcohol rehabilitation."

"Will you live in graduate housing or get an apartment?"

"Graduate housing. I want to avoid distractions and living in the dorm seems to offer that."

Sandi had become a mature, independent young lady.

"I'm going to be in town for a few days. Would you like to go out?"

"Sure."

Sal said, "Let's take in a movie and have dinner at Brutico's in Old Forge on Saturday. I'll come for you at 6 p.m."

On Friday, as planned, Sal got together with Mike and Jimmy at the Flame. They finished the night as they always did at the Main Diner in Exeter.

On Saturday, Sandi and Sal went to a movie, Frenzy, in Scranton.

"Are you enjoying the movie?" Sal said.

"No, it's weird."

"Let's leave."

They walked around Scranton. They found a park bench with a view of people learning to dance at an Arthur Murray Dance School. The class was on the second floor and the large windows were open. They could hear the music and could see students engaged in their dance class—it was more enjoyable watching them than watching the movie.

Sal stood up and said," Would you like to dance."

"I don't know how to dance."

"Just 'wing it.' "

They were in the middle of the sidewalk sort of dancing and tripping over each other. They laughed about stepping on each other's toes and talked about serious things. They talked about her plans after school, marriage, and relationships.

Sandi said, "I feel like I'm being interviewed for a job; the job of becoming your wife."

"I didn't realize I was conducting an 'interview.' I just wanted to see if there was a chance for a relationship since you will live in Tucson and I live near Chicago. Not your typical dating scenario."

On Sunday, they spent the day at Harvey's Lake. Sal didn't talk about anything serious since he didn't want Sandi to think he was "cross-examining" her. That night, they went to her parents for dinner. Sal liked her parents, her sister, and her brother. He especially liked her father who was a dentist.

Sal was comfortable at her house. Sandi was attractive, smart, and came from a nice family—all good things. He felt fortunate he met her and happy to be dating her. Finally, he found someone who had the potential of becoming "The One." The thought of meeting and falling in love with one of your students was romantic. Sal and Sandi decided to get together in Tucson after she settled in the graduate dorm. Tucson was an easy flight from Chicago.

Tucson, Arizona

IN LATE AUGUST, Sal flew to Tucson for a four-day visit with Sandi. After dinner the first night, he asked her, "Would you like to stay at the hotel with me?"

"I want to go back to the dorm. I want to save intimacy for marriage."

He respected that and went along. He remembered Mary Ann

and I waited for marriage to get intimate and our marriage went well.

Sal had never been to Tucson but he felt as if he had been there before.

Sandi and Sal went on a sightseeing binge--Old Tucson (a movie studio), the Desert Museum, Sabino Canyon, and Chiricahua National Monument. They suited each other. Their relationship was moving along briskly without any hitches. Sal didn't see any flags that concerned him.

He thought, "Can she be the one I've been waiting for?"

Lake Forest, Illinois

IN OCTOBER, SANDI visited Sal in Lake Forest.

Sal asked her again if she wanted to stay at his apartment, but she wanted to stay in a nearby hotel. The first night they went out for dinner with two other dentists, Brian Burns and David Slavkin and their wives. Sal had a good time, but Sandi told him afterward she didn't have a good time.

She didn't like one of the dentists because he was too controlling and didn't give his wife a chance to express her opinion. She didn't like the wife of the other dentist, because Sandi believed, she was flirting with Sal. Sal told her, if she didn't like them or get along with them, they would exclude them in future plans.

The next night, they went, by themselves, to a Greek restaurant, Diana's Delicatessen, downtown Chicago. After dinner, they went to Old Town to window shop. All went well.

Their conversation during the time Sandi was in Chicago was a little tense--not what Sal expected. She didn't like where he lived and questioned his choice of friends, people she thought were below her class.

She said, "I think Brian and David are 'rummy.' "

That statement put Sal on the defensive. He told her, "This is a temporary situation. I haven't had opportunities to find new friends other than coworkers. Brian wasn't shutting off his wife when he explained his plans to go into private practice and David's wife has no interest in me."

Sal didn't know if this was a sexual tension or if this was something he should worry about. He told her he needed to think about their conversations. He said, "Perhaps we should date others until I can sort it out." We could meet back in Wyoming Valley for Thanksgiving vacation."

After Sandi left for Tucson, Sal began to think about the incidents occurring over the last few days: they seemed to get along only when it was the two of them, she didn't like his friends, and she seemed to have a chip on her shoulder. Their relationship seemed more difficult than past relationships. Her good looks and mysterious personality clouded Sal's judgment.

The next day, Sal met a flight attendant at a club in Chicago. They went to her apartment and had sex. For the next three days, they went out and they slept together. The sex distracted him from Sandi but he was beginning to feel like dating was a waste of time and the only girls he met were loose chicks. Like I did before I met Mary Ann, he felt depressed. He was only screwing around and not getting what he wanted out of relationships.

Sal thought, "Maybe Christina is the one for me. She likes my family; she likes my friends. Why am I chasing someone else?"

November

SANDI PLANNED TO arrive in Wyoming Valley on Tuesday, November 21. Sal told her he would arrive on Wednesday,

November 22 and they would get together for Thanksgiving. Sal actually arrived on Tuesday and planned to go out with Christina on Wednesday night before he saw Sandi. Although he never lied to anyone with whom he had a relationship, he was concerned about his and Sandi's interaction in Chicago. He believed it was necessary to lie in this circumstance.

Sal's date with Christina went as expected—they had a good time and talked about the same things they talked about on their past dates. He was disappointed but moved on.

Sal went to the Slovenski's for Thanksgiving and all went well. Her father lit the fireplace and everyone sat in the living room talking about dental practice, the Navy, Sandi's graduate program, and her brother, who was a student at Wyoming Seminary. Things went well. Sandi's parents were very friendly and made Sal feel at home. The incidents in Lake Forest with his friends took a back seat to what was happening.

Christmas

LONG-DISTANCE ROMANCES are challenging. From the time Sal opened Sandi's letter last July until Christmas, they had only dated ten times during four weekends over the past six months. They were fifteen hundred miles apart. Under normal circumstances and over a period of six months, most couples would have dated more than fifty times.

Sal had difficulty establishing a relationship with Sandi as he had done with other women he dated in the past. Dating someone in your "back yard" over time, you see them interact with your friends and family, you see them during unexpected predicaments, and you see them react to your mood swings—yes, we all have them.

When Sal and Sandi got together, which was about once a

month, they were so excited to see each other and had so much to say, they didn't have time to assess their relationship or observe each other in a more relaxed atmosphere. Yet, they wanted to be with each other and wanted to plan a life together. The attraction had to be her looks and the mystery surrounding her personality.

They spent every day together while on Christmas vacation. They got a fresh Christmas tree; Sal had dinner at her house; she had dinner at his house. They went out to dinner and to the movies. They talked about the future without being "interviewed." They didn't go out with any of his friends.

Finally, Sal left for Great Lakes and Sandi left for Tucson.

On the serious side, U.S. Troops withdrew from Vietnam, and the Supreme Court decided "Roe v Wade" which gave women a Constitutional right for abortions.

On the lighter side, Billy Jean King defeated Bobby Riggs in the tennis match of the century, "Battle of the Sexes."

After the Vietnam War movies got "lighter." Two notable movies were "The Sting" and "American Graffiti."

We listened to love songs, "You are the Sunshine of my Life," "My Love," and "Touch Me in the Morning."

Chapter 16

The Third Decade Begins

1973

Wyoming Valley

DURING THE PAST eighteen months, Sal was under a lot of pressure in the Navy. He didn't get along with his superior officers—they wanted him to do dental procedures their way; he wanted to do them the way he learned in dental school. They wanted him to attend "Hail and Farewell" parties where there was a lot of drinking; he wanted them to leave him alone.

He was feeling pressure about not finding the "right one." He was tired of one-night stands and sleeping with women for which there was no future.

He wasn't sure Sandi was the "right one" but didn't like any of the alternatives.

Sal flew home in February. He went to the Flame and then to the Midway diner with Mike and Jimmy. The only friend he had from the original group was Mike. He was beginning to feel isolated.

At the Midway Diner, Sal said to Mike and Jimmy, "I want you to be the first to know that I'm getting married."

"What?" Mike asked.

"You're getting married! Did I hear that right?" Jimmy said.

They were both shocked.

"Who's the unlucky girl?"

"Sandi."

"I thought you broke up with her because she didn't like your family." Mike said,

"She certainly didn't like us," Jimmy said. "What changed your mind?"

"A few factors--we get along great when it's just the two of us; I'm almost thirty; I'm tired of dating; and I'm tired of sleeping around. I also don't want to return to Pittston and have my mother put pressure on me to live at home. I'm better off getting married and moving away from Wyoming Valley."

"When are you getting married?" asked Mike.

"Next August."

"Where are you going to live?"

"I'm not sure."

Mike had more questions but didn't ask them.

When Sal went to the men's room, Mike said to Jimmy, "It seems like a 'done deal' to me."

Jimmy said, "Yeah, we better not say any more or we'll push him away and we'll really lose him as our friend."

Sal told his parents that he and Sandi planned to get married in August with the wedding at Saint Jude's Church and the reception at Wyoming Valley Country Club. His mother wasn't happy with the arrangement to have the reception at the country club instead of at her brothers' restaurant, Il Primo Ristorante. She asked him to have the reception there. He told her it was the girl's decision.

Sal asked Mike to be his best man. As it turned out, Sal already had called Sandi after Christmas and asked her to marry him.

New York City

MARY ANN HAD BEEN working at the NYU student clinic for almost a year. She and Alexandra had become best friends.

Mary Ann said to me, "I don't know what's going on with Alexandra. She is more quiet than usual. This has been going on for the last three months. I don't know if I should say something to her."

"Perhaps you should ask some open ended questions. Be direct. Your friendship is strong enough to have a dialogue."

A few days later, Mary Ann said to Alexandra, "I noticed you've been quiet lately. Have I done something wrong?"

"No, you're a great partner, a great nurse practitioner, and I enjoy working with you. Over the past year, we have become good friends. Let's talk later."

Later in the afternoon after all the patients were gone, Alexandra offered Mary Ann some coffee.

She told Mary Ann, "Rick and I are having marital problems, mostly about responsibilities of two careers and children. Rick wants children and I don't. I suggested we adopt a baby to satisfy Rick and to save our marriage."

"I'm sorry you're having problems. Is there anything I can do?"

"No, thanks. We went to an adoption attorney three months ago. He completed paperwork and we wrote an escrow check. We also started marital counseling."

"That sounds promising."

"Although I was optimistic, I was worried because you can't predict the outcome of counseling. I don't know what effect adoption would have on us."

Mary Ann said, "I'm sorry to hear about this. Please let me know if I can help."

Transition from the Navy

OVER THE NEXT FEW months, Sandi and Sal flew back and forth to Cape Cod to arrange for an apartment, a counseling internship for her, and a dental office for him.

He had a silver Datsun 240Z sports car that he bought when he went into the Navy. Sandi thought it was more like a "playboy" car instead of a professional car. Since she didn't want women to get the wrong impression of Sal because of his sports car, she suggested he trade it for a silver Audi sedan.

He continued with his plans for a dental office in Hyannis and Sandi continued with her studies. His office would be ready in May. Sandi's internship would start in September.

Wyoming Valley

Sal's Wedding

SANDI AND SAL were married in Saint Jude's Catholic Church in August 1973. On the way from the church to Sandi's house, the air conditioner on their new Audi died. It was hot, humid, and very uncomfortable but they made it to Wyoming Valley Country Club for the reception. There seemed to be a black cloud over them—he traded his reliable Datsun for an Audi with defective air conditioning.

They went to Boston for their honeymoon.

Cape Cod

BY SEPTEMBER, SANDI AND SAL settled in their new apartment in Hyannis, in her internship, and in his dental

230

practice. One day Sal came home from work and piled on the bed were clothes Sandi bought with her newly acquired credit card. He told her his practice wasn't making money and they couldn't afford to buy new clothes. He asked her to return the clothes. After a hissy fit, she agreed to take the clothes back to the store.

October arrived and Sal's dental practice stalled. Most of the people who lived on the Cape during the summer returned to Boston for the winter. Within two weeks, he knew he couldn't make a living there and arranged to move his equipment to Wyoming, Pennsylvania to set up practice.

Pocono Mountains

IN OCTOBER, MARY ANN AND I were on our way to the Pocono Mountains to celebrate our two-year wedding anniversary, Mary Ann whispered in my ear, "I have a surprise for you—a special anniversary surprise."

I thought that perhaps she bought some new sexy lingerie.

"What's the surprise?"

"I can't tell you now or it won't be a surprise. I'll tell you when we get to Camelback."

"You can tell me now!"

"No, you can wait."

"OK, be that way."

When we arrived at Camelback and checked in, the receptionist told us our room wasn't quite ready but would be ready in ten minutes. We waited in the lounge for a bellman to take us to our room.

Ten minutes later, a bellman called to us and took us to our room. When we walked into our room, there was a light on in the bathroom. Mary Ann and I went into the bathroom and saw candles surrounding the tub and countertop.

Mary Ann arranged for the resort to have lighted candles around the tub in the bathroom when we arrived.

I said, "What a nice surprise. This is great!"

"No, this isn't the surprise; this is leading up to the surprise."

We filled the bathtub with water, undressed, and got in.

"Are you ready for the surprise?" asked Mary Ann.

"Yes, I can't wait any longer."

Mary Ann gently kissed me on the lips a few times, kissed my ear, and whispered, "I haven't taken my birth control pills this month."

I instantly got the biggest hard-on of my life; I was so excited I almost had an orgasm.

I said, "Let's get to work! Let's not waste any time."

As I tried to get out of the tub, Mary Ann held me down. She wanted to savor the moment. After an excruciating amount of time, maybe two or three minutes, we got out of the tub. We dried off, jumped into bed, and made love.

This time was different--it wasn't about two people who loved each other making love; it was about two people in love, making a baby as an expression of their love.

A feeling of calm came over us. We had never been to this place before. We felt good. Well, better than good, great. We were ecstatic.

We must have made love six times that weekend—we didn't want to miss the opportunity. Actually, we almost wore out "little Jeffrey."

Surely, we would make a baby this weekend.

Wilkes-Barre

BY NOVEMBER, SAL AND SANDI had moved into their apartment in Wilkes-Barre. They went out with a few of his friends and she reacted negatively. She didn't like Mike or me—two friends with whom Sal had made a pact, twenty-five years ago, to remain friends, no matter what! She believed Jimmy Kane was a bad influence on Sal and didn't want to be around him.

Sandi was not fond of Sal's family either because she believed they didn't like her. Apparently, there were daily arguments about his family. She believed they were trying to run their lives. She was only happy when the two of them were alone.

When Sal and Sandi moved to Wyoming Valley, they moved into a townhouse in Wilkes-Barre. At the end of one argument, Sandi went upstairs to the bedroom, packed a suitcase, and came downstairs.

Sal said, "Where are you going?"

"I'm going back home to my parents. You don't love me; otherwise, you would take my side with your friends and your family."

Sal didn't say a word as she stepped outside and began to close the door.

The door hadn't closed completely when it opened again.

Sandi walked into the apartment and said, "You were just going to sit there and let me go?"

Sal said, "If that's what you want to do, I can't stop you."

She came back into the apartment and cried.

She said, "You should have stopped me. I need to know you love me."

Sal said, "I love you, but I can't disown my friends and family to prove my love for you. You need to deal with your insecurities. It's not my family or my friends interfering with your happiness, you're interfering with your own happiness."

Sal knew he made a mistake marrying Sandi. He was blinded by her looks, blinded by love, blinded by the need to make his marriage work, blinded by the worry of what people would say or think if his marriage failed, and blinded by a future without a partner.

However, guilt was the main culprit keeping Sal in his marriage. Sandi continually reminded Sal every time they argued that she "saved" herself for him and she would be "used goods" if they divorced. He was literally screwed--he was in a no win situation! Divorce meant he would have stolen her virginity. Sounded like blackmail to me.

New York

MARY ANN WAS LATE for her period. It had been five weeks.

She wondered, "Am I pregnant or is this the result of stopping the pill after two years?"

I tried to calm her suggesting she make an appointment with her physician.

"Let's wait another week," Mary Ann said.

Mary Ann went to the library to look up false positives after stopping the pill. There was nothing in the literature to explain the absence of a period. Certainly, she must be pregnant!

A week later, still no period.

I said, "Christmas is almost a month away, we'll know by then. What good news to give our families. What a wonderful Christmas present for us and for them."

Mary Ann decided to go to her doctor for an evaluation. After his examination, he said, "Congratulations, you're pregnant."

Mary Ann and I talked about how we would tell our parents the good news.

At the Cusano's Christmas party, we announced Mary Ann's pregnancy. Everyone was elated with the good news. Patricia asked if we had picked a name. We said, "No!" simultaneously.

Wyoming Valley

THINGS HAD SETTLED down a little. Sandi and Sal were always happy around the holidays. However, her parents always looked stressed, especially around the holidays, but he never said anything.

The House Judiciary Committee recommended impeachment for President Richard Nixon.

He resigned. After Nixon resigned, President Gerald Ford pardoned him. So goes politics!

"The Godfather, Part II" mesmerized us.

We listened to "The Way We Were," "Sunshine on My Shoulders," "Annie's Song." We also listened to "I Honestly Love You," "You're Having My Baby," and "Can't Get Enough of Your Love, Babe."

Chapter 17

The Third Decade Continues...

1974

New York

FIRST THING, MONDAY morning, January 7, 1974, Mary Ann noticed some bleeding when she went to the bathroom. She didn't know if the bleeding was serious or something that happened from time to time during pregnancy. She didn't tell me about it so I wouldn't worry. When she arrived at work, she called her gynecologist, and he told her to come in right away so he could examine her. She told Alexandra what had happened. Alexandra told her to go to the doctor immediately.

Mary Ann called me and said, "I had some bleeding this morning and I'm on my way to the gynecologist."

"I'll meet you there."

While at the doctor's office, she miscarried. The gynecologist did a thorough examination and delivered the bad news, "I found some anatomical anomalies that were not visible during my pre-marital examination. I don't think you should risk having children."

We were devastated. All we talked about since we decided to get married was having a family. Now, having a family was impossible. What were we going to do?

That night, we talked; we cried; we talked more; and we cried more. How would we ever get over our disappointment? A profound silence ensued.

During the past six years, we developed a plan for a family. That was our culture—to get married, to have children, and to raise a family. We were Sicilian for God's sake! Well, half Sicilian in my case.

Mary Ann thought, "Jeffrey has wanted children from as far back as he could remember. All he and his friends ever talked about was finding the 'right one' and having a family. He ended more than one relationship when he believed his girlfriend wouldn't want children, couldn't have children, or wouldn't make a good mother.

"If I'm not able to have children, does that breach our contract—would we get an annulment? Suppose Jeffrey doesn't want me any more now that I can't have children. Does he want children more than he wants me?

"If he stays with me, will he always resent me and have regrets. At twenty-seven and infertile, I'm 'over the hill.' Who would want a divorced woman who couldn't have babies? Who would want me?"

As Mary Ann was allowing a barrage of negative thoughts to go through her mind, I was also thinking about our situation.

I thought, "I have always wanted children and a family. I wanted a son with whom I could play catch and play golf as I did with my father. I wanted a daughter with whom I could take shopping and walk up the isle on her wedding day.

"I knew, given an abstract choice of dating someone who *wanted* children or someone who didn't want children, I would pick the former.

"I knew, given an abstract choice of dating someone who *could* have children or someone who couldn't have children, I would pick the one who could have children.

"However, life is not about abstract decisions; it's about actual breathing, thinking, walking, and talking human beings. You don't get to choose abstractly. Life is real and doesn't fit neatly on paper.

"I knew my life with Mary Ann was better than I ever expected. She was my soul mate—everything I ever wanted in a wife and partner. If life threw me a curve, I knew I wouldn't walk away. I was never a quitter and wasn't about to become one. I just didn't know how to make it right."

I said to Mary Ann, "We've loved each other from the moment we met, from the moment when we danced at Joe's wedding. Our love has grown deeper and wider with each minute we've been together. How often does that happen with people?"

"But you want children so badly; I don't know what to do!"

"I don't know what to do about children, but I do know what to do about you and about us. All you have to do is continue loving me. In many marriages, couples marry to have children—that's their primary purpose--their love is secondary. With us, our love is crucial, and if children followed, they would only enhance our love. I could spend the rest of my life with only you. There's a reason why we can't have any children. We don't know the reason right now, but we must trust God's plan."

Mary Ann thought, "I've never heard him talk like that. He sounds deeply religious."

She agreed, "I love you as much as you love me, and you're all I need. After get through this ordeal, we'll think about what to do about a family. Alexandra and Rick are adopting. Maybe we need to think about that."

Mary Ann called Alexandra and told her what happened.

Alexandra told Mary Ann, "Take a few days off and grieve over the loss of your baby." Alexandra comforted Mary Ann with her understanding—she was truly a good friend.

I took the day off to be with Mary Ann. We talked all morning and were reconciling the issues about the miscarriage and about choices for the future. Mary Ann's mother, Patricia and her father, Joseph, senior, volunteered to bring some baked ziti for lunch. After lunch, Joseph and I went to the pro shop at the club to look at golf clubs—neither of us needed golf clubs. We thought Mary Ann would want to talk with her mother alone—you know girl talk!

"Is Jeffrey OK?" Patricia asked.

"Yes, better than I expected. We had a long conversation about love and marriage. We love each other more than anything in the world. Nothing will change that. We need to get past this catastrophe so we can think clearly about our future."

"I think this is a good plan. Take your time. Dad and I know you and Jeffrey have good heads on your shoulders and we're confident you will emerge better than ever."

The Clinic

THE BIRTH OF ALEXANDRA AND RICK'S adoptive baby was due at the end of January. All the paperwork, fees, and related issues were good-to-go. The due date was January 21.

On Thursday, Mary Ann went to work. She was still smarting from the mental anguish of her miscarriage. She had lunch with Alexandra who supported her. They talked about possibilities for raising a family. Alexandra suggested they consider adoption.

Alexandra said, "I know you and Jeffrey never considered adoption because you both believed you could have children. Maybe you need to be open minded about this now. We could love adopted children as much as we can love our own children—maybe more. We raise children to be moral, ethical, loving, caring, and engaging—creating a substantial human being who can contribute to society. How does this process differ in children who are your own versus children who you adopt?"

"Your point is well taken. I don't know if Jeffrey will feel the same way."

"He will. He's a man of substance. You don't have to be around him very long to know that."

Mary Ann asked, "How is your relationship going?"

"Everything is the same."

"How is the adoption going?

"Everyone is doing well. Mom and baby are healthy. The only problem is with Rick and me. I wanted to adopt this baby to 'glue' our family together, but we're more apart than ever. Our problems seem to grow exponentially, as we approach the expected day of delivery. We'll see."

Mary Ann told me about her conversation with Alexandra especially the part of "your own baby versus an adopted baby."

I said, "If we adopted a baby, we would both participate in raising him or her. We would instill our values, our beliefs, and our perspective on the world to him or her. We would teach our child about life, love, and caring. We would teach him or her how to interact with us, with our families, with our friends, and with the world. Think about whom we would create. Would our creation be flesh and blood—our flesh and blood-- or would our child be the very essence of a good human being?"

"You're right. If we can't have our own children, we should consider adopting. The baby would be our own, if not from our genes."

On Monday, Mary Ann went to work, but Alexandra wasn't there yet. It was unusual for her not to be at work early and before Mary Ann. Thirty minutes later, Alexandra arrived frazzled.

"Rick and I had a fight, he stormed out of the apartment Friday night, and I haven't seen him since."

Mary Ann didn't know if she should just listen or ask questions. She and I never had a quarrel after which I left the room for a minute, let alone for an entire weekend.

Alexandra said, "I'm so stressed! If he leaves me, what am I going to do? What am I going to do with a baby I don't want? I

241

can't take this pressure."

This was the first time Mary Ann heard Alexandra express her feelings about the baby in this way. She stood there without saying a word. She waited for Alexandra to complete her thoughts. A few minutes later, Alexandra said, "I don't think our marriage is going to work. All we do is fight. I was the one who came up with the ridiculous idea of adopting a baby thinking that would solve our problems. I take full responsibility for that decision. I realize that more responsibility won't fix the many problems we have. I couldn't call him over the weekend since I didn't know where he was. I called him at work this morning and his secretary said he was in a meeting. The lying bitch. I'm sorry. I shouldn't take it out on her; he told her what to say. Hopefully, we'll talk tonight when I get home."

Alexandra didn't hear from Rick at all during the day. When she got home, he had moved all his stuff out of the apartment. There was a note on the island where they kept their house keys.

Alexandra,

I don't know where to start so I'll start in the beginning. Ten years ago when we began dating during your senior year in medical school, it was obvious to me you were in financial trouble and needed someone to fund your education. I was OK with that since I believed we were mutually building a relationship and a life together. As time went on, you made decisions based on your needs and your wants. I wanted a stay-at-home wife; you wanted a career. I wanted children; you wanted a career. You chose to adopt a baby because you didn't want to ruin your figure by having a baby.

I can't take your self-centered attitude any more. I want out of our marriage and I want out of the contract to adopt a baby. Since it was your idea to adopt, you can keep the baby and the adoption escrow money. I have engaged an attorney who will be in touch with you in the next few days.

The next morning, Alexandra called the attorney handling the adoption and made an appointment to see him that afternoon after work.

When she got to his office, she told him what had happened and gave him the letter. Alexandra asked the attorney, since it's a private adoption and the mother doesn't know who was getting the baby, could designate someone else to accept the baby.

He said this was highly unusual, and he had never known anyone to renege on an adoption for these reasons. He said he would look into it the next morning and get back to her as soon as possible.

"Before you leave, I'd like for you to fill out these papers with the proposed beneficiaries so that I have their information."

Alexandra filled out a form naming Jeffrey and Mary Ann Rosenbloom as the beneficiaries. She gave the attorney as much information as she knew about Jeffrey and Mary Ann. Since she suspected this petition would go to a judge for review, she indicated Jeffrey's status as a forensic artist and his participation and success in solving several high profile crimes over the past few years. She also told him about their crisis with the miscarriage.

She didn't want to tell Jeffrey and Mary Ann about her proposal, because if it backfired, she didn't want to inflict any additional distress on her friends.

Wednesday, January 17, 1974

THE ADOPTION ATTORNEY called the clinic late the next morning and talked with Alexandra. He did indeed pass the proposal through a judge and his decision was favorable. The judge knew Jeffrey personally through a trial in which he participated. "If they want the baby, the baby is theirs."

Alexandra asked Mary Ann, "Could you and Jeffrey have dinner with me in the city?"

"Of course, let me call Jeffrey and confirm."

Mary Ann was worried Alexandra was going to quit; Mary Ann couldn't practice without a supervising physician. She was sure NYU would replace Alexandra if she quit but Mary Ann liked Alexandra so much and they meshed so well in their practice philosophy. In addition, she would be without work until NYU could find a replacement for Alexandra.

We met at Ruggero Italian Restaurant on Grand Street. After ordering dinner, Alexandra said, "I have something important to talk about."

Mary Ann said, "You're not quitting are you?"

"No! This is not about the office. Rick and I are getting divorced. Apparently, his interpretation of our ten-year marriage differs completely from my interpretation, but this isn't about us; it's about you. Have you thought about adopting a baby?"

As Mary Ann nodded, I said, "Yes, we have and we decided adoption is an option."

Alexandra said, "The baby Rick and I were going to adopt is due Friday. All I know is the baby is healthy and is Western European—maybe Italian, Greek, or German and maybe a blend of these. I took the liberty of asking my attorney if I could designate someone else to adopt the baby. Are you interested?"

"Yes!" We said simultaneously. Mary Ann and I didn't know what to say. Alexandra answered prayers in a way neither of us expected.

Alexandra said, "I have some clothes and some baby furniture I bought recently and want to give them to you, if you'll take them."

"We'll be happy to have them," Mary Ann said. "We appreciate your gift."

We were so excited—we began to list the things we had to

do—shop for more baby furniture and baby clothes, and find a nanny.

Even though Mary Ann started to read about how to care for a newborn once she knew she was pregnant, she said, "I don't even know how to take care of a baby." As luck would have it, Mary Ann has two Sicilian women in her life--her mother, Patricia, and her mother-in-law, Rose. Problem solved!

Well, one problem solved—the problem about how to raise a baby. New problem--how do you deal with three Sicilian women, all of whom are independent, living under the same roof?

Mary Ann and I decided not to tell anyone until we had the baby. We arranged our schedule to be off the next week.

Thursday, January 18, 1974

BECAUSE OF THE EXCITEMENT, neither Mary Ann nor I could get any work done. We must have talked on the phone a million times. Each time we hung up, one or the other of us would call with a new question.

Friday, January 19, 1974

LATE FRIDAY MORNING, the adoption lawyer called and told me the birth mother was in New York Methodist Hospital with contractions and we should be prepared to go to the hospital later in the day to get the baby.

Alexandra volunteered to cover for Mary Ann.

At 3 p.m., the lawyer called and told us the baby had been born. He told us to go to the hospital where he would meet us.

When we arrived, twenty minutes later, a nurse took us to a room to meet with the lawyer and to wait for the baby.

Sheldon Parks, the adoption lawyer, was waiting in the room; he introduced himself to us. He handed us papers to sign making the adoption official.

The OB-GYN doctor came into the room and said, "We have a healthy birth. A delivery nurse will bring the baby in within the next thirty minutes. We want you to stay overnight so the nurses can monitor the baby and you can learn the fundamentals of caring for your new baby."

After everyone left the room, Mary Ann said, "No one told us if the baby is a boy or a girl."

I said, "We don't care if the baby is a boy or a girl—it's our baby!"

"I just want to know. The suspense is killing me."

As we were talking, the delivery nurse brought the baby into the room, and handed him to Mary Ann. The blue blanket told us the baby was a boy.

Mary Ann held her son. The baby opened his eyes for a moment. Mary Ann made eye contact; the baby yawned, and fell asleep as if he were satisfied with what he saw. Mary Ann knew they made the right decision. This was their baby, no doubt!

A clerk filled in all the information on the baby except for the baby's name. She asked Mary Ann for the baby's name.

Mary Ann said, "Jeffrey, what do you think?"

"Alexandra has been so wonderful to us; we should name him Alexander after her."

Mary Ann agreed, "So, we have a new baby in the family, Alexander Rosenbloom! Sounds like a winner to me." Mary Ann called her mother to tell her the news.

Mary Ann told Patricia, "Jeffrey and I adopted a baby boy."

"You did what?"

"We adopted a baby boy. His name is Alex and we're at the hospital to learn how to take care of him."

"I know what to do! I can tell you what to do."

"We're going to stay here overnight and then go home."

"I'm on my way!"

"OK. When you get here, ask the nurse to take you to our room. I don't know how long we'll be in this room."

Several hospital workers came into the room at different times—a nutritionist, a nurse, home health nurse, and an aide.

They taught us how to handle a baby, especially supporting the baby's neck, feeding and burping, dressing, changing diapers, cleaning, and taking the baby's temperature.

Back at Patricia's house, she turned to Joseph and said, "Put on your shoes, we have to go to the hospital."

"What are you talking about?"

"Just do as I say and come with me."

On the way to the hospital, Patricia told Joseph, "Jeffrey and Mary Ann adopted a baby."

"They what..."

"They adopted a baby boy."

"And, they didn't tell us. What's the matter with these kids?"

They couldn't wait to get a glimpse of their new grandson. Patricia said she was available to be a babysitter, nanny, or whatever we needed to help little Alex.

Saturday, January 20, 1974

WE BROUGHT ALEX HOME from the hospital. Alexandra brought the baby clothes and arranged to have the furniture brought to our apartment later in the day. Patricia was waiting at their apartment to take care of Alex.

Later, Mary Ann's brothers and their wives came to see their new nephew.

It was a joyous occasion for the Rosenblooms and the

Cusanos.

By July, we were comfortable traveling with Alexander, now six months old. We went to West Pittston and stayed with Levi and Rose who "hosted" a party for the little guy. Mike, his fiancé, Debbie, and Sal came to see our new family.

It had been seven months since we adopted Alex. We discussed moving to Long Island where we could be away from the city, Alex could have friends, and we could plant a vegetable garden. Mary Ann would look for a job with an internist, perhaps in upscale Great Neck or King's Point. She grew up in Bayside and her family lives in Bayside Hills. She was familiar with that part of the island and wanted to live around Bayside. There were many advantages to living near her parents and her brothers' families—"ample free babysitting and cooked meals."

We casually started looking around at houses.

With the help of Mary Ann's brother, a contractor, we looked at several fixer-uppers. We found a detached house in Syosset, New York—2275 square feet, three bedrooms, two and a half baths, family room, formal dining room, and an unfinished basement.

We made an offer, which was accepted. The house was near Saint Edwards Confessor Church. Mary Ann's brother would renovate the kitchen, laundry room, master bath, and finish the basement. The work would take about eight weeks during which time we would continue to rent our apartment on Park Avenue from Johanna and Stanley.

Wyoming Valley

THIS YEAR WENT BY quickly for Sandi and Sal. After Christmas, things went back to normal. Over the next few months, Sandi's behavior further strained their relationship. Sal felt more and more isolated from his family. He hardly saw his friends.

Every week, Sandi took issue with something he said, his parents said, or his friends said. He was no longer interacting with his aunts or uncles. Unexpectedly, they would be fighting again. The only way he could satisfy her insecurities was to give up anything competing with her—friends or family.

Once Sal gave in or gave up, she felt in control and everything was OK. However, he couldn't give himself up every time they had an argument. As they stopped visiting relatives or going out with friends, their relationship improved. However, Sal insisted on continuing a relationship with his parents even though Sandi didn't like his mother. He thought about divorce again but was convinced staying in his marriage was best because of his fear his family and friends would think he was a loser.

Sal's office was completed and he opened his practice. He did well from day one.

Mike's career was on track. His love life was also looking good. He was dating one of his trainees, a girl from Scranton named, Debbie Gilroy. Mike robbed the cradle and married Debbie on October 12, 1974. We told him he was a dirty old man; he didn't care what we said.

Mike and Debbie invited Sandi and Sal to their wedding. Mike told Sal he seated them with Barry Warren, his wife, Judy, and Sal's parents. Sandi didn't want to sit with his parents and pitched a fit so they ended up going to dinner at the Ryah House instead of going to Mike's wedding. Even though Sal apologized to Mike and Debbie for not attending their wedding, he has never forgiven himself.

Christmas, 1974

MARY ANN AND I got together with Mike, Debbie, Sandi, and Sal for dinner at Coccina Italiano in West Pittston. We rehashed growing up in Wyoming Valley and the places we had been. I had moved to New York and stayed there, Mike had moved to Philadelphia, and Sal, the big traveler, had been to Pittsburgh, Tucson, Chicago, Hyannis, and back to Wyoming Valley.

I talked about my various jobs in advertising, forensic art, and painting. I talked about my apartments in Greenwich Village and on Park Avenue. MaryAnn talked about her first career in nursing, her current career as a nurse practitioner, and her "career" as a mother.

Mike talked about his career as a buyer and merchandiser. Debbie talked about how Mike wooed her and robbed her from her proverbial cradle. He denied it!

Sal reminisced about his careers in a dress factory, in a restaurant, as a barber, a teacher, and, now, as a dentist. Sandi was obviously bored and didn't say much throughout the evening. Otherwise, we had a great dinner and had many laughs.

Sandi and Sal ate Christmas Eve dinner with his parents and spent Christmas Day with her parents. Sandi preferred that their parents didn't interact.

New York

MARY ANN AND I hosted the entire Cusano family for Christmas in our new renovated house. Of course, I was confident about the repairs since Mary Ann's brothers wouldn't want to hear any negative comments about the house at family functions.

On Becoming Us

The United States celebrated its Bicentennial. Margaret Thatcher became the first female Prime Minister for the British Conservative Party.

Bill Gates and Paul Allen created Microsoft, Steve Jobs and Steve Wozniak formed Apple Computer. The Apple IIe became the first Apple computer sold to the masses. IBM introduced the first commercial laser printer, and Motorola introduced the first hand-held cellular phone.

We listened to John Denver's "Thank God I'm a Country Boy" and "I'm Sorry"; Olivia Newton John's, "Have You Never Been Mellow"; Neil Sedaka's "Laughter in the Rain" and "Bad Blood"; Barry Manilow's, "I Write the Songs"; Diana Ross's, "Theme from Mahogany" and "Love Hangover"; and the Bee Gees' "You Should be Dancing" and "How Deep is Your Love."

We watched movies, "Star Wars," "Saturday Night Fever," "Close Encounters of the Third Kind," "Rocky," "One Flew Over the Cuckoo's Nest," and "Taxi Driver."

Chapter 18

The Unsettled Years

1975-1978

I FINALLY ACCOMPLISHED my dreams from over twenty-five years ago—I have a "big deal" career, I have a goddess, and I now have a family. Our little family--Mary Ann, Alex, and I-- were contented in our house on Long Island.

During dinner one night, Mary Ann told me she was thinking about a career change—more a location change than a career change.

"Jeffrey, the biggest stress we have is commuting to the city every day for work. I don't have time to cook, I don't see Alex as much as I want, and I'm far away if there's ever an emergency. I like my job in the clinic, but I think I'd like a job closer to home."

"I agree about the stress. Why don't you look for an opportunity closer to home? I believe you would be happier, and we would have more time together. I've been working from the house two days a week and I can increase to three days. I would enjoy more time around you and Alex as well."

"OK. I'll ask a few pharmaceutical reps who call on us about opportunities on the Island. Some of them call on internists in private practice as well as our clinic."

Mary Ann interviewed with three internal medicine practices in Great Neck, New York. The first was a brand new practice with two male internists, the second was a twenty-year old practice with three male internists, and the third was a ten-year old practice, Village Internal Medicine, with two men who started the practice and a woman who joined the group five years later. None of the practices had a nurse practitioner.

Village Internal Medicine was conveniently located on the Syosset side of Great Neck and would be less than a thirty-minute commute. The doctors, Martin Samuelson, Paul Volpetti, and Gina Romanoski, were young and the practice was growing. Mary Ann liked Gina. All the doctors wanted to hire a nurse practitioner.

Village Internal Medicine offered Mary Ann a job contingent on their investigation of her credentials and her references. Mary Ann wanted to give Alexandra a three-month notice so that it would be easy for her to find a replacement. She asked her for a meeting.

At the meeting with Alexandra, Mary Ann said, "Over the past five years, you've changed my life in so many ways; I can't begin to list all of them. When most doctors were reluctant to hire nurse practitioners, you gave me a job that I loved. You've taught me so many things about medicine and about life, we've meshed in ways I never expected, and you respected me as a nurse practitioner. You've given Jeffrey and me a child who has brightened our lives and has fulfilled our dream of a family. I will forever be grateful for your kindness and thoughtfulness."

"Uh, oh, do I see something unpleasant coming or do you just want a raise?"

"No. Over the past few years, commuting has become more stressful—I don't see Alex as much as I want, I can't spend enough time cooking, and I'm spending most of my life on the subway. I thought about getting a job closer to home, and I interviewed at three internal medicine offices. One of them, Village Internal Medicine, offered me a job."

"I knew I couldn't keep you forever. You've been a godsend to me and have helped me get through the worst time of my life. I thank you for that. I'll truly miss you. When do you want to start with them?"

"I thought July First. That would give you enough time to find a replacement especially when many nurse practitioners are finishing their programs at the end of June."

"OK. I'll begin my search. I'll miss you."

In July 1976, Mary Ann started work at Village Internal Medicine. Their plan was to build her practice by booking urgent work-in patients with her and new patients not related to existing patients. Most patients Mary Ann saw urgently wanted to see her in follow-up. Her schedule for patient care was Monday-Thursday. On Friday morning, she would do paperwork or follow up on lab orders.

Mary Ann liked this schedule because it gave her a long weekend to be with Jeffrey and Alex.

For the past year, Mary Ann was working at Village Internal Medicine and had been building her practice. We enjoyed the extra time we had to spend with Alex and Mary Ann's parents. Patricia was thrilled to babysit and to bring lasagna, baked ziti, or chicken potpie for dinner.

I got along well with Mary Ann's family.

New Jersey

IN MARCH 1977, someone from the Red Bull Inn, a motel in Bridgewater, New Jersey, called the police. When they arrived, they found Johnny Cokes Lardiere, a business agent for the Teamsters Local 945, shot to death. The police found a .22 pistol with a silencer and a .38 revolver at the scene.

At a previous trial, Lardiere refused to testify about organized crime activity in New Jersey. During the trial, he and his "paisanos" took the Fifth. The judge charged them with Contempt of Court and put them in the "slammer." The judge incarcerated him at the Clinton Reformatory. Johnny Cokes, a big mouth and an in-your-face type, was constantly in fights with fellow prisoners.

Although a women's prison, Clinton housed a number of male inmates. Authorities furloughed him for Easter to be with his family. After checking into the Red Bull Inn, he moved his car closer to his room, and walked to the trunk of the car to get his suitcase. He saw a shadow and turned to see Michael Coppola holding a .22 automatic pistol with a silencer. Coppola pointed the gun at Lardiere and squeezed the trigger.

To their surprise, the gun didn't fire. Coppola pulled the trigger again and the weapon, again, didn't fire. Lardiere's shock turned into contempt.

Lardiere said, "Hey, asshole, how could you come to a hit with a defective weapon? What's the matter with you?" Then he said in his typical manner, "Wada you gonna do now, tough guy?"

Coppola threw the .22 pistol on the ground, reached into an ankle holster where he had the .38 revolver, and killed Lardiere.

"That's what I'm gonna do, asshole!" Coppola said.

After hearing shots, someone called the police. The police arrived shortly after and investigated. They took several "witnesses" to the police station.

The police captain called me to the police station. When I arrived, sergeant Cotter told me all the witnesses denied seeing anyone shoot Lardiere and they didn't need me anymore. The Sergeant apologized for asking me to come to the station before they realized no one was talking.

Wyoming Valley

SANDI AND SAL WENT to her parents' house for Christmas; her parents seemed stressed. Often they wouldn't speak to each other--sometimes for months. Sal wasn't aware of any of this behavior until after Sandi and he married, then, wasn't sure what to make of it.

A few days after Christmas, Mike, Sal, and I had lunch. At lunch, Sal told us of the problems at Sandi's house.

Sal said, "Sandi's parents are always fighting, usually over money, or who controls their money. Sandi's mother wants her own money in a separate account, and her father wants to keep a joint account."

"That pretty progressive for a woman in the 1970s.

"What are they like? Sandi's father, Jim Slovenski, is a big man, 6'2" and is a first generation Czechoslovakian. Family is important to him and he wants to take care of his them. He had a good family life. His parents, although not well to do, did well enough."

"What's her mother like?"

"Anna Fagan is Irish—"Shanty Irish," as she refers to herself—and not from a well off family."

"I hadn't heard that term before," Sal said. "She's very attractive. In old pictures of her when she was young, she was a knockout. It's easy to see how Sandi's father found her irresistible and how she had the upper hand in their relationship. My father would describe her as 'easy on the eyes.' However, she seems preoccupied with money, especially a potential inheritance from an aunt, Anna Marie, who she ceaselessly wants to please in order to stay in her will.

"According to Sandi, at times when she, her sister, and her brother came home from school, her mother had their bags packed and announced they were moving out. She would take her children to a hotel or to her aunt's house until Jim gave her what she wanted. The demands were usually about money. Apparently, this scenario played out several times a year--more often before holidays when her mother thought she had a better chance of getting what she wanted."

"How are her siblings dealing with this?"

"Poorly. Neither Sandi nor her sister, Loretta, wants children. Her brother is too young to figure out what he wants. When her sister was engaged to a nice man, she insisted he have a vasectomy before marriage. He got the vasectomy, married Loretta, and she divorced him."

"It seems like you have your work cut out for you," Mike said.

For the past two years, Sal had been leasing his dental office from Tom Chiampi. Tom owned the building on the corner of Wyoming Avenue and Eighth Street and three additional connected buildings on Eighth Street toward West Wyoming, the last of which was Sal's office. Tom wanted to sell the building to Sal, but he declined.

Sal instead bought a house on the corner of Wyoming Avenue and Ninth Street where Dr. Pyne had his OB-GYN medical practice. Eventually he would renovate the office space for a dental office.

Sandi's mother gave her father an ultimatum, "If you put $50,000 in a separate account in my name, I'll stay with you."

Apparently, he had all he could take of this type of behavior. He told her, "I won't be asking you to stay. I'd like you to move out of the house."

She moved into an apartment in Wilkes-Barre.

When Sandi's parents separated, the allegiance of Sandi's brother and sister went with her mother, and Sandi's allegiance went with her father. Sandi and Sal often had her father and his girlfriend over for dinner. She was pleasant enough but not the knockout his wife was. Sandi and Sal attempted to reconcile the siblings but lost that battle.

Both men and women have the potential to use sex to get what they want from their spouses. We learned about this with my friends in high school. The world has many master-manipulators, but it's sad when a mother puts her children in the middle of the battle.

Mike was traveling with his job. Often, he was gone from Monday morning to Thursday night. Debbie, being a good wife, never complained about Mike's schedule. Mike and Debbie celebrated their second anniversary. They went to Disneyland for a few days.

Sal's practice was going well; his marriage was not going well. His marriage was unchanged over the past four years.

Abroad--The Ayatollah Khomeini returned to Iran from exile and students immediately took 63 American Hostages in the American Embassy. The Solidarity Trade Union formed in Poland and the shipyard workers went on strike.

At home—Ronald Reagan became president. When the U.S. air traffic controllers went on strike, he fired them. We learned the first test tube baby was born. Sally Ride was the first American woman in space.

In technology—Silicon Valley introduced smaller, faster, and more affordable devices. Sony introduced the "Walkman," IBM introduced its desktop computer, and Microsoft introduced the word processing program.

We went to the movies to see "James Bond," "Star Wars," "Star Trek," "Rocky II," "Rocky III," and "Kramer vs. Kramer."

On TV, we watched "Taxi," "M*A*S*H*," "Happy Days," and the beginning of T & A, "Three's Company."

We listened to Donna Summer, Michael Jackson, Bee Gee's, Olivia Newton-John, and Diana Ross.

Chapter 19

Marital Disharmony

1979-1983

New York

ANGEL SANTIAGO HAD BEEN in trouble with the law in Mexico, Arizona, and New York. He was in trouble many times during his incarceration. Mandatory hearings for his parole occurred over the past three years. The court denied parole every time.

On Friday, October 19, 1979, Santiago completed his full prison sentence. Police officials informed FBI Agent Thomas Martin of Santiago's release. Agent Martin was responsible for informing Carmelitta Vega and me of the release of Santiago, two people threatened by Santiago in the courtroom after the verdict. Agent Martin searched for Carmelitta Vega in Westchester County but was unable to locate her. She had quit her job several years ago and did not leave a forwarding address. "She could be back in Mexico for all we know," a local Westchester county policeman told him.

I was at a trial in Westchester County. At the end of the court session, I left the courtroom with my briefcase and sketchpad, and walked to my car.

Agent Martin entered the main entrance to the courtroom as I left through the side door. He asked for me and the security guard told him I had just walked out the side door. Agent Martin hurried to the parking lot.

I was carrying my sketchpad and my briefcase, and, in the darkness, I was having trouble opening my car. I finally got the car unlocked, put my keys in my pocket, and put my briefcase and sketch pad in the trunk. I sensed someone behind me and started to turn around.

Instantly, the person behind me slammed the trunk on my right hand. The man yelled, **"Te dije que iba a venir por ti , y ahora voy a matar Carmelitta."**

It was Angel Santiago. He said, "I told you I would come for you, and now I'm going to kill Carmelitta."

Agent Martin heard the yelling in Spanish and ran over to my car. Santiago pulled a knife and lunged toward Agent Martin who pulled his service revolver and shot Santiago between his eyes.

I was in intense pain and Agent Martin drove me to the hospital.

Once I arrived there, the ER called the "on-call" orthopedic surgeon. Luckily, the orthopedic surgeon on call was the hand surgeon, Phillip Zimmerman, MD, who rushed to the Emergency Room to perform surgery on my hand. The operation took three hours. Afterward, Dr. Zimmerman told me I would likely lose most of the fine motor skills in my right hand and would have months or even years of physical therapy to gain any use of my right hand again.

Once my hand had healed, I started rehab at Queens Physical Therapy every Monday, Wednesday, and Friday. Each one-hour session consisted of stretching and lifting weights with each finger of my right hand. The session ended with a ten-minute ice wrap. My friends teased me about my "workout" program with weights. The weights ranged from one to four ounces. They had never heard of weight therapy like that; I guess its relative.

Mary Ann, Alex, and I alternated with whom we spent

Christmas between Wyoming Valley and New York.

By 1982, I was gaining movement in my right hand because of diligent physical therapy. I could sketch but not as well as I could before my attack. Dr. Zimmerman changed his prognosis and became optimistic that I would regain eighty-five percent of my fine motor movements. Although this sounds great, eighty-five percent for an artist is not good enough.

As I progressed with rehab, ·I could sketch outlines and details and fill in with watercolors. I began a new media—a combination of sketching and watercolor painting. I was pleased with how it looked. Watercolors were becoming a large part of my art. I continued to be involved in forensic art.

Wyoming Valley

IN APRIL 1979, Sal had an asthma attack after turning on the HVAC in his newly renovated dental office. Within a few days, he started coughing and wheezing. An internist, who diagnosed him with "extrinsic asthma," sent him to an allergist. The allergist prescribed steroids and he recovered.

A few months later, Sal began feeling weak and shaky most mornings as if he didn't have enough fuel—most likely from the medication. He had a small "tremor" and was worried patients would think something was wrong with him—like alcohol or drug abuse.

So began a long, drawn out saga of doctor hopping for the next five years to determine what was wrong with Sal. He went to doctors in preventive medicine, endocrinology, gastroenterology, homeopathy, and immunology. He also went to a nutritionist. His health declined to the point where he was allergic to everything and lived in a porcelain and stainless steel trailer.

In September 1980, Sal spent eleven days at Presbyterian Hospital in Denver for tests to environmental irritants including dental materials and for Dr. Kendall Gerdes to evaluate him. Dr. Gerdes recommended changes to his dental practice to minimize exposures. He said if these measures didn't help, Sal might need to leave dentistry.

The next spring and because Sal's asthma symptoms got worse, he quit practicing dentistry.

In August 1981, he closed his dental practice and moved to Tucson, which his physician considered more environmentally healthy. Sandi and Sal lived there for a year and then moved to the Pocono Mountains.

While living in the Pocono Mountains in fall 1982, Sandi applied to law school. Sal's health had not improved.

Sandi and Sal moved to Springfield, Massachusetts, and she began her first year of law school. Sal's health issues continued. They flew to Denver for a follow up with Dr. Gerdes. It had been two years since Sal closed his practice and he had not regained his health. Dr. Gerdes spent an hour discussing his health.

Dr. Gerdes said, "I don't know what's keeping your immune system in high gear now that you've removed yourself from dental materials."

Over the past five years, some health issues resolved and others began anew. Sal thought he was spinning his wheels.

Mike finally got his big break. G Fox offered him a position, and he and Debbie moved to Hartford, Connecticut. This marked the first time he and Debbie lived outside of Pennsylvania, but they adjusted well.

In 1980, Ted divorced Joan, his first wife. We didn't know what happened since our contact with Ted was only an occasional Christmas card and rumors along the grapevine since that fateful night in the Baptist Church when Ted got married. Finally, we would get to see Ted again.

Two years later, Ted was living in Atlanta and dating Anne

who he met in a "Divorced and Separated" group. He went to work for Alcan as a project manager.

Apple introduced the Macintosh personal computer and Sony introduced the 3 ½-inch computer disk.

Scientists identified the AIDS virus.

Geneticists developed Genetic finger printing- -DNA profiling was now possible.

Seventy banks failed during the recession in the United States.

We watched movies "Star Trek III—The Search for Spock," "Indiana Jones and the Temple of Doom," "Romancing the Stone," and "The Terminator."

We listened to Madonna, Cyndi Lauper, Tina Turner, and Lionel Richie.

Chapter 20

Back to the Beginning

1984

Friday, October 12, 1984

MY ART EXHIBITION HAD ended and it was a success. During three hours, I sold sixteen of my twenty watercolors and received critical acclaim for my new medium.

The time was 4:30 p.m. and family and friends were leaving to head home. Mike and Debbie left for Philadelphia. Ted took a cab to JFK Airport to fly to Atlanta. Sal drove back to Springfield, Massachusetts.

I was talking with my assistant, Kelly, who was wrapping paintings when the lady in the black dress reappeared holding a bag. She walked over to me and said, "My name is Izzy, Isabelle Rosenthal. I'm sorry to bother you, but I was here earlier and noticed a pen-and-ink portrait of a lady. I looked at it several times because it was quite similar to a smaller portrait I had in my apartment. Would you take a look at it for me?"

"It's no bother, let's take a look."

Izzy opened the bag and removed a framed, eight by ten pen-and-ink drawing of a woman. Uniquely inscribed initials, "JR," were in the lower left corner.

I immediately recognized the portrait of Paula Cohen, a girl I knew at Wilkes College. I felt flush and my upper lip began sweating, but I didn't know why. I was, at the same time, apprehensive and intrigued about the connection between Izzy and the drawing.

"This is my work; I recognize it. How did you happen upon it?"

"My aunt gave it to me."

I was somewhat calmed by what she said.

"What's your aunt's name?"

"Pamela Rosenthal."

I plausibly had a "deer in the headlights" look on my face.

"I don't think I know her. Does she know me?

"I don't think so ...Well; I don't know ...I came upon your exhibition by accident. I interviewed for a modeling job during lunch and walked by your exhibition on my way out. I saw the watercolors and, since I had time, I came in to take a closer look. As I was walking around the room, I saw a large pen-and-ink portrait that looked familiar. I stopped to look at it, walked away and then, because I was drawn to the portrait, I walked back to take a closer look."

I said, "Tell me about Aunt Pamela."

"Aunt Pamela is my mother's older sister. She's in real estate."

"Here in New York?"

"No, in San Francisco."

I must have had a puzzled look on my face by the way Izzy looked at me. I couldn't figure out the uncertainty of the portrait. I needed more information.

"Tell me about the portrait."

"It's complicated."

"Well, I have time. Simplify it for me."

"Aunt Pamela gave the portrait to me when I was a little girl and told me this was a drawing of my mother. I've had it on my dresser forever. I was inspired to go to art school by this painting."

"Tell me about Izzy Rosenthal."

"Not much to tell—I haven't lived that long. I was born in San Francisco on March 15, 1966—the Ides of March. My mother died when I was born, and my aunt adopted me since she was the only living relative. Although I consider her "my mother," she prefers I call her Aunt Pamela out of respect for my 'real mother.' "

"Where did you grow up?"

"I grew up in San Francisco. I went to private school there and came to New York to study fine art."

"Where do you go to school now? How far along are you?"

"I'm in my last year at the *New School* on West 12th Street. I love pen-and-ink."

"You mentioned you were looking for a modeling job. Tell me about that."

"I work as a model, mostly in fashion."

I intensely listened to Izzy's every word. People usually feel at ease and comfortable around me, they often will tell me about their secrets.

I said, "Who's your father?"

"We don't know my father. My mother, so Aunt Pamela tells me, was a 'free spirit.' I'm not sure exactly what that means—it was a 1960s term. When my mother was young, she fell in love and got pregnant. During her entire pregnancy, she never told anyone my father's name. Perhaps she intended to tell my grandparents who he was after I was born. Nevertheless, we'll never know since she didn't survive childbirth. All these years, I've felt incomplete not knowing this one piece of information."

"Who was your mother?"

"Paula Cohen."

I broke into a serious sweat. I wiped my forehead and asked, "Do you know where your mother went to college?"

"Yes, she went to Wilkes College, a small college in Wilkes-Barre, Pennsylvania."

With a catch in his voice, he said, "I think I may have known your mother. I went to Wilkes College and dated a girl named Paula Cohen. We dated the last semester of our senior year—we were young then, and neither of us was serious about relationships. I sketched the portrait you have in your hand and gave it to her as a present. At the end of school, she returned to San Francisco, I moved to New York for graduate school, and we lost touch."

I wondered, "Just how many senior girls at Wilkes College in 1965 were named Paula Cohen? I silently counted the months from the last week of May 1965 to the middle of March 1966. Paula and I had sex the last night we were together--during our last week in college. The timing is right."

Could Izzy be my daughter?

Oh God, if she is my daughter, what will Mary Ann think. Is this a good thing or is this the end of my happy life with Mary Ann? If she is my daughter, it was out of a relationship occurring years before I met Mary Ann. It isn't as if I had an affair and had a child while engaged or while married to her! There's a difference between this and an affair. I hope that Mary Ann will see that! It isn't the same. Surely, she's smart enough and compassionate enough to understand the difference.

Wait a second. I'm getting ahead of myself. I'm not necessarily Izzy's father. Someone else could be the father, someone from San Francisco who had sex with Paula when she returned to the Bay Area—a week later. On the other hand, I don't know how much weight I can put into the theory of a second man since Paula wasn't a loose chick, and wouldn't have slept around—it took us four months to have sex and that was seeing each other all the time.

I don't know if Mary Ann is going to be OK with this. Apparently, no one knows who the father is—not Izzy, not Pamela. No one would ever think I'm the father; no one knows my connection to Paula—except for the drawing. No one would suspect I could be the father except Mike, Ted, and Sal who know about Paula and the drawing.

How could I know for sure if Izzy is my daughter? I look ethnic and so does she; I'm artistic and so is she. The circumstances surrounding my sexual experience with Paula and Izzy's birth are compelling, the timing is perfect, and she has my drawing of her mother, Paula.

Is there a way to be sure? I don't know. I need to know with certainty if Izzy is my daughter. If she is, I want to know her and have a relationship with her. I'm not interested in hiding my relationship with Paula or with Izzy or walking away from her. My God, people have been convicted and executed for murder with less circumstantial evidence than this.

I asked Izzy, "Can we have lunch next week and talk more?"

"Yes, I'd like that."

They exchanged phone numbers and Izzy left.

Mary Ann and I had dinner reservations and wanted to eat before we went home. We talked about how successful the exhibition had been. This was truly our first awkward moment together since we met at Joe's wedding.

After ordering dinner, Mary Ann asked, in a quiet, little voice, a voice I never heard before, "Who was the lady in the black dress?"

I remembered something my father, Levi, and my mother, Rose, said to me. "Always be totally honest with those you love. If you aren't totally honest, you put yourself at risk to go down a long and slippery slope ending in a hole from which you can never get out." Of course, I had always been honest with Mary Ann and would never consider anything else.

"It appears she's the daughter of a girl I dated in college."

"Are you going to tell me about her?"

I told Mary Ann about Paula--everything about Paula--from the minute she tapped me on the shoulder to ask me to dance to when she left college to return to San Francisco.

We met at a college dance—she asked me to dance.

She was a "free spirit"; I was a serious student.

She wasn't interested in me since I wasn't "fully" Jewish; I wasn't interested in her because she seemed like the "fly-by-the-seat-of-your pants" type.

We dated during the last semester in college and had fun together.

I told Mary Ann I enjoyed dating Paula but it would never have worked out—it was just a "fun" relationship in college. I said, "She was my first sexual experience, and it was on the last day we were together before leaving Wilkes College."

As I was telling Mary Ann the story, she sat there with her eyes glued to mine and didn't say a word, not one word. She just sat there thinking, so, he dated this girl for months...*months!* ...and, even though he was sure she wasn't "the one," he had sex with her. I'll never understand men!

He said he didn't want to be with her; however, he liked her enough to have sex with her... *They had sex!*

He liked her enough to have a baby with her. What kind of man does that? Just who the hell did I marry?

He said "fun relationship." Just what does *that* mean? Just how much "fun" did he have before he met me? His first time was during his senior year in college and then what—every night with a different girl until he met me. We're talking three years—May 1965 to August 1968—and that's a whole lot of women; that's a whole lot of sex!

I want to know why my brother introduced us! Certainly, Joe knew what type of guy he was. I always thought Jeffrey wasn't like other men; he was a nice, sincere person. I was sure he wasn't a "player." Just how many of his "seeds" did he spread around Pennsylvania and New York before we met? Are there more little 'Jefferies' running around? How many? Do I really know the man I married?

I told Mary Ann all the details Izzy told me: Her mother was

Paula Cohen, she was born in San Francisco, her mother died during childbirth, her mother's sister, Pamela, adopted her, and no one knows her father's identity.

I said, "I know this is circumstantial evidence—strong circumstantial evidence—but there is a possibility Izzy may be my daughter. I never anticipated the possibility of a child out there. If I thought it were a possibility, I certainly would have told you."

Although Mary Ann did not say one word during the entire dinner conversation, she just listened to me as her mind generated questions at mach speed:

"What if Izzy is his child? Will he still love me? Will he still love Alex? Will he want to leave me? Men have jumped ship for lesser reasons than this.

What does this Izzy want from us? Will she want to move in? Will Jeffrey want her to move in? Perhaps she needs money. I mean, we don't have a lot of money—we're OK, but not rich! How am I going to tell Alex he has a twenty-year-old sister? Christ! Am I going to tell Alex that Izzy is his 'aunt' or his 'sister?' He'll ask who her parents are—he's smart, that kid. What do I tell him when he asks if I'm her mommy? Oh boy! Do we look like white trash or what? Will we headline in the National Enquirer?

"OK. I have to get a grip! I have three older brothers and I've heard them talk about the "girls" they've dated, the overnight trips to the Poconos, the request not to come to their apartments without calling first, and the teasing of each other about their "dates." I know they didn't "save themselves" for marriage. I knew Jeffrey didn't save himself for marriage. Is this a "guy" thing? Does it matter?

"It just doesn't seem fair!"

Mary Ann and I arrived home. Mary Ann did not utter one word, except when she yelled, "Stop, red light!" when I almost ran one.

I sheepishly asked, "Are we OK? Are you thinking of leaving me? Please talk to me!"

Mary Ann responded, "I don't know what I think; I don't know what to say; I don't know what to do. I need time to think. Can we just sleep on it?"

"Yes, we can sleep on it, but I need to know if you still love me."

"I love you. Nothing is going to change that, nothing is going to take away my love. This is such a surprise; I just need to assimilate it and sort it in my mind—to put together the pieces of the puzzle."

We went to Alex's room to say good night before we got ready for bed. Both went to the master bedroom, got ready for bed, and got into bed.

I thought this is a good sign. I'm going to take this as a good sign. We are getting into the same bed together--the same bed in which we always sleep. That has to be a good thing.

We lay in bed on our backs—our "thinking position." After a minute, I moved my foot over to touch Mary Ann's foot. She didn't move her foot away from mine. "Whew, good sign!" I thought.

We lay awake for a long time--twisting, turning, more twisting, fixing the pillows, getting up to pee, blowing our noses, and looking at the clock. Finally, we fell asleep.

At about 2:30 a.m., Mary Ann woke me and said, "I'd like to talk now."

"OK."

I was tired, but I needed to talk when Mary Ann was willing to talk.

We got up, went to the kitchen, and sat on stools at the island--our favorite place to discuss important things—both happy and sad. It was where we talked when Mary Ann had a miscarriage. It was where we talked when we found out they could adopt baby Alexander. It was where we talked when we found out I couldn't use my right hand any more.

Mary Ann said to me, "I apologize for everything. I wasn't behaving like a very good wife..."

I interrupted, "I'm the one who needs to apologize for...

Mary Ann interrupted him, as she never did before, "Hear me out."

"Sorry."

"If Izzy is your daughter, I'm afraid you might love her more than Alex since she's 'blood' and he's adopted. I'm afraid you might stop loving me because I can't give you any children of your own. I'm afraid you may have had a lot of sexual experience and I don't measure up to the others. I'm afraid I wasn't the type of girl you really wanted and you preferred someone like Paula—a 'free spirit.' I can't be me and be her at the same time! I'm afraid there may be more children we don't know about. I'm afraid our relationship will never be the same. I'm just afraid!"

I said, "I married you because I fell in love with you. It was love at first sight! You were pretty, smart, kind, compassionate, and I felt a connection as I never felt before. You're my soul mate. I didn't fall in love with anyone else. People 'love' in many different ways: We love our parents, our brothers and sisters, our families, our children, and we love our friends. We even love our dog—even when he pees on the floor. We fall in love with our spouse, and that love is stronger than all other types of love. All are love but are dramatically and essentially different. We sometimes believe our love is finite but it isn't. You could try to explain love as a waterfall spilling an unending supply of water or explain love as a shower of heat coming from the sun. We have infinite capacity to love—the more we love, the more love we have to give.

"I'm in love with you and I love you, I love Alex, and I may grow to love Izzy. If we had a dozen children, I would love them as well. If Izzy is my daughter, we will find love in our hearts for her and our love for her will not in any way diminish the love we have for each other or for Alex. We'll never run out of love. Please don't worry I picked wrong when I asked you to marry me. I picked exactly whom I wanted and exactly whom I needed. *You're everything to me.*

"As far as Izzy is concerned, let's meet with her next week and talk about what we think is going on. You can rest assured there are no other children wandering around."

Mary Ann said, "OK. This is why I love you. Even in the middle of the night, you can think clearly. I know I'm very lucky you picked me. We will get through this stronger than we are now. I'm not afraid any more. I love you."

"I love you. Let's get some sleep."

Saturday, October 20, 1984

MARY ANN AND I invited Izzy to our house for lunch. We hoped she liked Italian food—three-quarters Jewish, one-quarter Italian. Certainly, the small Italian part will like Italian food.

We greeted Izzy at the front door just before noon. I introduced Izzy to Mary Ann. Izzy's black hair was pulled back into a ponytail; she looked like a million dollars in her jeans and Yankees sweatshirt. She carried a vase with a bouquet of flowers.

We made some small talk about the Yankees, New York, art school, and living on the east coast after growing up in California. Mary Ann served lasagna she had made that morning, salad, and Italian bread.

After a while when everyone was comfortable, I asked, "Izzy, have you thought more about what we talked about last week?"

"I have. Based on the time line, I know my mother, who was

unmarried, got pregnant in May 1965 when she lived in Wilkes-Barre. She told neither my father nor my grandparents she was pregnant. She didn't tell my grandparents the name of my father. When she died, the secret went with her to her grave. I believe that if she knew she would die, she would have told someone. I don't believe I burdened Aunt Pamela since she wanted more children and couldn't have any more. I don't know for sure who my father is."

I said, "Your Aunt Pamela was correct when she told you your mother was a 'free spirit' but not in a way you would expect by the definition in the dictionary. Paula was fun loving, carefree, eccentric, and a non-conformist. Although her characteristics don't tell you who she was, I would like to tell you who she was. Paula was always upbeat and happy. She was never judgmental—only saw the good in everything and never had a bad word to say about anyone or anything. She loved to be outside with nature. She was happy watching the birds fly or rabbits hop around. She always did things she wanted despite what others thought—she was her own person.

"The phrase 'free spirit' is misleading. Paula was not a loose woman, as the term would imply or like many young people today. During a time when it was common to have sex with multiple partners, we dated four months before we slept with each other and it was only once. Sex just happened between two people who liked each other and had a relationship. She was a good woman, someone of whom you could be proud."

Izzy said, "Do you think you may be my father?"

"I don't know for sure. The timing is right for me to be your father. We look enough like each other. I know Paula didn't sleep with anyone else while we dated in Wilkes-Barre, and it would have been too late for someone in San Francisco to be your father had she slept with someone there. We're both 'artsy.' We know the drawing is of your mother, and I did it because I remember it and it has my initials on it. I don't know if we'll ever be sure. More importantly, do you want a relationship with me and my family in the future?"

Izzy expressed herself beyond her years when she said, "I've been happy with my life. I have a nice family who cares for me; I'm on track for the career I love. I've been fortunate to have enough money-with my mother's life insurance and my modeling jobs--not to worry about those things. I would like to have known my mother and father. Someday, I'll fall in love and start a family of my own. I would be happy to get to know you whether or not we are related because you are a nice, caring man, and I feel close to you even though I don't know why. Oh, I forgot, you're also very talented and I like your work."

She turned to Mary Ann, "I feel like an intruder, and I'm sorry if I have caused any pain or discomfort for you. I want to know what you think."

Mary Ann remained silent up to now. Although hesitant, she said, "You seem like a very nice young lady--a quality person and I want you to be part of our family. I couldn't have children and we adopted a baby boy. I would've been happy with more."

I said, "I couldn't have said it better; I'm so relieved. I think we should spend some time together and get to know each other. The worst that could happen is we have a new friend; the best that could happen is we have a new family member."

Mary Ann said to Izzy, "We're going fly-fishing next weekend. I don't suppose you know how to fly-fish."

Izzy said, "I do! I had a boyfriend last year who taught me. I'm not saying I'm good at it, but I can cast a line. Are you asking me to join you?"

"Yes, we would love to have you come with us."

Christmas, 1984

MARY ANN AND I were going to the Cusano's for

Christmas—they invited Izzy. I told Izzy she didn't have to go to church with us. She said, "I want to participate in the whole thing."

Microsoft introduced the Windows Operating System.

The Domain Name System named the first ".com" name, "Symbolics.com."

We listened to Madonna, Phil Collins, Whitney Houston, and Lionel Ritchie.

We went to see popular movies: "Rambo," "Rocky IV," and "Cocoon."

Chapter 21

Moving Forward

1985

New York

MARY ANN AND I were busy building a relationship with Izzy. Often Izzy came to our house for Sunday dinner. We met Izzy for dinner and theater in the city. We drove to the Pocono Mountains a few times. Izzy and Alex bonded.

Mary Ann, Izzy, and I agreed it wasn't important if Izzy was truly my daughter. We had a bond and got along well. Izzy felt at home and Mary Ann was happy with her new friend.

Jeffrey took Izzy to court with him to learn how to sketch courtroom participants. She became interested in forensics.

We all went to Disneyland for spring break. Like most adults, Mary Ann and I enjoyed the rides. Izzy and Alex liked the characters.

In May, Izzy and a friend of hers, Katherine Koslowski, an analyst on Wall Street, leased an apartment in Queens. They planned to move in the day before graduation. The new apartment was close to their work in Manhattan and convenient to our house.

The New School of Art was to graduate seniors on Sunday, May 26. Mary Ann and I arranged a graduation party afterward at the North Hills Country Club in Bayside. We invited the Cusano's, my parents, Pamela and her husband, Morton, their daughter, Elaine, and a few close friends of Izzy's.

Pamela, Morton, and Elaine Rosenthal arrived three days before Izzy's graduation. The next night, Mary Ann and I hosted them for dinner at our house. Izzy was there; Alex went to the Cusano's house for "vacation." All agreed that they wanted to find out as much information as they could to find closure about Izzy and my relationship.

On Saturday, May 25, Joe, Rene Elise, and Izzy met at our house. I rented a U-Haul truck to move Izzy from her old apartment to her new apartment. There wasn't a lot of furniture—a bed, sofa, odd chairs, dining room table and chairs, pots and pans, dishes, books, photos, drawings, sketches, and clothes. Izzy bought the bed, sofa, and dining room furniture when she moved to New York.

Izzy, Mary Ann, and Rene Elise carried the small stuff while Joe and I carried the heavier stuff. When we arrived at Izzy's new apartment, we had lunch. After lunch, while unloading the furniture and other things, an accident happened.

Rene Elise dropped the framed portrait of Paula and broke the glass. The frame and portrait were undamaged. She was so sorry this happened. I told Izzy I had glass and glasscutters at my house, and we would fix it as soon as they returned the U-Haul truck.

Izzy, Mary Ann, and I went to our house. Joe and Rene Elise went home. Rene Elise kept apologizing for dropping the portrait. Mary Ann, Izzy, and I went to the workshop in the garage to fix the portrait.

I gathered the tools and glass for the repair. I needed to remove the glass and portrait so I could repair the portrait. I removed the paper seal and padding from the back of the portrait and found a sealed envelope. The address on the envelope was, "To my son or daughter." All three of them looked at each other, and for a moment, no one knew what to do.

I gave the envelope to Izzy. "If you want to open it in private, you can."

"No, I believe we're 'family' and this appears to be a family matter." Izzy opened the letter and started reading it:

My darling son or daughter:

If you are reading my letter, it means something serious has happened to me and I want you to know about me and about us.

When I was a senior at Wilkes College, I met a handsome man named Jeffrey Rosenbloom. We spent the last semester of our senior year as friends--dating friends. We bonded on many levels; we had fun in school, at dances, and at the movies. When we were alone, we discussed the important things in life—love, goals, and ambitions.

Jeffrey was a very serious student—you know, a nerd, but a nice nerd. He was also a serious and responsible person.

I, on the other hand, was a "free spirit" who knew how to flit around more than how to invest in the stock market. I knew I didn't have to study and get a well-paying job to make a living—your grandparents would take care of that. As you know, they're wealthy San Francisco real estate barons.

Our family is Jewish. They raised us as Jews with our parent's expectation we would marry Jews and raise children in the Jewish faith.

Jeffrey was half-Jewish and half-Catholic, but more importantly, he was raised Catholic. Your grandparents would never have been OK with that.

I knew from the start that I loved Jeffrey—from the time we first slow-danced when he held me as if I were a bird about to fly away--but I never told him. I knew he was too serious and I was too adventurous for us to have a meaningful, long-term relationship.

On the last night we spent together, we made love. I really wanted to have a baby with him, but I knew better. As it turned

*out, God had other plans, and I got pregnant. I never told
Jeffrey that I was pregnant.*

*A little more than half way into my pregnancy, I had
complications and the doctor told me I might not survive if I
continued my pregnancy. By that time, I loved you and
couldn't end your life to save my own. I wanted to take a
chance on us. If it didn't work out the way I hoped, there was
Aunt Pamela who, I believed, would be willing to raise you.
The doctor put me on bed-rest to give us a chance.*

*I want you to know I love you and, if anything happens to
me, I will watch over you for the rest of your life.*

We all cried. We had a group hug for almost an eternity. We
couldn't say anything.

Finally, Izzy said, "I found the missing piece."

Mary Ann said, "I have a daughter."

I said, "Thank God."

Mary Ann couldn't believe Izzy could read the letter aloud. I
recognized Paula's handwriting. There was no doubt Izzy was
my child. It didn't matter to Mary Ann, Izzy or me. What always
mattered was we bonded like family.

Izzy had found the missing piece in her life. She had a father.
Mary Ann and I had a daughter. Alex had a sister.

On Becoming Us

Chernobyl Nuclear Power Station exploded in Russia. It was the worst nuclear disaster in history.

"Mad Cow" disease, which led to major farm reform, occurred in The United Kingdom.

The space shuttle Challenger *exploded shortly after takeoff.*

IBM introduced the first laptop computer.

We listened to Michael Jackson, Whitney Houston, and Lionel Ritchie.

We watched "Good Morning Vietnam," "Dirty Dancing," "Moonstruck," and "Big."

Chapter 22

Moving On

Late 1980s

ALL FOUR OF US were living in different ends of the world. Although geography separated us, we still had an emotional connection. After all, we made a pact when we were in Cub Scouts to stay friends for life. We were still alive and still friends.

Springfield, Massachusetts

DURING HER THIRD year in law school, Sandi received an offer to clerk for an Arizona Supreme Court Judge in Phoenix. As soon as she received the job offer, Sandi announced she no longer wanted to be married.

Tucson, Arizona

SAL MOVED TO Tucson and his health improved. The improvement couldn't be solely from the Tucson weather because he lived there with Sandi three years ago and didn't feel any better; actually, he got worse.

Sal felt healthy enough to attend graduate school at the

University of Arizona for a Master's degree in Exercise and Sport Science. This seemed like the perfect fit for him. For someone who wanted to open a pizza parlor instead of going to college, he spent eleven years in college and graduate school.

In graduate school, Sal learned how the mind influences the body and how people can make themselves sick if they were in a toxic relationship or in a toxic job. It was clear to Sal—his first marriage got him sick, and his divorce got him well again. Unfortunately, some of the damage remained--damage to relationships with his friends and family. He mended as many fences as he could.

He taught classes at the University of Arizona and Pima County Health Department.

At a gathering of fellow graduate students, Sal met a thirty-three year old pediatrician, Heather McGrath, studying neonatology at the Medical Center of the University of Arizona. Heather had an appealing Southern twang. She was from the Southeast—as if her accent wouldn't have revealed that! Heather was cute ...real cute—cuter than anyone he had expected to meet. She was 5' 4" with curly red hair—looked like Shirley Temple when she was a kid in the movies. She had a warm smile and was very personable. He thought, "How lucky is this?"

Sal began dating Heather—dinner, hiking, golf, and exploring Arizona. They went out every weekend and once or twice during the week. It seemed like they knew each other forever.

Heather and Sal became close quickly. For Christmas, Sal gave her a large print of two children bowing to each other with the boy handing flowers to the girl. It pretty much summed up how he felt. He asked her to marry him and she accepted. They planned a Spring Wedding.

Heather's father, Earle McGrath, came to Tucson to "see who's taking my little girl from me." Since he was a big golf fan, Sal arranged for them to play golf with LPGA golf pro. He thought this would distract him and he would pay more attention to her and less attention to Sal.

With his psychology training, he thought he would put the cards on the table. On the second hole, Sal said, "Earle, I'm forty-five, divorced, Italian, and Catholic, do you have any questions?"

Earle smiled and said, "A few."

By the end of the round of golf, they were friends.

In April, Heather and Sal flew into Greenville, South Carolina a few days before the wedding. They planned a small wedding with just family and friends and a reception at her father's house. Once they selected the date, they sent invitations to guests. They didn't realize the date they picked was the Saturday of the Masters Golf Tournament—big mistake.

"Don't they know the Saturday of the first full week of April is an important day in the Carolinas and Georgia—almost a holiday?" said one of Earle's friends.

"I guess not."

However, on the day they got married, it rained nonstop. Perhaps the rain gave those guests who would have gone to the Masters Tournament a chance to attend their wedding reception. When the guests got to Earle's house, they weren't as angry as when they received the invitation—they couldn't have gone to the Masters after all.

The next day, Heather and Sal flew to Wyoming Valley to have a reception for his family at Il Primo Ristorante in Pittston. That weekend, Eastern Airlines went on strike and instead of going straight to Wyoming Valley they went via of Pittsburgh with Allegheny Airlines. They made it to the reception just in time to change their clothes and greet their guests.

They flew back to Tucson and went to Sedona and the Grand Canyon for their honeymoon. Sal was finally happy with his life and his health.

Philadelphia

MIKE HAD BEEN working for G Fox in Hartford, Connecticut, for five years. It was time to move again. For two people glued to Wyoming Valley, they had sprouted wings. His new job was with Snyder's in Richmond, Virginia. Wow, they had become Southerners!

Debbie went with the flow. Each time Mike got a promotion, she went with him and found a job. She was a trainee at Pomeroys and worked there for many years. During the past decade, she had numerous jobs including customer service representative for Ethan Allen.

They moved to Toronto in 1988. In May 1989, after Mike and Debbie lived in Toronto for his work, they moved to a suburb of Philadelphia. They couldn't take the winters in Toronto. They had learned French during their time in Canada. Mike was fortunate to have met the love of his life the first time. They celebrated their fifteenth year wedding anniversary.

Atlanta

TED MARRIED ANNE who was personable, sociable, and a nice person. He deserved to be happy with someone he liked. Perhaps we will lay our eyes on him every now and then.

New York

IZZY BEGAN A new job as a children's book illustrator with publisher, "Sticks and Stones." Her first assignment was as an illustrator for a book in production, "Growing up in the Forest."

I left the advertising agency, ABZ Advertising, to open a studio, "Jeffrey Rosenbloom Creations," full time but continued my involvement in forensics. My new art studio was successful. In addition to selling my paintings, clients commissioned me to paint for them.

After Izzy finished her illustration project, a major publishing company published the book. She increasingly got involved in my work and developed her own interest in forensics. She often came to court with me.

***

IN THE LATE 1980S, Mike and I were still married to our first wives. Ted and Sal were in their second marriages. All of us had achieved "big deal" careers. All of us had found our "goddesses." Out of the four of us, only I had a family with children.

Although our lives didn't turn out exactly as we dreamed as children and young adults, we were healthy, happy and still friends.

The End

Afterword

In Cub Scouts at Saint Rocco's Catholic Church, Pittston, Pennsylvania, four friends made a pact to be "friends-for-life." They were optimistic about their friendship and their future. They expected to be strong enough to deal with everything that would interfere with their friendship.

They didn't expect love and marriage to sidetrack their friendship but it did. They didn't expect their religion to be a deterrent to finding the love of their lives but it was. They didn't expect illness to separate them geographically but it did.

Through it all, they retained their core values, their deep-seated principles, and their ability to reinvent themselves when reinvention became necessary.

Jeffrey Rosenbloom reinvented himself when a criminal he helped put in jail attacked him. He transformed from a pen-and-ink artist to a watercolor artist.

Mike Costanzo's job caused him to relocate multiple times to climb the ladder of success.

Ted Mosconi changed careers and locations to become successful.

Sal Greco reinvented himself many times--when he changed career goals from medicine to teaching, from teaching to dentistry, and from dentistry to healthcare management. When he quit dentistry due to illness, he traveled to find a safe place in which to live.

What made these changes possible were the lessons they learned from observing their families and the work ethic under which they operated.

After seventy years, they're still friends. The Rosenblooms live on Long Island, New York; the Costanzos live outside Philadelphia; The Mosconis live in Williamsport, Pennsylvania; and the Grecos live in Greenville, South Carolina. They all get together when they can and they enjoy hearing from each other.

On Becoming Us

They've all worked hard "On Becoming Us."
They hope you enjoyed their story.

About the Author

Guy S. Fasciana has always enjoyed writing. At first, college term papers created on a typewriter he borrowed from his next-door neighbor. They didn't have computers then.

When he started dental practice, he wrote a patient pamphlet entitled, "Does Your Lifestyle Promote or Prevent Health." The booklet was about health in general and dentistry in particular.

After he developed asthma due to exposure to dental materials, he terminated his dental practice. He wrote a non-fiction book, "Are Your Dental Fillings Poisoning You?" He was a columnist for the *Journal of Environmental Medicine*, "The EI Dentist."

In graduate school, he wrote term papers about health, wellness, exercise, and the effect your thoughts have on your health. Some of the articles included:

"The Relationship between Stress and Health,"

"How Stress Affects the Immune System,"

"How Exercise Intensity Affects the Immune System,"

"The Psychological Benefits of Exercise in Rehabilitation,"

"Can Subliminal Communication Enhance Performance," and

"Overdoing Exercise Can Make You Sick."

He elected to write two-master's theses instead of oral exams.

After graduate school, he wrote his second non-fiction book, "Golf's Mental Magic: Four Strategies for Mental Toughness."

He has had numerous editorials about health and medicine published in newspapers.

"On Becoming Us" is his first fiction book.

You can find more information about his life or about his writing on his website, guysfasciana.com.